D0734939

SOMETHING IN THE WAY

JESSICA HAWKINS

© 2017 JESSICA HAWKINS
www.JESSICAHAWKINS.net

Editing by Elizabeth London Editing
Beta by Underline This Editing
Proofreading by Tamara Mataya Editing
Cover Design © R.B.A. Designs
Cover Photo by Perrywinkle Photography

SOMETHING IN THE WAY

All rights reserved. Except as permitted under the U.S. Copyright Act of 1976, no part of this publication may be reproduced, distributed, or transmitted in any form or by any means, or stored in a database or retrieval system without the prior written permission of the author.

This book is a work of fiction. Names, characters, places, and incidents either are products of the author's imagination or are used fictitiously. Any resemblance to actual persons, living or dead, events, or locales is entirely coincidental.

ISBN: 0-9978691-9-4
ISBN-13: 978-0-9978691-9-4

TITLES BY
JESSICA HAWKINS

LEARN MORE AT JESSICAHAWKINS.NET/BOOKS

SLIP OF THE TONGUE
THE FIRST TASTE
YOURS TO BARE

SOMETHING IN THE WAY SERIES
SOMETHING IN THE WAY
SOMEBODY ELSE'S SKY
MOVE THE STARS

THE CITYSCAPE SERIES
COME UNDONE
COME ALIVE
COME TOGETHER

EXPLICITLY YOURS SERIES
POSSESSION
DOMINATION
PROVOCATION
OBSESSION

1
LAKE, 1993

It seemed unfair, spending three hours a day in a classroom during summer, only to wait another thirty minutes in the parking lot. There were things I could do about that, like walk home, or tell my parents my older sister was always late to pick me up—but either of those would inevitably lead to an argument or two. Dad would yell at Tiffany. She'd take her punishment out on me.

It wouldn't do much good now anyway, with only two days of summer school left. I hadn't gotten my license yet, so what right did I have to complain? Instead, I did what I had every other afternoon and took out one of the books I needed to read before summer ended.

Some pages later, Tiffany came around the corner, screeching to a stop at the curb. "Get in," she said, as if I were making her late for something—even though I'd done nothing but wait in that same spot for forty-five minutes. "Come on. Hurry up."

Gainfully unemployed, my nineteen-year-old sister lived at home, ate Mom and Dad's food, and had an allowance my dad constantly threatened to cut off. She had one job only—take me to and from school.

Rolling through stop signs on the drive home, she explained the rush. "If Brad calls, I don't want to miss it. I've been waiting ages for him to ask me out."

It would've been easy not to care that she was driving fifteen miles over the speed limit—the windows were down, the breeze warm, and there were still six weeks left of summer. But Tiffany knew better. "You're going to get pulled over, and Dad'll take your car away," I said.

"Maybe for a day, but I'd get it back."

"Can't you just call Brad and ask *him* out?"

"Not unless I want to look desperate," she said with an air of knowing, as if she were imparting wisdom. In a way, she was. I had no idea about these things. "You want to watch music videos later?"

"I have reading to do."

"You've been reading or doing homework all summer," she said. "Your class is practically over. Relax."

University of Southern California wasn't looking for 'relaxed' students. According to Dad, summers were for "weeding out the lazy kids"—like my friends, who were probably at the beach. "I will, in two days."

"Then we should do something this weekend. Something cheesy, like the Fun Zone at Balboa. Get ice cream bars, like we used to when we were kids."

One thing about Tiffany, I could never predict what she'd say next. Most days, she didn't want me anywhere near her. Others, she'd burst into my room, hop on my bed, and ramble on about her day. She had only two speeds—annoyed older sister or best friend. I preferred the latter . . . unless I was in the middle of studying for something important. "Maybe," I said.

With an eye-roll, she turned up the radio for "Runaway Train" and sang all the way home. She parked along the curb of our cul-de-sac, close to the next-door lot where they were doing construction.

One of the hard-hatted men whistled at us. "Hey. Blondie."

Tiffany looked through her window. "What?"

"Come here a sec."

Why should it surprise me that Tiffany responded? If a man had eyes and they were aimed in her direction, she noticed. That might not have meant much if it only happened once in a while, but Tiffany was a California beauty through and through.

There'd been a lot of arguments about the construction since it'd started earlier that summer. My father didn't like the noise, the dust, or the men he was sure were looking at my mom and sister. It hadn't involved me, so I hadn't paid much attention. But if he'd been that upset about the men looking at Tiffany, he definitely wouldn't want her talking to them.

Tiffany slanted the rearview mirror, brushing her bangs side to side and forward again. She puckered her lips. "You have any lipstick?"

I carried tins of Candy Kisses lip balm in my backpack, flavors like cherry vanilla, bubblegum, and my favorite—watermelon. Here I was, entering junior year of high school, and I was still "too young" for makeup. Even though my friends wore it. Even though Tiffany had been granted that privilege the summer *before* her freshman year. I didn't care too much about stuff like that, but I was still a little protective of my lip balm. My allowance was finite.

I rummaged through my pencil pouch until I found cherry vanilla and handed it over. It was nothing to Tiffany, who dug her finger into it, spread a ton over her lips, smacked them together, and tossed it into my lap. "Thanks."

She got out of the car, her Steve Madden platforms wobbling as she stepped over the curb into the dirt lot.

I slung my backpack over my shoulder and went to interrupt her conversation with the construction worker. "We're not supposed to be over here."

"Then why don't you go inside?" she asked without looking at me. It wasn't a suggestion.

The man looked down her top.

"And leave you out here alone?" I asked.

She'd rolled the waistband of her black denim skirt dangerously high. A short skirt and platforms didn't seem like the kind of thing you wore around a construction site, but what did I know? Less than most sixteen-year-olds, Tiffany would say. Nineteen-year-olds, though—they knew a lot about a lot. Particularly how to dress around men.

"How long's it take to build a house?" she asked him, sweeping her bangs aside. Realizing her mistake, she fixed them again. She spent at least ten minutes in the bathroom every morning plucking at them, fashioning them into a casual curl.

"Depends. We're pretty quick." He laughed into his fist. I looked behind us to see why. One of the workers had cocked an electric drill in front of his crotch. It spun around as he jutted his hips back and forth. It was stupid, but the other men on the site laughed.

I fingered the thin, gold bracelet around my wrist, a birthday gift from Dad. Tiffany and I didn't always get along, but I didn't want to leave her in a dangerous situation. These men were big and dirty.

They were making me nervous. "I thought you were waiting for Brad's call."

Tiffany opened her mouth, probably to tell me to go away, but then shut it. "I have to go," she told him, whirling around.

"Hey, wait," he called after us.

We went up the brick and concrete walkway to the front door. My parents' house wasn't a mansion or anything, but my classmates gawked when they came over. With palm trees, a perfectly manicured lawn, and a three-car garage, our two-story home fit in with the upscale Newport Beach neighborhood. It curved gracefully at the end of the cul-de-sac and even had a pool, despite the beach being a ten-minute drive away.

"Why were you talking to him?" I asked Tiffany. "We're not supposed to."

"Are you going to tell Dad?"

He'd said to stay away, but when did Tiffany ever listen to him? Or anyone who knew better? If I brought it up, it'd only start a war at the dinner table. "No."

"Good." She unlocked the house. "Problem solved."

———

The next day, Tiffany forgot to pick me up altogether. After an hour passed, I hoisted my book bag and wandered home. It was hot outside, but summer was supposed to be hot, so it felt good. Living miles from the beach, we got some breeze, and our neighborhood was safe, even by my dad's standards.

I could've walked home with my eyes closed. I'd grown up here, had explored nooks and crannies with friends who'd come and gone, played baseball in the cul-de-sac, run away to the Reynolds' treehouse when I'd gotten a B-minus on a math test. Aside from all that, though, had my eyes been closed, I would've known I was home by the telltale sounds of the construction site.

My heart rate kicked up as I approached the lot. At dinner the night before, Mom'd asked why my bracelet wasn't on my wrist since I rarely took it off. The most likely explanation was that I'd lost it while fidgeting yesterday. Dad had warned me it was expensive when he'd given it to me.

I kept my eyes down, even though there was no reason for the men to notice me. Mom had told me years ago that one day I'd look like my older sister. That day hadn't come yet. My limbs were too gangly, my dishwater-blonde hair wasn't highlighted. I didn't even have breasts. My mom had gotten hers at seventeen and kept assuring me they'd come.

Retracing my steps from where Tiffany had parked the day before to the dirt lot, I bent at the waist and searched for hints of gold.

"Hey," one of the men said. His voice was so deep, it gave me goosebumps on the inside, if that was even possible. "I found it. Here."

7

Slowly, I turned. The enormous hand in front of me had dirt under the nails and my delicate gold chain coiled in its deep valley.

"It looks valuable," he said.

I squinted up, and up, and up at him. I had only two concepts of men—ones my father's age, like my teachers, and the boys I went to school with. This one didn't fit into either category. He was bigger than my dad, bigger, even, than our vice-principal, who was the tallest man I knew. I couldn't quite see his eyes under his hardhat, so I looked at the rest of his face. Black scruff nearly hid the dent in his chin. His nose was strong and hard with a noticeable bump.

"It is," I said.

He held it out. The sleeves of his charcoal-gray t-shirt had been ripped off at the seams. His arms were like the guns Dad displayed in his study—hard, defined, chillingly powerful. The more my father warned me off the weapons he kept locked behind glass, the more I just wanted to touch one to see how it'd feel.

I didn't move an inch, my heart beating harder.

"It's all right," he said, nodding. "It's safe."

I opened my hand. He poured the bracelet into it, and I put it in my pocket.

He removed his hardhat. He'd rolled and knotted a red bandana around his head, but it didn't seem to do much; he had a lot of thick, black hair that spilled over. Picking up his shirt, he wiped his temples, giving me a glimpse of his hard, rippled stomach, and a smattering of fine dark hair. He dropped the hem immediately, but I averted my eyes anyway.

"Sorry," he said.

"For what?" I asked the pavement.

"If I made you uncomfortable." He removed the bandana and used that on his face instead. Dirt smeared across his olive skin. He was making it worse. I could see his eyes better now, dark brown like soda pop, but against the sun, there were lighter flecks, gold as the chain in my pocket.

My stomach tightened. I *was* uncomfortable, but him knowing that made it worse.

He pulled a pack of cigarettes from his back pocket and hit it against his palm. "You should get the clasp checked," he said before he walked away.

I made it all the way to the front door when I remembered I didn't have my house keys. I could picture them on my desk between my phone and a stack of *Sassy* magazines. I hadn't even thought to take them this morning. Why would I? Tiffany was supposed to be with me. Even the gate into the backyard was locked. Dad had been extra diligent about securing the house since construction had started.

I shuffled back down the walkway, sat on the curb, and took out my book. Somehow, I could sense the man watching me. I wanted to look back. I liked his dark eyes, and how he looked scary, but he'd done something nice for me. I read the same paragraph three times and still didn't know what it said, so I

JESSICA HAWKINS

gave in and glanced up. He sat on a brick wall that surrounded the lot, his hand cupped around a lighter as he lit the cigarette between his lips. He wasn't looking at me.

I realized what was bothering me. I hadn't thanked him for returning the bracelet, and that was rude. I closed my book and got up. This time, he did watch as I walked back along the street toward him.

"Thanks," I said from the curb.

"For?"

I put my book under one arm, took out the bracelet, and showed it to him. "You could've kept it. I wouldn't've known."

"What would I do with women's jewelry?" he asked.

"Give it to your girlfriend." I pretended to concentrate on getting the bracelet on so he wouldn't see me blushing. The longer he was silent, the more uncomfortable I got. I had no idea how he'd taken the comment. Unable to help myself, I finally glanced up at him. "Or your mom. Or sister."

"If I'd kept your bracelet, I would've taken it to a pawn shop."

Heat soared up my chest, right to my cheeks. A *porn* shop? If he hadn't seen me blushing before, he definitely did now. I'd never heard of a porn shop. Well, I knew what porn was. Boys at my school bragged about looking at it. My dad got Playboy in the mail. But what kind of things did a shop sell?

"You get locked out?" he asked.

I stepped onto the lot. "My sister has the key."

He nodded. I wasn't sure what to make of him. Because he was older and bigger, he seemed unapproachable, but I wanted to talk to him anyway. He took a drag of his cigarette. "What're you reading?"

I gave up trying to get the bracelet on. "*The Grapes of Wrath.*"

"The one with the farmers?"

"It's about the Great Depression," I said.

"Why'd you pick that?"

"Because it was next on the list."

His forehead wrinkled. "The list?"

I walked a little closer to him, holding my unclasped bracelet in place. "Required summer reading."

He stubbed out the cigarette he'd just lit. "You want to sit?"

The wall probably only came up to his waist, but for me, it was tall enough that I wasn't going to embarrass myself by trying to get up. "I'll stand."

"So this list . . . you just go in order, one by one?" he asked. "What if you're in the mood for something different?"

Was anyone ever in the mood for the Great Depression? This paperback had taken me longer to read than any other book so far and not just because it was almost five hundred pages. I hadn't thought to tackle the list any other way. "I guess I could try something else."

"You're not enjoying it?"

My mouth went dry just thinking about all the lengthy descriptions—traveling across country, drought, dust. "There's a lot of . . . information."

"Put it down for a while. Try something else. Maybe something not on the list."

"Can't. School starts in six weeks, and there are more books after this."

"You could always do what I did and watch the movie."

I balked. "I can't do that."

"Why not?"

"That's cheating."

"Huh." The ends of his grease-smudged jeans grazed the bottoms of his worn boots. Where did they carry pants long enough for so much leg? His t-shirt must've been through the wash hundreds of times, faded to the point I could barely make out a rainbow streak across it.

I squinted to read it. "What's Pink Floyd?"

"What?" He glanced at me and then down, pulling the fabric taut with one hand. "It's a band. You never heard of them?"

I shook my head as my cheeks warmed. I shouldn't have asked. Tiffany knew all the latest bands, watched all the music videos, and I tried to keep up, but there were so many. Nirvana was the one Tiffany loved most. Why couldn't he have been wearing a Nirvana shirt? I knew most of their songs—I'd heard them through the wall enough times. "I don't listen to the radio much."

"Me, neither. There's some pretty bad stuff out there."

I smiled a little. Tiffany was all about her CDs. Saying you didn't like music was like admitting you weren't cool. Everybody had something to say about the latest album or some underground band or the 'song of the summer.' "I play a little piano," I said. "But I'll probably stop."

"How come?"

"I'm not any good. Anyway, my sister says piano's for geeks."

He studied me a few seconds and then nodded toward my parents' house. "Was that your sister yesterday?"

Of course he wanted to know about Tiffany. It should've occurred to me earlier that she was the reason he'd talked to me, but for some reason it hadn't. Even though I was pretty sure he was around Tiffany's age, he seemed more mature.

I nodded. "Tiffany. She'll probably go out with you."

"Yeah? How do you know?"

"She goes out with lots of guys."

His heavy black brows fell. "What do you know about who she goes out with?"

"She tells me."

"Tells you what?"

"About who she likes and stuff."

"And stuff." With a grunt, he reached into his back pocket, took out another cigarette, and stuck it in his mouth without lighting it. "You should stay out of your sister's business."

I jutted my chin out. He sounded just like my dad, except when Dad said it, it was an order, not a suggestion. Dad made Tiffany's business sound filthy, like I might go looking for it in the garbage cans out back.

"Look at that." The cigarette sagged from between his lips as he glanced at my feet. "You dropped it again."

I followed his eyes to where my bracelet had fallen in the dirt. *Damn.* I picked it up and tried again to get it back on.

"Come over here," he said. "Let me do that."

I breathed through my mouth. "What?"

"The clasp," he said.

My heart skipped as he beckoned me. I took a few tentative steps and held out my arm, the chain dangling precariously. He moved the unlit cigarette from his mouth to behind his ear, then leaned forward and turned my forearm face-up. He could crush my wrist with one hand, I was sure of it. It took him several tries to even get the two ends between his huge fingers. He squinted, muttering under his breath. His callused palms brushed over the thin skin of my wrist until goosebumps traveled up my arm and my insides tightened up. The ends slipped from between his fingers over and over.

14

His knee brushed my ribs, and I flinched.

"Sorry," he said.

I was pretty sure with a little more focus, I'd have better luck with the bracelet than he was having, but I didn't want to stop him. An unfamiliar tingle made the hair on the back of my neck stand up. It wasn't as if I'd never had a crush. Like my friends, I blushed when a senior said *hi* in the hall. I got giddy when someone like Corbin Swenson, the most popular boy in school, acknowledged our table in the cafeteria. But the boys at school were just that—boys. Tiffany liked to tear out pictures of celebrities and tape them to her wall—Andrew Keegan, Luke Perry, Kurt Cobain— and this man was as wall-worthy as he was sweaty, dusty, and quiet.

He grasped me, his tanned hand covering more than half of my white forearm. "Hold still."

Men of his age or size were never this close to me. I hadn't moved; I was certain of it.

Finally, he got the two pieces to connect. "How's that?"

I gave my wrist a shake to make sure the bracelet was secure. "Good, I think."

"You walk home from school a lot?"

"What?"

He nodded at my backpack. "Didn't you walk?"

"Today was the first time."

He tilted his head back, looking down his nose at me. "Probably shouldn't be walking home alone. Or at all, maybe."

15

"It's not far. I don't have my license yet."

He knocked the heel of his boot against the brick, looking anywhere but at me. "But you're old enough?"

I almost asked how old he thought I was so I could tack "what about you?" on to the end, but what if he guessed too young? I suddenly regretted my t-shirt, high-necked and white cotton with a round, yellow happy face in the center. I'd bought it from a record store, so it wasn't really childish, unless, I realized, a child was wearing it. On Tiffany, it would look cool, but I was flat-chested. Suddenly, a year seemed like a lifetime to wait for breasts.

"I'm old enough . . ." I said. He looked as though he expected me to continue. "I'm sixteen, but I have to get a certain number of behind-the-wheel hours with my parents." Tiffany was a licensed driver and could take me, but she'd had two speeding tickets and a fender bender in the last year alone. My dad would never allow her to teach me. I shifted feet. "We started, but I haven't had time lately."

"You haven't? Or your parents?"

I went to answer but stopped. Dad usually worked until past seven. Mom was probably showing houses or at some meeting. I had time now, but there were a hundred other things I should be doing, like reading from the list, studying for SATs, or volunteering. "We've all got stuff going on."

"What keeps a sixteen-year-old so busy?"

"College prep," I said in the same tone Tiff said *duh.* "Do you go to school?"

"At night."

"Oh. Like community college?"

"Yeah." He let his posture fall and laced his hands between his knees. "You sure you don't want to get up here? That backpack's as big as you."

I looked around, as if someone might be watching. "I don't think I can."

He gestured for me to come closer. When I was at his feet, he took my backpack off and dropped it. It landed on the ground with a *thud,* disturbing the sand into a cloud. "Christ. What's in there? Rocks?"

I unzipped it to put *The Grapes of Wrath* away and showed him the inside. "More books."

"Figures. You need to lighten your load, like me." From his back pocket he pulled a paperback small enough to fit in one of his big hands.

I read the title—*The Metamorphosis.* "What's that about?"

The cover had what looked like a huge cockroach on it. He studied it, his eyebrows drawn. "To be honest, I'm not sure yet. It's weird. I'll get back to you."

I wrinkled my nose. Nobody I knew ever called a book *weird.* My English teacher and classmates were always using words like *abstract, poignant,* or *metaphorical.* It was so unheard of that I started to laugh.

Without any warning, not even a grunt or word to prepare me, he lifted me by my waist and sat me on the wall like I weighed a hundred pounds.

Well, I about did, but that wasn't the point. He was strong, all dirt and grime, long and lean, his face and arms bronzed by the sun. He could pick me up. He could throw me if he wanted to. He could probably put me over his shoulder and walk a thousand miles without running out of breath. My urge to slide closer to him was as strong as my urge to jump down, run inside, and hide in the house where men like him only existed in my glossy magazines.

The hard brick didn't give much of a welcome. All at once, I was an absolute and nervous mess about sitting next to a man. I didn't think of my dad as a man, and certainly the boys I went to school with weren't. The sun beat down on us, and he smelled of heat and sweat. It wasn't bad.

"What's your name?" he asked.

"What's yours?"

He wiped his palms on his jeans. "Manning."

"Lake."

The cigarette was back in his hands. He rolled it, flipped it around, tapped it against his knee. Everything but smoked it. "Are you trying to quit?" I asked.

"Quit what?"

"Smoking." My feet dangled over the wall. "You look like you really want to smoke it."

He returned it behind his ear. "Lake," he said as if trying the word out. "And your middle name?"

That, I'd never reveal. "I hate it."

He turned his whole body to me. "Tell me."

"It's ugly."

"How can a name be ugly?"

"Trust me, it can," I said simply. Mom liked to remind me it was a family name when I talked like that, but I didn't care. Family or not, Dolly seemed like a babyish name, and it was no better than the stuffy-sounding Dolores from which it came.

He half-smiled, one corner of his mouth lifting. That was the first I saw of his straight, white teeth. My heart skipped. Under the dirt, the sweat, the calluses, he was handsome. I'd known it already, peripherally, as I knew the direction of the beach or the artwork hanging in my dad's office. But now it was right in front of me—I couldn't miss it.

His forehead creased with lines. "Careful, or it'll come off a third time," he said.

It took me a second to realize I'd been twisting my bracelet around my wrist.

"This time, I might not give it back," he said.

"You'd take it to the porn shop?" It came out fast, breezily, before I could think about it. But it was probably the most brazen thing I'd ever said.

"The *what?*" he asked, pulling his entire upper body away.

"The . . ." I widened my eyes at his incredulous stare. "You said you'd take it to a porn shop."

19

"*Pawn*," he pronounced slowly. "P-a-w-n."

I shook my head. I was still confused. "I—I don't know what that is."

He blew out a sigh and glanced up at the sky. "It's a place you can take valuables for quick cash. Never mind."

"Oh." My embarrassment was palpable, like an anvil on my chest. The silence made it worse.

"You can go if you want," he finally said.

Did I want to? My impulses since I'd come over here had ping-ponged between smiling and shaking and lots else. Everything felt different. Even the house they were building looked further along than it'd been yesterday. Nobody seemed to think it was weird, me sitting here with him. "Do you want me to?"

He kept his eyes forward. "You remind me of my younger sister."

"I thought you said you didn't have one."

"When?"

I thought back to the conversation earlier. I'd suggested he might've given the bracelet to someone like a girlfriend or sister. Maybe I hadn't said sister. I shook my head. "Never mind."

With the squeal of tires against pavement, I checked over my shoulder. Tiffany's BMW zoomed in our direction. I wasn't supposed to be out here. I didn't think Tiffany would tell Dad, but I didn't want her to see me and come over. I also wasn't ready to go inside.

Tiffany parked at the curb. I sucked in a breath and held it, sitting as still as possible, hoping to blend in with my surroundings. After all, Tiffany overlooked me all the time.

I should've known she wasn't in the habit of overlooking attractive men.

2
LAKE

Tiffany shut the driver's side door of her BMW and started across the construction lot to where Manning and I sat on the wall.

Manning leaned his elbows onto his knees and watched her approach. My sister had that effect on men. They were always looking over or around me to see her. What'd he think when he looked at her? What'd he notice first?

I'd spent my life hearing how beautiful my sister and mother were and had been told I looked like them enough times to believe I might also be attractive. Some day. What I didn't have usually didn't bother me. Things like lipstick and hairspray and shopping had always seemed stupid compared to books and grades and college applications. Watching

Manning's face as Tiffany approached, I began to wonder if that was true. I'd never doubted my own attractiveness more.

"Sorry I was late," she said to me as she looked Manning over. "I went by the school."

"I walked."

She stopped in front of us, shielded her eyes, and put a hand on her hip. "What are you doing out here?"

I shrugged casually, but inside, fervently prayed she wouldn't send me home. "He found my bracelet."

"I didn't know you lost it." Tiffany glanced from my wrist to the cigarette in Manning's hand. "You're smoking?"

I shifted on the brick wall. "No. Of course not."

"You can tell me. I smoked sometimes at your age. It's normal."

"She wasn't," Manning said, his voice smooth. Deep. "And smoking at her age isn't normal."

Tiffany wrinkled her nose. "It was for me and my friends. I'm Tiffany, by the way."

"Manning."

The three of us went quiet.

"Where were you?" I asked.

She squinted against the sun behind us. It was obviously hurting her eyes. "The mall. Nordstrom's Anniversary Sale is next month, so I was making a list of what I'm going to get. As Daddy says, it's good to be prepared." She glanced between the two of us.

"I'm sorry if she was bothering you. She's not supposed to be out here."

My hairline prickled. Being made to sound like a child might be worse than getting sent back inside.

Manning shook his head fractionally. "She wasn't bothering me."

It didn't sound convincing. My stomach clenched at the realization that maybe I *was* annoying him, and he'd just been too polite to say anything. My butt began to ache from the wall, but I stayed put. Tiffany was about to pull the plug on my afternoon, and I wanted to soak this up. The sun on my back. The sweat and dirt. Manning. I hadn't realized until now how little I'd been outside this summer because of studying.

"You work out here?" Tiffany asked. "One of your crew whistled at me yesterday."

"I saw," Manning said. "Did you hit it off?"

"With him? God, no. He's not my type."

Manning nodded. "Then it won't happen again. The catcalling."

"Oh. It was no big deal." She shrugged, running a light fingertip along her collarbone. "Manning. That's a cool name."

"I had no say in it."

She laughed. "What about you, Manning? You have a girlfriend?"

"No."

"You live around here?"

"Not that close."

"How old are you?"

"Twenty-three."

My gaze had been bouncing back and forth between them, and I did a double take. He wasn't even close to Tiffany's age. He might even be too old for her.

"Want to come inside for a beer?" Tiffany asked.

We weren't allowed to drink our parents' alcohol. It should've gone without mentioning since Tiffany wouldn't be twenty-one for two more years, but it *had* been said, more than once, since Tiffany had stolen from their stash before.

I didn't know what would be a worse offense in my parents' eyes—drinking their alcohol or inviting one of the workers into their home. I would be sworn to secrecy afterward. I didn't like lying to my parents, but sometimes, a teenage girl like my sister could be more menacing than anyone.

"I'm working," Manning answered.

Tiffany closed one eye against the sun and smiled. "Doesn't look like it."

"Lunch break."

I looked up at him. "But you have no food."

"I'm on a diet."

Tiffany laughed. I drew my brows together. Was that a joke? He didn't seem like the funny type but it was even less likely he'd go on a diet. I forced a chuckle as well.

"Come inside," Tiffany said. "Lake'll make you a sandwich. She makes the best ones."

"Sorry," he said. His eyes stayed on me. "I don't think your parents would like it."

I must've stared at him like I was seeing the sun for the first time, but I didn't know how to help that. I knew he shouldn't come in. I wanted him to. If he didn't, either Tiffany would leave and make me go with her or she'd want to be alone with him.

"I'll make you a sandwich," I blurted.

Manning looked over my head. "I can't."

"Okay, fine." Tiffany turned to nod at me. "Don't you have homework or something? Get lost."

Manning's dark eyes narrowed on Tiffany. "You talk to your sister that way?"

She brushed hair from her neck, visibly reddening. "She knows I'm joking. Don't you, sis?"

I nodded. Tiffany wasn't joking. Her thin smile and rigid back were a silent warning—go away, or else. It wasn't fair, though. I'd been here first. "I don't have any more homework. Tomorrow's my last day."

"Oh." Tiffany shifted feet. "I bet Manning would like if you brought him a sandwich then."

I figured Manning probably *would* like that. I didn't want to go, but Tiffany would find a way to get what she wanted, and at least this way, I'd be doing something for Manning, too. "Okay."

Manning sighed. He looked down at me and then over at Tiffany. "I'll come in, but I only have twenty minutes."

Tiffany grinned. "Cool."

Manning jumped down from the wall. I started to slide off, too, but he caught my waist at the last minute. His hands were so large, they nearly wrapped all the way around me. I got hot and cold all at once, doing everything in my power not to shiver so I wouldn't give myself away. He set me on the ground gently, like a porcelain statue on a shelf. "It's not good for your ankles if you don't know how to jump," he told me.

"But you did it."

He smiled a little. "You always argue with someone who's looking out for you?"

Tiffany pulled on Manning's elbow. "Come on."

I followed them across the lot toward the house, the feel of his hands on my waist lingering. They were enormous. And hot. They made *me* hot—my cheeks, my chest, all the way down, between my legs. This time I did shiver, just replaying it in my head. Thankfully I was behind them, out of sight. Tiffany would think I was ridiculous for getting so excited over being helped off a wall.

Just now, in less than five minutes, she'd gotten more information out of him than I had all afternoon. It was as if they were speaking a language I only sort of understood, like when the Brazilian exchange student in my Spanish class spoke Portuguese to confuse the teacher.

In the entryway, Manning looked around. He seemed even bigger inside. We had vaulted ceilings, but I was sure if he stretched hard enough and

28

jumped high enough, he could touch them. He looked as uncomfortable as I felt. I needed something to do with my hands. I needed to stop staring.

Tiffany called us into the living room where she was hunched over the mini-refrigerator behind Dad's bar. "We have Corona or Budweiser."

"Should you be drinking when you're working?" I asked.

Manning had tipped his head back to take in my dad's impressive selection of liquor, but he dropped just his eyes to mine. "No. I'll take a Coke if you've got it."

"Go make the sandwich, Lake," Tiffany said.

"What kind do you want?" I asked him.

He spread his long fingers over his stomach and for the first time, he grinned. "I'll eat anything you make."

I couldn't help responding with my own smile. "All right. I'll make the Lake Special."

Coined by my dad, the Lake Special consisted of sliced turkey and ham layered between cheddar and provolone cheese, smothered in mayonnaise and barbecue sauce, topped with lettuce, tomato, and avocado. For Manning, I'd add extra meat, since he had a hard job and looked big enough for two sandwiches.

I pulled ingredients from the fridge, trying unsuccessfully to catch words from the conversation in the next room. I didn't want Tiffany to know more about him than I did. What if they talked about something personal? Got closer, while I was in here fussing with deli meat? Once everything was laid out in front of me and I could no longer stand the idea of them alone together, I called out, "It's almost ready."

Manning entered the kitchen and walked around the island where I stood slicing an avocado. For one brief moment, his heat warmed my back, and then it was gone. He washed his hands, took a stool on the opposite side of the island, and nodded approvingly. "That is a monster sandwich."

"Well, you're a big person," I said without thinking. "Not that you're fat. Obviously, you're not." I focused on placing the avocado in neat slices across the meat to disguise my awkwardness. Nobody in my life was double my size, but pointing it out felt rude. "You don't have to eat it all."

"I won't leave a crumb."

I looked up at him. Manning sat still, just watching as I built his sandwich. We exchanged a smile right before Tiffany came in, set the sodas down, and reached across the island to pluck some avocado from the sandwich. "Are you from here, Manning?" she asked, taking the seat next to him.

With a frown, I took a fresh avocado from the fruit basket. Tiffany never made her own food, so she didn't respect the art of presentation.

I cut into the gnarly skin as Manning eyed the knife in my hand. "Want me to do that?" he asked.

"I do it all the time."

"Los Angeles area," he answered Tiffany.

"Really?" she pressed.

"Sort of. Pasadena."

"Do you have family here?"

"No."

I pretended to mind my own business. It hadn't crossed my mind to ask where he was from. I placed a slice of sourdough bread on top of the sandwich, cut it down the middle, and admired my work. In two halves, the sandwich nearly toppled over.

"You might not be able to hear it, but my stomach's grumbling," Manning said.

Tiffany giggled.

"Almost done." I took a jar of pickles from the fridge, gripped the lid, and twisted. Nothing happened. I flexed my hand and tried again, putting more muscle behind it. The top didn't budge.

"So no girlfriend and no family. Why Orange County? When did you move here?"

Manning took the jar from me, popped it open, and handed it back. "When I turned eighteen. I like the weather."

"I loosened it for you," I said as I concentrated on selecting the best pickle in the jar.

"I know," he said.

"What do you like to do for fun?" Tiffany asked.

"What d'you mean?" Manning cracked his neck, his eyes conspicuously on the sandwich, as if it might grow legs and make a run for it.

"You're annoying him," I said to Tiffany.

"*I'm* annoying him?" she shot back. "What do you know about anything, Lake?"

I ignored her. For some reason, making Manning's food had made me brave. Invincible. I had something he wanted. Once I was happy with the placement and position of everything on the plate, I slid it across the counter.

Manning grabbed the sandwich and dug in.

I watched, rapt, as he finished half in four bites.

After swallowing, he took one long swig of soda, his Adam's apple bobbing up and down. He must've downed half of it. "This is the best sandwich I've ever had."

The way I grinned, I probably looked like an idiot, but I didn't even care.

"I told you she makes a good sandwich." Tiffany leaned over and bumped her shoulder against Manning's. "Didn't I tell you?"

Manning nodded and wiped his mouth on his shoulder sleeve. I handed him a paper towel.

"Are you in college?" Tiffany asked.

I couldn't believe she was so brazen—touching him like he belonged to her. Asking him personal questions. I'd put up with my sister for sixteen years, but suddenly I found her unbearably obnoxious. "Are *you*?" I asked.

"Shut up, Lake. Why don't you go play with your dolls?"

My face heated. Manning looked between both of us as he chewed.

"I don't play with dolls," I told him.

"You have stuffed animals on your bed," Tiffany said. "You're like a five-year-old—"

"No, I'm not," I said in a panic. I didn't need Manning thinking I was any more childish than he probably already did. "Mom put those there. I don't even like them."

"Just go away already," Tiffany said.

Manning chewed his food calmly, but when he spoke, his words were sharp, delivered in a level, deep voice that left no room for argument. "I told you before, don't talk to your sister like that."

We both shut our mouths, but Tiffany glared at me. I felt it, even when I looked away.

"You must not have siblings," Tiffany said airily, glancing sideways at him. "We fight like that all the time. It doesn't mean anything."

"He has a sister," I said, excited to be in possession of information Tiffany wasn't.

"Is she in L.A.?" Tiffany asked, giving me her shoulder to face Manning.

"No." He wiped his mouth with the paper towel and finished off his soda. His plate was empty. "I should get back to work."

My heart dropped into my stomach. It was over already? I wasn't ready to say goodbye. "Do you want another sandwich?"

He stood and rubbed his stomach. "I don't want to say no, but no. Thanks, though."

33

"Okay." I shifted on my feet. "Need some help out there?"

He raised his brows at me. Again, I noticed the flecks in his eyes, as if they were sparkling. "What are you gonna do?" he teased. "You can't even lift most of the tools out there, forget the materials."

I basked in the glow of his rare playfulness.

Tiffany followed as he left the kitchen. I went to a window at the front of the house. Manning stood at the end of the drive with her. I willed him to acknowledge me. I was greedy. I'd spent a lot of time with him today, but I wanted more.

He didn't look up, though. Instead, he said something to Tiffany.

Whatever it was, it made her smile.

3
LAKE

Just because my dad wasn't necessarily a large man didn't mean he wasn't scary. Chief operating officer at a pharmaceutical company, he was second-in-command at work and had final say on all things concerning the Kaplan family here at home.

That worked okay for my mom and me. Mom knew how to manage his temperaments, sometimes with just a simple word or gesture. She said he had a sense of humor that most people didn't get. And I just did what he said. He was my dad. He knew better than I did.

Tiffany was a different story. That night, after I'd helped Mom clear the dinner table, I passed by his study on my way to my room. It wasn't unusual for me to hear them arguing in there, but the mention of my name made me stop.

"Lake deserves a night off," Tiffany was saying. "More than that. She's been doing schoolwork all summer."

"I don't expect you to understand the value of hard work," he said calmly. "But your sister does. Don't interfere."

"One night at the Fun Zone is hardly interfering," she said.

Over dinner, Tiffany had mentioned she was taking me to the fair that weekend. Dad had shut it down, worried I was losing focus because I was still reading *The Grapes of Wrath* after two weeks.

After a weighty silence, my dad said, "Do you think I'm stupid, Tiffany? You honestly expect me to believe you want to spend a Saturday night playing arcade games with your little sister?"

"Yes," she said. Tiffany acted tough most of the time, but I heard the hurt in her voice.

"God only knows what you really have planned. Probably some unsupervised party at one of your degenerate friends' houses. The answer is no."

I frowned. Tiffany didn't have to be in there sticking up for me. She was telling the truth after all.

"She couldn't possibly be a better student, so why can't she have fun, too?" Tiffany asked. "I swear, we'll go right to Balboa and come home."

"I don't believe you. And I tell you something, if I'd ever lied to my father, I would've gotten a beating for it."

"Go ahead, then. Beat me."

With a gasp, I put my hand on the doorknob to intervene. Fear made me hesitate. I rarely stood up to my dad. I wasn't even sure how he'd take it if I did.

"Don't be ridiculous," he responded. "Your mother and I have never lain a hand on you. In fact, we let you do whatever the hell you want. All I'm asking is that you leave your sister alone. She's on track to get everything she wants, and I'll kick you out of this house before I let you drag her down."

"You're such a jerk," Tiffany said. "All you care about is Lake. If I left tomorrow, you wouldn't even notice."

"I certainly would, but you won't. You need money and a job to move out. That shouldn't be too hard, or so one would think."

My heart beat double-time. I didn't want Tiffany to leave. She could be difficult, yes, but I liked knowing she was in the next room. I knew no matter what, if I really truly needed her, she'd be there.

I jumped back as Tiffany blew out of the study and upstairs. After a few seconds, her door slammed. I wasn't sure what to do—comfort her or keep my distance.

Mom appeared from the kitchen, wiping her hands on a dishtowel. "Everything all right?"

"They got in a fight," I said.

She glanced toward the staircase. "Give your sister some space," she said, turning back. "She'll calm down."

"Lake?" Dad called. "Get in here."

I had no reason to be nervous, but my mouth went suddenly dry. Tiffany was both stupid and brave for regularly picking fights with my dad. I didn't consider myself either of those things.

I peered into the study. Dad sat at his desk, tinkering with his new computer. We were only allowed in there when he was home. He had important papers and files that couldn't be disturbed, and as of a few weeks ago, we were most definitely not to go near the study. He'd purchased the IBM he said was worth more than me. After a month of debate over whether he actually needed a personal computer, he'd let me go with him to pick it out. He'd spent two days just setting it up, and that night, he'd let me watch as he'd moved icons around, opening them, showing me what he'd called "the future in a box."

I crept into the room.

"When will you get your summer school grades?" he asked, rubbing the bridge of his nose. "It's unacceptable that we have to wait at all."

"Not for a couple weeks," I said. "But I'll get an A-plus in both classes."

"You're sure?"

"Yes."

He breathed in so deeply, his chest expanded. With his exhale, he relaxed back into his leather chair. "That's my girl. What would I do without you?"

I furrowed my brows. "What do you mean?"

"Just that I don't think I would've survived another emotional teenager. You're like me. Focused. Logical." He leaned his elbows on the desk. "Now, let's talk about the reading list. You're falling behind?"

I wasn't as dramatic as my sister, but I hadn't considered I might be more like my dad. If I was a little of both, where did that put me? "This book is just longer than the others," I said.

"You had no trouble with *Catch-22*. That's a big one."

"Because I liked it."

"You liked it?" For whatever reason, that seemed to surprise him. "So did I. But not liking a book isn't a reason to hold up the whole list."

I recalled my conversation with Manning earlier about reading what I wanted, not what was required. "Maybe I could take a break and read something for fun."

"There'll be a lot you won't want to read in college. Just push through, Lake." He turned back to his computer, effectively dismissing me. "Besides, I'd like you to finish so I can give you my own list."

That was my summer in a nutshell. I didn't need to ask why it had to be packed with schoolwork; I already knew. USC wasn't looking for the type of student who finished *some* or *most* of her reading list. They wanted the ones who went above and beyond. Who had a second list. And it wasn't that I didn't want to do it—I loved to read. But maybe Manning and Tiffany were right. Would it be so bad if I did something that wasn't mandated by my dad, like picked up a book that interested me or took a night off?

"I want to go to the fair," I said. "With Tiffany."

He inspected the bottom of the handheld bulbous device that attached to the computer—a *mouse*, he'd called it, which had made me giggle. "I already said no."

"I've been working really hard, Dad. I did summer school, I've been reading or studying non-stop, and next month, I'm volunteering to be a camp counselor again. Shouldn't I get to have a little fun before summer ends?"

He looked up. "You know who has fun? Your sister. Do you want to turn out like her, no job, no money, living with us after high school? She had a chance to read the same books and get the same education you are, but she chose to goof off instead."

At times, his disappointment in her seemed unfair. As long as I could remember, he'd expected little of her and a lot of me. I was just fulfilling his expectations—wasn't it possible she was doing the same?

Before I could decide whether or not to defend her, he sighed. "You can go to Balboa and that's it. Come straight home after."

I smiled. "Thanks, Daddy. I'll finish the book by then, promise."

I went directly from his study to knock on Tiffany's door. Her music was up loud, so I had to pound a little harder.

"Go away," she said.

"It's me."

"I know."

I entered, even though Tiffany might eviscerate me, to tell her the good news.

She lay on her bed, a pillow over her face. "What do you want?"

I stayed by the door in case she threw anything. She'd once broken the receiver of her touchtone because Dad had blown up over the phone bill. I couldn't tell if she was crying. Usually when she did, it was loud enough for all of us to hear. Tiffany didn't really see the point of crying if nobody knew about it.

"Dad's letting us go out Saturday night."

"I should've just had you ask in the first place. Duh. You always get what you want."

I'd tried to do something nice, and now I was the bad guy. "Because *I* actually had something to bargain with. I'm doing well in school, so I get to ask for things. Maybe you should try to do something, too."

She grabbed the pillow and flopped it on the bed next to her. "Like what?"

"I don't know . . . get a job?"

"I barely got through high school."

"You're exaggerating," I said. "Your grades just weren't up to Dad's impossible standards. You should just try to find something, even if it's part-time."

"Where?"

I rubbed my nose. "How about Nordstrom? You spend enough time there anyway."

She blinked up at the ceiling. I thought I saw a hint of a smile. "At the mall the other day, this guy asked if I was a model. Maybe I could do that."

"Like . . . as a career?"

"Um, have you heard of Claudia Schiffer?" she asked. "Or Linda Evangelista? She doesn't wake up for less than ten thousand dollars a day."

Tiffany was beautiful, there was no denying it. Truthfully, I couldn't think of anyone I knew personally who was prettier than my older sister. But I wasn't sure I could picture her walking the runways like the models in her coveted magazines. "I think you have to be, like, five-eight," I said. "Or at *least* five-seven like Kate Moss."

"I *am* five-seven." She balked at me. "You and I are the same height."

I wasn't getting into that argument again. Mom had measured us both months ago, but despite the evidence, Tiffany insisted she wasn't a half inch shorter than me. "Maybe you could model for Nordstrom, like in their catalogues," I suggested.

"You think?" Her eyes lit up. "Then I'd get free stuff."

"I don't think you get free stuff," I pointed out, although I wasn't sure. "Do you?"

"You get an employee discount, so it's practically free."

"So you'll try then? Maybe go down there and see how it works?"

She didn't answer. I picked up the CD case next to her stereo. Gin Blossoms. The bands she listened to always had strange names. Like Pink Floyd. Was Floyd a person or a thing? If it was a thing, was it always pink, or did it come in different colors? I wanted to ask but she might've noticed Manning's shirt, too, and then she'd want to know why I cared. But if it meant not embarrassing myself in front of him again, then I'd take that risk. "Do you know who Pink Floyd is?"

"Yep," she said.

"Do you have their CD?" I asked.

"I might have a tape I took from this guy I used to see. He was into them."

"Will you play it for me?"

"What am I, your *servant?*" she asked but smiled. "Maybe later. Where'd you hear about them?"

She must not've noticed Manning's shirt after all. "At school."

"Of *course.* I hate when good stuff goes mainstream, you know?"

I didn't know. "Are they new?"

43

"No. Even Mom and Dad know Pink Floyd. But when high school kids start talking about it, then it's really not cool."

I guess Tiffany had forgotten she only graduated high school a year ago.

She sniffled, staring up at the ceiling.

"Are you okay?" I asked.

"Why?"

"Because of what Dad said."

"Oh. Yeah. He can be such an asshole."

I put the CD down and went to sit on the edge of her bed. "He just has a bad way of showing he cares."

"Whatever," Tiffany muttered. "Honestly, it could be worse. I could be you."

"*Me*?" I asked. "What's that mean?"

"At least he mostly leaves me alone." That was true. Dad and Tiffany fought, but he'd stopped trying to get her to do most things. She no longer came home by curfew or pretended she didn't drink or paid for her own gas—that had lasted less than a month. "But you," she continued, "he'll be on your case nonstop for at least six more years, all the way through college. It's only going to get worse as you start applying to schools."

I didn't think of it like that. I was lucky to have someone who cared as much as I did, more even, about getting me in to the school of my dreams. "Maybe once I get in to USC, he'll back off both of us," I said.

"Have you thought about any other schools?"

Her hair looked soft, fanned out over the comforter. I ran my fingers through it. "Not really."

"Maybe you should just to be sure. There are a lot more options than 'SC."

I shook my head. "It's always been my first choice."

"I know." She looked away. "As long as it's what *you* want, and you're not doing it just for Dad."

She sounded concerned, and that didn't happen a lot. But she'd grown up in the room next to mine; she knew I had a drawer full of USC merchandise and that Dad and I had toured the campus once a year since I was ten. "It is."

She turned back to me. "By the way, Manning's coming to the fair with us."

My fingers stilled in her hair. "What?"

"He's so serious. I was hoping he'd ask me out, but when he didn't, I told him about Saturday and he's never been to Balboa Island. Can you believe it?"

I needed to blink or swallow. I just stared at her with a dry mouth. An evening with Manning excited me, but were they going on a date? No. He hadn't asked her, and brave as Tiffany was, she didn't want to seem desperate. That's what she'd said earlier about making the first move, anyway. "What about Brad?"

"Who?"

"The guy you were hoping would call."

45

"Oh." She shrugged. "I talked to him this afternoon. I'm not sure how I feel about him."

I didn't ask if that had anything to do with Manning, afraid she'd say yes. How would I respond to that?

She sat up. "Isn't Manning *gorgeous*? I should hang around you more often. You're good luck."

My neck and cheeks flushed. I loved my sister—she probably knew me as well as my mom. Regardless, hearing her call Manning gorgeous made my ears hot. I'd thought he was handsome before she'd even met him. Didn't that count for something? Just because I didn't fawn all over him didn't mean it was okay for her to.

"I can't believe he's from Los Angeles," Tiffany said. "It sounds so glamorous."

"Pasadena's outside of L.A."

"Guys my age just don't get me, you know? It's bad when you have more experience than a guy."

"What do you mean?"

Tiffany smiled a little, watching me. "Sex."

My face got even hotter. I didn't know what to say. Last year, I'd aced an AP English test most of my classmates had flunked. I could recite Pi to the fifteenth digit. I'd made Principal's Honor Roll the last two years. But on this topic, I knew hardly anything. I didn't hang around with any girls who'd had sex yet. They weren't in my classes. They didn't belong to the clubs I did. They were like Tiffany. "I don't want to know," I said. "I'm not interested."

"You will be soon." She grinned as she looked over my face, which was surely red. I could never hide my blushing. "I started that stuff around the time I was your age."

A knot formed in my throat. What did that mean—"stuff"? I mean, I knew the logistics of it. At least, I thought I did. I tried not to think about it, though . . . sex. Girls like me worried about different things.

"Manning just looks like he knows what he's doing," she added wistfully.

That made me think of his hands, how they'd enveloped my waist and my forearm earlier, of his fingers, the way they'd set my skin prickling. I didn't want him to touch Tiffany the way he had me.

I bent my leg under me, picking at my sock. "So he said he'd come to the fair?"

"Yep."

"What about dad?" I asked. "I doubt he'd want you going out with one of the workers."

"Imagine how he'd react if I brought home someone who's older *and* a construction worker," she said.

I didn't understand her sudden, strange smile. "So then maybe you should think about, uh, not going out with him."

"Why?"

"If it'll make Dad mad . . ."

Tiffany pulled me down onto the bed, hugging me as she laughed. "You have so much to learn about

47

life. Don't you realize part of Manning's appeal is that he'd piss Dad off? A blind person could see that, Lake."

It was lot to wrap my head around. In one afternoon, everything about my small, easy world had changed. Tiffany was talking to me about sex. I'd met Manning, who fascinated me beyond my understanding. And the three of us were going to the fair.

But I couldn't shake the feeling that even though I'd met Manning first, for some reason, Tiffany thought he belonged to her.

4
LAKE

Tiffany thought she had the better room between us and didn't often let me forget it. That's because she didn't know what she was missing. My window opened to a flat part of the first floor's roof. Saturday night, I crawled through, sat, and pulled my knees up to my chest to wait.

Already, Tiffany was breaking the rules. She'd told Dad we were getting a ride with her friend Sarah instead of Manning, who was on his way to pick us up. I didn't like lying to my dad, but to spend time with Manning, I was willing to do it.

I set my chin on my knee. I'd been ready for hours, not that getting ready meant the same to me as it did to Tiffany. I'd put on shorts and Converse before running a brush through my hair. My fitted, pink-and-purple paisley tee came from Wet Seal. I never shopped there, but it was a hand-me-down from Tiffany. She'd been in our bathroom for an hour doing her hair and makeup, but that wasn't unusual.

I'd been to Balboa Park lots growing up. It was a small amusement park on the water. It'd never sounded romantic until now. It was known for its Ferris wheel, games, and chocolate-covered ice cream bars with sprinkles. There were always young couples holding hands and making out. I'd always thought that was gross, two people French kissing against a wall where others could see. I wouldn't have minded holding Manning's hand, though.

Headlights appeared at the corner as a white truck pulled up outside. I got off the roof to knock on the bathroom separating Tiffany's room from mine.

"What?" she asked.

I opened my door and leaned in. "I think he's here."

Her hair was coiled around a curling iron. The drawer between our sinks had been pulled all the way open, sagging as if it were about to fall out. It held countless lipsticks, all kinds of eye makeup, bobby pins, compacts, and more. Up until recently, the only interest I'd had in that drawer was the urge to organize it. I'd never wanted to play with makeup like Mom and Tiffany. They knew just how to apply lipstick, dab perfume, shop designer, balance in high heels. All that made their beauty rituals more intimidating than exciting.

Tiff looked at me in the reflection of the mirror. "Go tell him I'll be right down."

"What if Dad says something?"

"Like what?" she asked. "Just lie."

He might stop me on my way out and ask if Sarah was out front. Or want to make sure she wasn't drinking—he'd done that with Tiffany's friends before. Then what? I'd omitted the truth so I could go tonight, but I wasn't sure I could lie to his face. If I got caught scheming with Tiffany, I'd be grounded for good. Then again, these next few minutes might be the only time I got alone with Manning tonight.

I went downstairs. The foyer fed into the living room, where my parents sat on the couch watching some action movie. Their backs were to the windows overlooking the front yard. I tiptoed past.

"Lake?" Mom called, looking over.

"We're leaving for the fair," I blurted.

I couldn't see my dad from where I stood. "Where's Tiffany?" he asked.

"Finishing her makeup."

"What's Lake wearing?" I heard Dad ask.

Mom playfully rolled her eyes at me. "Shorts and sneakers, Charlie. Hardly party attire."

She turned forward again. Every second I stood here was less time talking to Manning, but if I sounded too eager to leave, Dad might suspect something. The clock in the entryway ticked. A car exploded on the TV screen.

"Fine," Dad said. "Home by ten, all right?"

I was relieved, but not off the hook until we were driving away. "Okay," I said on my way out the door.

The truck was parked at the curb of the lot next to ours, the construction site. It looked like an older model, but it was clean. A large, shadowy figure leaned against the driver's side.

I smelled smoke before I saw the cigarette. "Manning?"

He turned his head but didn't speak.

I pushed some hair off my face. I should've brushed it one last time. Because it was long, it got tangled easily. "Tiffany will be ready soon."

He took a long drag of his cigarette. The little orange tip flared before he dropped the butt on the street and stamped it out. "Come over here."

I went to stand next to him. The glare of my parents' TV flashed in the window. I still worried they'd look out and see me standing with Manning, but not so much that I wasn't going to do it. "Is this your car?" I asked.

"Yeah." He put his hands in his pockets. "Sorry about the smoke."

I shrugged. "I don't care."

"You should. It's bad for you. Anyone offers you one, say no. All it takes is that first time, and you're hooked. For life. Got it?"

I nodded as if I hadn't been told so a thousand times by teachers, parents, PSAs on TV. I didn't have the guts to try it, but that didn't stop me from being curious. "I'll say no," I promised.

"Good. Did you finish the book?"

"I had to if I wanted to come tonight."

"Yeah? How was it?"

"Depressing. I probably should've watched the movie."

"But you pushed through? Just to go ride a Ferris wheel?"

To spend an evening with you, I wanted to say. I didn't have the guts. "No. I don't go on the Ferris wheel."

"How come?"

Something like that, you could fall off at any time, I was sure. It probably happened all the time. I didn't want to admit I was scared, though. "I get sick."

"You throw up?" he asked.

"*No*. Gross."

"What then?"

I nudged the curb with the toe of my sneaker. The ashes of his cigarette were like silver confetti on the concrete. Big, dark Manning would've blended right in with the night if not for his bleach-white t-shirt.

"If you're scared, it's okay to admit it."

Tiffany had snuck me onto a pendulum ride at a carnival when I was little and I'd peed my pants, terrified. My Dad had spanked her and we'd gone home early. "I don't think *scared* is the right word . . . I just don't trust it."

He checked his watch. "What's your curfew?"

"How do you know I have one?"

He raised his eyes to mine. "You don't?"

I wished I didn't. Not that I planned to stay out all night with my sister and him, but it bothered me that Manning might think I was childish. "Ten," I said.

"Your parents know I'm taking you guys?"

"No."

With a grunt, he tilted his head toward the sky, but quickly looked back at the house. Sawdust and cigarette smoke lingered in the air, but standing close to him, I mostly smelled men's deodorant and soap.

"How about the bumper cars?" he asked.

"What?"

"Are you afraid of a little turbulence?"

I smiled. "No."

Tiffany came outside. In the porch light, her blonde hair yellowed. Her denim shorts were a few inches shorter than mine, her ponytail and hoop earrings swinging. For all the time and effort it took her to get ready, she looked breezy. Confident.

Manning kept his eyes on the pavement as she approached.

"Why're you guys standing in the dark?" She was chewing gum. "Hi, Manning."

"Hey." He pushed off the side of the car, rounding

the hood to open the passenger's side door. "Should we get going?"

Tiffany and I followed. There was no backseat in the truck, just one long bench. I didn't even have a limb inside when Tiffany cut in to climb between Manning and me. Considering his size, I wasn't even sure all three of us would fit, but that didn't turn out to be a problem. Tiffany slid as close to Manning as she could get without sitting in his lap. "Oh, I want to make one stop," Tiffany said when he started the car.

He sat back and looked over at her. "Where?"

"There's this party—"

"We're not going to a party," he said.

"But Lake's never been to one." She looked over her shoulder at me. "It's huge. I bet even your loser friends will be there."

Mona and Vickie actually looked up to Tiffany. There was no reason to call them losers except that they were my friends, not hers. "Dad specifically told us not to," I reminded her.

"Five minutes. I just want you to see what it's like."

Manning pulled away from the curb. "She doesn't want to."

"But she will. Soon. And it's better if she goes with me her first time rather than her friends." She pointed to an upcoming stop sign. "Take a right here. It's on the way."

Manning stuck his elbow on the window ledge and steered with one hand. Tiffany's knee knocked against Manning's every time the truck bounced. She murmured directions to him. With each turn, envy grew in me, unwelcome and unfamiliar. I couldn't stop watching their legs. What would it feel like, to have Manning's jeans scrape against my bare outer thigh? The hair on my legs prickled to life. I should've shaved all the way up my leg. I didn't always, since the hair on my thighs was fine and blonde. But Tiffany's smooth, tan skin made me realize mine was white and furry. I angled my offensive legs toward the car door, away from the cozy couple.

"I can't shift," Manning said.

"Oops." Tiffany peeled her shoulder from his, but her knee stayed put.

Manning kept a strong grip on the steering wheel. His forearms were all dark, thick hair and corded veins, his skin brown from working in the sun.

"Turn here, on Marigold," Tiffany said. "See?"

Parked cars lined the curb all the way up and down both sides of the block. People loitered on a lawn in an otherwise quiet neighborhood. Tiffany said my friends might be here, but what if they weren't? What if Tiffany ditched me as we walked in the door? I'd never been to a party for reasons that had nothing to do with my strict dad—I had no desire to get drunk and stupid. It was dumb how Tiffany and her friends wore hangovers like gold medals. But that didn't mean I wanted to stand alone in a corner drinking water.

Manning pulled in front of the driveway and put the car in park, looking past both of us into the party. A group of seniors stood by the mailbox with red cups in their hands.

I looked back at my sister. I didn't want to go in. Even though everyone there would know Tiffany, they wouldn't know me. They'd try to get me to drink. I'd be embarrassed in front of my classmates, in front of Manning.

A varsity water polo player leaned over and puked in the street, ten feet from the truck. His teammate picked up a cheerleader by her waist. She squealed and squirmed as he threatened to drop her in it.

Manning watched it all and finally said, "We're not going in there."

"Why not?" Tiffany asked, sounding genuinely confused.

He shifted out of park.

Tiffany grabbed his arm. "Lake needs this. She can't study in her bedroom her whole life."

"Let go of my arm."

Tiffany pulled back. "But——"

"If you want to go inside so bad, I won't stop you. Your sister and I will go to the fair. How's that sound, Lake?"

"I don't care about some lame high school party," Tiffany said defensively. "I'm doing this for her."

He drove away. "You don't know what your sister wants."

Manning was right. Either Tiffany didn't know or care what I wanted. But *he* did.

Tiffany glared at Manning. I braced for an explosion. She didn't respond well to being told no. It didn't happen often, not since our father had learned she'd fight him tooth and nail to get what she wanted, and if she lost, find a way to do it anyway.

She sulked, but she stayed quiet. I almost couldn't believe it. Since when did she give in so easily? Wasn't she going to wear Manning down until he agreed to go back to the party?

Gently, she touched Manning's bicep. "Are you mad?"

After a few tense seconds, Manning shook his head. "We can have fun without all that," he said.

She relaxed against the back of the seat. We rode in relative silence the rest of the way, except for the low din of the radio. Manning turned it up slightly for one song. When it ended and the DJ said the name, I committed "Black" by Pearl Jam to memory.

Manning parked, and we walked across the street toward the entrance. The Fun Zone at Balboa Park was one long strip with an arcade, bumper cars, and the biggest draw—for *some* people—a Ferris wheel.

Tiffany stopped at the first carnival game we walked by and clasped both hands around Manning's bicep, her fingers barely touching. "Win me a stuffed animal," she pleaded. "I know you can."

I responded before Manning could. "I thought you said stuffed toys were childish?"

Tiffany turned to me with a slight sneer. "Not when your boyfriend wins it for you. Come talk to me when you have one of *those*."

The insult was so ridiculous, I couldn't stop myself from laughing. "He's not your boyfriend," I said, glancing at Manning. "Just to warn you, sometimes you have to repeat yourself with Tiffany. She doesn't always *get* it."

Tiffany's face paled. She'd certainly said worse to me in front of my friends, but as soon as the words were out, I regretted them. She wasn't dumb, but Dad treated her that way sometimes.

"It's so typical of you to act like you're better than everyone," Tiffany said, looking like she was about to lunge for me.

I didn't think that about myself. Tiffany was the one who did what she wanted, breaking rules and hurting people but still getting everything handed to her. "I do not."

"Do to. I did you a favor bringing you along tonight—"

"Hey." Manning put his hands on her shoulders, drawing her backward. "Take a minute. Both of you."

Tiffany balked. "She's implying that I'm an idiot."

He turned Tiffany around to face him. "So what?" he asked. "Is it true?"

"*No.*"

"Then who cares?"

I just stood there while they looked at each other, having some kind of moment.

"Yeah," she said finally, looking over her shoulder at me. "Who cares what you think?"

Manning sighed and ran his hand down his face. "Why don't you go get us some ice cream, Tiffany? Give each other a second to cool off."

"Ice cream?" she asked.

He arched an eyebrow. "You went on and on about it when you invited me."

She took a step back and sniffed. "Oh. Okay. Will you come with me?"

He glanced briefly at me and back. "No. You can take care of yourself."

Even with Tiffany's back to me, I could sense her disappointment. If Manning kept telling her *no*, it could be good for her. Either she'd learn she couldn't always get her way or she'd get bored and move on.

Tiffany left in pursuit of something sweet.

Once alone, Manning turned his full attention on me, putting us face to face.

"You're good with her," I said, looking up at him.

"Why's that?"

"Normally, she does the opposite of what people tell her."

Manning ran a hand through his hair, left it sticking up. I could see him better now in the bright, colorful, blinking lights of the fair. He'd rolled up the sleeves of his white t-shirt, the cuffs hugging his muscles. He had a cigarette behind his ear again, stark against his soft black hair. He could've walked straight out of *The Outsiders*, which I only knew because it'd been on last summer's reading list.

"She does it on purpose." I was beginning to notice how Manning's voice, always deep, seemed to get even lower when he was about to lecture me or impart wisdom. "Don't let her goad you on. You're young, and you're better than what you just said to her. Aren't you?"

I suddenly felt half my size. Although my dad was demanding, I didn't often get scolded. Not like Tiffany. I was the good kid. "What does being young have to do with it?" I asked. "I don't need a babysitter."

"Your sister's different from you. She's impulsive. She says what pops into her head, but you think things through. I see you. I see you thinking."

I had no idea what to make of Manning. He was hot and cold. Sometimes, I thought there was something between us, but then he went and treated me like a five-year-old. "Why do you care what I do?" I asked.

He laid a heavy hand on my shoulder and it spanned all the way to my neck. His fingertips brushed my skin, his palm warming me. He shook me gently, my entire body swaying. "I'm not attacking you. All I'm saying is be better than that. We're at a fair. This is supposed to be fun."

"For who? I feel like I'm tagging along on one of Tiffany's dates."

Manning took his hand back and crooked one corner of his mouth. "Trust me. If this was a real date, you wouldn't be here. She asked if I wanted to go to a carnival with you guys, and it sounded like the kind of innocent fun I haven't had in a while." He nodded backward. "So let's go on a ride. How about the Ferris wheel?"

I widened my eyes. "I told you I can't."

"Nah. You're scared, but I'm going to go with you. You'll see there's nothing to be afraid of."

My heart raced. Not just because Manning had touched me. Not just because he was looking out for me. Mostly because no part of me wanted to get on that ride, but I was considering it just to have some time alone with him. "What about Tiffany?"

"She'll find us."

He strolled away. I had to hurry to keep up. Two kids darted between us, nearly knocking me over. "We can do the bumper cars," I said. "Those are way more fun."

He looked sidelong at me. "What scares you about the wheel?" he asked. "You don't like heights?"

It wasn't that. I sat on the roof all the time. So what *was* holding me back? I glanced at the ground as we walked. "I don't know. What if something happens up there and you can't get out? How do you know it won't break down or the seat won't fall off?"

"You just have to trust it."

"Trust what?" I asked, pointing to the operator. "That guy looks like he's in high school. How can he be in charge of lives?"

Manning laughed. "I think I understand the issue."

I furrowed my brows. "What issue?"

"You don't like to feel out of control. I'm the same, but you have to know when to let go or you'll drive yourself crazy."

Sometimes, Tiffany called Dad a control freak. Nobody had ever referred to me that way, though. I was diligent about my schoolwork and when it came to my future. Did that mean I needed to be in control? I wasn't sure.

We stopped at the ticket booth. Manning leaned into the window and said, "Two adults." He looked back at me. "You are an adult, right?"

I frowned. "I don't know—"

"Fourteen and over," said the ticket taker.

He handed her a ten. "Then two adults."

"I mean, I don't know if I can do it," I said. "I don't want you to spend the money if—"

"Don't worry about the money. But try to look younger next time. Save me a few bucks."

Because his brows weren't as low and heavy as usual, I was pretty sure he was teasing me. He didn't do it often enough for me to know.

As we got in line, I tilted my head back to take in the behemoth of a ride—the creaks of the machinery, the gum-chewing, spaced-out attendant, the kids tilting their car in the sky to see how far forward they could make it swing. Adults just stood around, smiling at them. You had to be a certain height to ride. Manning was probably twice that. Unfortunately, I came in with plenty of room, too.

If I was going to get on this thing, I had to distract myself. Already, my stomach felt uneasy. There were a lot of people out tonight, waiting in line for corndogs, getting quarters for the arcade games, spinning postcard stands outside a souvenir shop. "What would you normally be doing tonight?" I asked Manning.

"Some nights I have class. Since it's the weekend, I'd probably be at a bar."

"Oh." College and bars—that was a whole other world to me. "What's your class for?"

"Criminal justice. I want to be a cop."

Even though my mouth popped open, I hoped I didn't look as shocked as I felt. I couldn't picture him in uniform. "Like a police officer?" I asked.

"Yeah." He scratched his chin. It might've been the first time he didn't look at me like I was from a different planet. "Why?"

I wasn't sure how to respond. He was mysterious. Rugged. Hard to pin down. To be honest, he seemed more like an outlaw than a peacekeeper. I didn't want to insult him, though, so I tried to think of something else to say.

"Lake?"

I blinked. The way he said my name brought me back to Earth. I thought I could be on a rocket to the moon and come crashing back in an instant when he called for me. "What?"

"You can tell me what you're thinking. I don't have a lot of friends, but the ones I do have, I like them to be honest."

Was it dishonest not to volunteer information? People did it all the time. Tiffany'd sneak out in the middle of the night and pretend she hadn't the next morning. Or Mom would take us shopping and hide the receipts from Dad. I looked away. Every time the Ferris wheel stopped, seats rocked.

"I'm honest." I couldn't think of many times in my life when I hadn't been.

Manning tilted his head. He'd returned to looking at me like I was a science project. A very young one. "I know you are."

"How?"

"I just do."

"All right." I fidgeted under his stare. "What was your question?"

"Why'd you look so surprised that I want to go into law?"

"You don't really look like the type. I mean, physically, you definitely do."

Almost imperceptibly, he raised one eyebrow. But it was true. He looked strong enough to take on criminals. Capable. "What other way is there?" he asked.

"Something about how you are. Inside." When I realized I was staring him straight in the eye, I stopped. I'd forgotten, for a moment, how intimidating he was, how much his opinion was beginning to mean to me. "I'm sorry."

"Never apologize for being honest."

"Does that hurt your feelings?"

He laughed, and I relaxed a little. "No. It would take a lot more than that."

"I don't know anything," I said. "I haven't been around that many policemen in my life."

"That's a good thing."

"Why do you want to be one?"

"Cops have a lot of power. They can abuse it, or they can make a difference in people's lives. Not everyone has the resources to help themselves. They need someone on their side who does."

"You want to help people?"

"I do."

I felt bad if I'd implied he wasn't the type to make a positive difference. It was obviously important to him if he planned to spend his life helping others.

"How about you? You thought about what you want to do yet?"

"A little." I wished I knew with the same confidence he did. I studied hard to get into a good school because it was expected of me, and because top universities were bound to have students who cared about more than drinking, gossip, and sex like

66

my sister and my friends. I just wasn't sure what I'd do once I got there. "I'm going to college."

"Well, that I guessed," he said. "I bet you'll like college. It's different from high school. But what about after?"

"My dad says I can major in business, law, or medicine."

He scratched his chin. "Your dad says? What's it to him?"

That answer was easy. "Everything."

"I see. So he wants you to do something big."

"Pretty much."

"And what do you want?"

"I guess I want to love what I do, I'm just not sure what that is yet. It doesn't have to be for money as long as it's worthwhile."

Manning looked forward, squinting over everyone in line in front of us. Just when I thought he'd change the topic, he said, "That could be lots of different things. Things you never even thought of." He scratched his chest. "How about if I get you some books from the library? You make me a list of your interests, and I'll see what I can find."

I smiled. If nothing else, it was a reason to see him again. "Okay."

"Next," the attendant said, holding his hand out for our tickets.

My stomach dropped. Manning had done a good job distracting me, but the ride loomed huge. A couple kids with windswept hair spilled out of their car, which swung back and forth long after they'd left. The ride had one seat for two people and a bar that came down. That was it. Not even seatbelts.

Manning handed the kid our tickets and climbed on the ride. He stood in the center of the carriage, hunched to keep from hitting his head on the roof. "See? It's no big deal. It's designed to be able to swing and move." He nodded for me to get on. "I'll be by your side the whole time."

I took a step. Adrenaline jolted through me. He was going through a lot of trouble to make me feel safe. That meant he cared, didn't it? And if he cared, he wouldn't want me to get hurt. I repeated his words in my head: *I'll be by your side.* With a shaky inhale, I wiped my palms on my shorts and walked toward the pile of metal parts that was supposed to carry me into the sky.

"Wait," Tiffany cried. I looked back. She waved two colorful spools of cloud-like cotton candy at us. "I'm here. Wait." She shoved one of the confections at me, pushed me out of the way, and jumped into the car with Manning. "How's that for timing?"

I looked from her to the cotton candy. "What?" I asked.

She plopped onto the plastic bench. "The line for ice cream was too long."

Manning looked at me. My hands began to shake with relief, but I couldn't deny my disappointment. What could he say? What could *I* say? There wasn't room for three people, and Tiffany would surely make a scene if she didn't get her way. Some of the parents waiting for their kids looked over. "What am I supposed to do with this?" I asked.

"Eat it, silly." Tiffany tried and failed to pull Manning onto the seat with her. "What are you doing?" she asked him. "She won't get on. She's afraid of heights. Come on."

He sat and pulled the metal bar over their laps. As the wheel moved forward, hot tears pierced the backs of my eyes. Something about all of this was beginning to feel cruel and unfair, and that made me feel helpless. Maybe that was what Manning had been talking about earlier—injustice.

"You got a ticket?" the attendant asked me.

"Oh. No." There was no way in hell I was getting on without Manning, I retreated and ran right into the person behind me. I whirled around, backing away. "Sorry. Go ahead."

Manning and Tiffany rose into the night sky together. Neither of them looked back at me.

5

MANNING

If someone'd asked me a week ago what a typical Saturday night looked like for me, it wouldn't've involved any of this. A Ferris wheel, pink cotton candy, and a pair of girls, one of which was only sixteen.

The wheel churned forward and stopped a few times. Tiffany tore off some cotton candy and put it in her mouth. I didn't know what I should expect during twenty minutes alone with her, but she'd become shyer without an audience.

"I don't know what my sister told you, but I'm not stupid," she said gently. "I can get a job, but nothing's really interested me so far."

"She didn't say that."

"She's annoying. Sometimes she doesn't even do anything and she still annoys me."

It wasn't a word I'd use to describe Lake, who was relatively quiet compared to Tiffany. "How come?"

"It's like she thinks she's better than me. Just the way she talks or the things she does."

"Yeah but what?" I asked. "What does she do?"

"She just, like, gets straight A's and it's all my parents can talk about for a month. It's lame. If I'd really wanted to be a nerd, I could've been, you know? I'd rather enjoy my life."

I looked Tiffany over. That might've been true to some degree, but I didn't buy all of it. "You don't think your sister enjoys life?"

"Everything she does has a purpose. She only takes piano lessons to be 'well-rounded.' And so she doesn't disappoint my dad like I have."

Up until this moment, I'd only really seen Lake as smart, driven, and curious. Maybe because I'd only really seen Lake. I hadn't stopped to wonder how many dinners Tiffany must've sat through hearing about Lake's accomplishments. "I'm sure that's not true."

"It is." She shuffled her feet on the floor of the car. "Whatever."

The wheel jerked into motion, sending us higher. "I think Lake looks up to you," I said.

"Why would she?"

"You're her older sister." If I'd been better at expressing myself, I would've told her how much it bothered me to see siblings not getting along. But that wasn't something you thought about until you'd lost one, and then it was too late for that kind of lesson. "Cut her some slack. She probably just wants you to be nice to her."

Tiffany scowled. "Nice?"

"Yeah. Like inviting her to come here. That was nice."

Her expression eased as she twisted her lips. "I see. Okay. Maybe."

A girl in the car above us laughed loudly at something the man with her said. She launched forward to kiss him. Tiffany noticed and smiled.

I preferred Tiffany this way, without all the drama. It made me uncomfortable when she was forward, the way she'd been in the car on the way over. I wasn't sure how I felt about her. With long blonde hair and even longer legs, and blue eyes a shade icier than her sister's, she was attractive as hell. I just wasn't all that attracted *to* her. Her attitude'd put me off that first day.

I should've probably walked away. I would've by now if I hadn't felt so confused the past few days, and since I'd really only existed since Maddy's death, nothing more, feeling anything was a welcome change. Losing my little sister had brought on the kind of darkness you don't ever really come back from. Even day to day, there wasn't much to my life. I went to work. Construction was good for me, it kept my hands busy, but it was hard. The men I worked with had seen shit, too. Some of them were ex-convicts, and others probably should've been behind bars—I'd almost gotten into it with some of them on Friday when I'd warned them not to catcall the girls. Then, I either spent my nights at the community college with other overworked, tired classmates, at a bar drinking by myself, or at home. I preferred it that way, I guess. I wanted to focus on graduating so I could be in a position to help others the way they'd helped me when I'd needed it, even though I hadn't deserved it.

Lake was the only person I'd come across since Maddy who still hadn't seen anything bad out of life. She was good. You could sense it just being around her. Not yet jaded. She had dreams, and she believed they'd come true. She was easy to talk to, ambitious, thoughtful. None of that meant she was uncomplicated. That day we met, when she'd sat on a curb with *The Grapes of Wrath*, I could tell she was having a hard time concentrating. I remembered Maddy reading a lot, but I'd forgotten that expression she made when she was trying to figure out a new word or when something went over her head. Lake made it, too. There were layers to her you might miss if you weren't paying attention.

My sister's death had turned my world dark, but Lake was light. By her age, I'd done all sorts of shit—drugs, alcohol, sex. Lake seemed so far away from that. Pure, naïve, like Maddy would've been. I'd have seen to it. Maybe wanting that in my life, someone to look over, to shield from the bad stuff, was wrong considering she was sixteen. Then again, if I'd done a better job of that with Madison, she might still be around to do things like this, to take in the night sky from the top of a Ferris wheel. To taste dyed-pink sugar melting on her tongue. To ask her big brother for advice.

"What do you want to do after this?" Tiffany asked.

I looked over at her, wondering how long I'd been in my trance. We were moving now, going in circles, the breeze warm on my face. "Take you home," I said.

"I don't have a curfew."

"Lake does."

"Oh. Yeah."

People became pins stuck in a 3D map as the buildings below us got smaller, more like a model of a fair than an actual one. The ocean stretched on one side of us. Carnival lights reflected orange, purple, green, and red on the water by the dock. But there wasn't anything but black beyond that.

"We could just drop Lake off." Tiffany put her hand on my thigh and left it there, as if deciding her next move. "Drive around for a while."

If this'd been a date, I would've put my arm around her, pulled her close, kissed her. If I gave her what she wanted now, she'd give me what I wanted later. I wasn't in the business of turning down sex from pretty girls. And Tiffany *was* pretty. A California beach girl, the kind men dreamed about. No doubt she was also experienced. I wouldn't have to go slow with her. Not that I minded going slow sometimes. I might've liked being with a woman for more than sex if I'd ever found it. Had Tiffany had that before? Did she want it?

I put my hand over Tiffany's to see how it'd feel. It didn't answer anything, but it didn't give me more questions, either. Maybe that was good. I was pretty sure if I tried to hold Lake's hand, I'd feel something about it. We'd both be worse off for it.

With the reservations I had, hand-holding was as much as I was ready for tonight. "I'll take you home after this," I said. "Wouldn't want your dad to worry."

"He wouldn't," she said softly, looking up at the sky. "Not about me."

I got the feeling this was the real Tiffany. That her bravado was a front for some insecurities that probably came from her dad. She needed someone in her corner. "You really think that?"

"We don't get along so well," she said. "In case you didn't pick that up."

I was beginning to. "That's a shame."

"Look how pretty the stars are," she said.

Even though the shift in topic was sudden, it didn't stop a lump from forming in my throat. I kept my eyes forward. The fucking stars. That was a place reserved for Maddy. I wasn't willing to go there. "What's pretty about them?"

She looked at me funny. "What kind of a question is that? They twinkle. They're . . ." She couldn't come up with anything else. "They're just pretty. Did you look?"

"I've seen them."

"So if you're going to drop me off early . . . when will I see you again?"

I didn't have an answer. I stretched my arm along the back of the seat. She took it as an invitation to move into my side. "I'll be back on the lot Monday."

"I don't mean like that. I was hoping we could, you know, go out."

I knew what she'd meant. I could just say no. I didn't want to lead her on. But there was no reason, not one, that I should ever see Lake again if her sister wasn't around.

As the wheel took us around, silence stretched between us.

I didn't tell Tiffany I'd see her again.

I didn't tell her I wouldn't, either.

6
LAKE

Standing under the Ferris wheel, watching it go round and round, made me ill. I did it until I lost track of Manning and Tiffany, then crossed the pathway and sat on a step eating tufts of cotton candy while I waited.

A pair of ripped blue jeans stepped in front of me. "Hey."

I looked up into sharp, crystal blue eyes that were a trademark of the very good-looking, very popular Swenson brothers, Cane, Corey, and the one blocking my view, Corbin. Blond hair curled out from under a Billabong hat that sat low on his head, its rigid bill almost shadowing his face.

Corbin was closest to my age. He stood with a skateboard behind his head, propped lengthwise on his shoulders, wheels out. He'd covered the underbelly in stickers. "Don't you go to my high school?" he asked.

Even though I was fairly sure he thought I was someone else, I nodded.

He tapped his chin. "You have, uh, stuff . . ."

Quickly, I wiped my face with my sleeve. "Thanks."

"And your tongue is blue." He grinned. "Why aren't you at that party on Marigold?"

I sat up a little. "Why aren't you? I'm sure all your friends are there."

"I was. It's no big deal." Absentmindedly, he spun one of the skateboard's wheels with a long finger. A cartoon sticker of a naked woman peeled at one corner. "So you know who I am?"

I blinked back to his face. "Corbin."

"What's your name?"

"Lake."

"Cool. You skate?"

I ate more of my cotton candy. "No."

"Surf?"

Tiffany and I had gone to a few surf camps over the years. I could barely stand. Tiffany was better, but she preferred dry land for sunbathing with her Walkman and magazines.

I figured I'd surfed more than the average teenager, so I shrugged. "Kind of."

"You should come out with me and my brothers sometime. We could use some chicks in the lineup."

"Maybe."

"You here by yourself?"

I still wasn't sure if he thought he was talking to someone else. I hadn't seen Corbin with any specific girl I could remember, but guys like him always had a girlfriend. "With my sister."

"Who's your sister?"

"Tiffany."

"Kaplan?" He swung his skateboard in front of his legs and laughed. "Yeah. Makes sense. I see the resemblance now."

I had no idea why that was funny. It happened a lot, people finding out we were sisters and mentioning "the resemblance." Whether or not it was just something people said, I usually took it as a compliment. With Corbin, I wasn't so sure. "How do you know Tiffany?"

"From school. And she's friends with my older brother."

"I'm a year below you."

"I know."

Only then did my heart skip a beat, once I realized the most popular guy in school really *was* talking to me. Corbin had noticed me. Our high school wasn't that big, but there were hundreds of students.

"I've seen you around," he added with a smile. It was a nice smile, too—since he was so tan, his teeth looked unnaturally white. Everyone knew who the Swensons were. Their dad worked with mine, so the name even came up a time or two at the dinner table. I could see why girls liked the brothers with their perpetual surfer tans, their tall and lean muscular bodies. If I'd thought much about talking to Corbin, I would've guessed it'd be a bumbling, muttering, stomach-butterflies kind of thing, but it wasn't. I liked him, and I liked that he didn't make nervous.

The Ferris wheel stopped. I tried to see around Corbin, then through his legs, past his skinned knees, but he blocked my view with the skateboard.

"We went to camp together when we were kids."

"What?"

"Young Cubs," he said. "You know? Camp?"

I looked up at him again. I remembered, but it seemed so long ago. We were different people then. Kids. "I'm going back this year as a junior counselor," I said.

"Cool. I'll be there for a day to coach a baseball game, show them how it's done." He winked. "I'd stay longer, but I have baseball camp that week."

"Sounds fun," I said, leaning so far to the side I almost toppled over.

"Looking for Tiffany?" he asked.

"She's on the Ferris wheel."

"Alone?"

Manning's height gave them away. He was at least a head taller than any adult, and in a crowd of kids, he verged on giant status. "She's with a friend."

"Who? Sarah?"

Manning's eyes locked on Corbin's back, and he came over, Tiffany on his heels.

The cotton candy made my mouth tacky. I ran my tongue over my teeth, worried they might be blue. I was suddenly aware of my breathing, of the fact that my shorts had ridden up when I sat.

"Hello?" Corbin asked.

"Huh?" I asked without looking away from Manning.

Corbin checked over his shoulder just as Tiffany spotted us.

"Hey, Corbin," Tiffany said, looking a bit off balance in her platforms. "Looking for me?"

"Nope." Corbin turned back to me. "Just saying what's up to your sister."

Tiffany grabbed Corbin's forearm, pulling him away. "Have you met Manning?" she asked. "He's in college."

"Cool." Corbin dropped the skateboard on the ground and planted a big, fat Airwalk sneaker on it to stop it from rolling away. "I should get back to my friends. We'll be surfing Huntington Pier all next week, Lake. South side, in the mornings. If you want to come watch."

I waved. "See ya."

Manning watched Corbin skate off, his eyes narrowed. "Who was that?"

"Corbin Swenson," Tiffany and I answered at the same time.

"What'd he want?" Manning asked.

I shrugged. "Just saying hi."

Tiffany tightened her ponytail. "Are you friends?"

Both Tiffany and Manning towered over me. For just getting off a carnival ride, neither of them looked very happy. Had they fought? I could almost convince myself I'd heard something like jealousy in Manning's questions just now.

I pulled my knees against my chest. "I wouldn't say *friends*. More like acquaintances."

"Oh." Tiffany sat next to me on the stairs. "I went out with his brother once. I always thought Corbin had a crush on me."

That was a typical thing for Tiffany to assume. "So?"

"So just keep in mind that some guys might look at you and see me."

"Meaning?"

She brushed some of my hair off my neck, glancing up at Manning as if checking to see if she should proceed. "You and I are different. I cut class. Went to bonfires on the beach, drank, smoked weed."

I wanted to relax into the feeling of Tiffany's fingers in my hair, but I worried an insult was coming. "And?"

"And you do homework for fun."

I made a face. "I do not."

"Just don't be naïve. Corbin's a nice guy, but he can have any girl he wants, which means he probably does. He's a heartbreaker."

Maybe I *did* focus too much on school, and maybe I had no clue about boys like Tiffany thought. But I didn't want Manning to know that. "I'm not as innocent as you think," I said.

Tiffany laughed and hugged me from the side. "Yes, you are."

Okay, so she was right. I'd experienced embarrassingly little—less, even, than my friends, and they were mild compared to most girls at my school.

"Innocence is good," Manning said, sounding funny, as if his teeth were clenched. "She has the rest of her life for parties. For punks like that guy."

Tiffany ruffled my hair as if I were her child, not her high school-aged sister. "What should we ride next, Manning?"

"You want that stuffed animal?" he asked.

Her eyes lit up. "Do you really think you can win it?"

I tasted metal. It was as if I wasn't even there. They acted like they were my babysitters. I should've paid more attention to the guys Tiffany had dated in the past. How long did it take for her to lose interest and move on to the next? To me, Manning seemed as untouchable as the glossy celebrities taped to Tiffany's wall, so why did she get to touch him?

Manning and Tiffany turned to the booth with the stuffed animals, ignoring me. As long as I sat there being my quiet, innocent self, they could carry on with their lives.

I stood, brushing dirt off the seat of my shorts. "I'm going to see if Corbin wants to ride the Ferris wheel with me."

Manning turned around first. "What?"

"I said—"

"I heard you." He glanced at the ride and back at me. "I thought you were scared."

"I was, but you said I could do it, so I think I'm ready." I wasn't ready. Not to go it alone, and if I wasn't riding with Manning, I might as well be by myself.

Manning's expression didn't change, but he cracked a knuckle. "Maybe it's better to wait."

I crossed my arms over myself. When Manning ignored me, everything hurt, but when he looked right at me, like now, the contents of my stomach turned upside down, as if my insides were doing acrobatics. "I'm going to do it now. With Corbin."

"You *like* him," Tiffany teased. "I don't blame you. All the Swensons are totally gorgeous."

Manning put a firm hand on my shoulder, physically keeping me where I stood. "I'll go with you."

I cocked my head. I had no intention of hunting down Corbin—maybe he wasn't as intimidating as I thought, but I wasn't about to approach one of the most popular guys in school for a kiddie ride. Manning didn't want me to do it, though, and fighting with him was better than being ignored by him. "You already went. With Tiffany. Remember?"

His hand warmed the entire left side of my body. By the look on his face, the sarcasm in my comment didn't amuse him. "Do you want to ride it or not?"

"Yes. With Corbin."

Manning shook his head. "You're too young to be alone with someone his age—"

I opened my mouth to protest, but Tiffany beat me to it. "It's a *Ferris wheel*, not Seven Minutes in Heaven. Don't you remember being sixteen?"

"Too well. That's why I'm saying no."

"You can't tell me no." I scoffed. "I'm not a kid, and even if I were, you still couldn't tell me no."

He looked at me a moment, then pulled me to his side with one strong, heavy arm around my shoulders. It wasn't an intimate gesture. I wouldn't be surprised if he took a page out of Tiffany's book and rumpled my hair. Still, I was pressed against him, surrounded in his soapy scent, his hip against my side, his enormous hand squeezing my shoulder.

"I'm going to win you a prize," he said. "Anything you want. Pick it, and I'll get it for you. No matter how big it is."

He no longer sounded angry or jealous or even cautious, and that was a first. Was this how Tiffany always got what she wanted from men—by doing what they told her not to? "Really?" I asked.

"What's your favorite animal? Frogs?"

I couldn't help my laugh. As kids, my friends and I used to catch and release toads in the street. But I wasn't a kid anymore. "Whose favorite animal is a frog? They're slimy."

He shrugged one shoulder and pulled me along with him toward a hit-the-target game. "So, nothing slimy then."

Manning paid the carnie, received three baseballs and missed the target three times.

I smiled at his effort. Just that alone was worth being happy over. "It's okay if—"

"No it's not. I promised you." Manning called the man over again. "Another round."

I almost missed Tiffany's glare, but when I caught it, I just about told her to take a hike. To go find Corbin Swenson, her number one admirer. Being the center of Manning's attention was as heady as I thought it would be, and I didn't want to share the spotlight.

Tiffany turned away on her own, though, leaving us to go talk to the man operating the booth.

Right as I turned back, Manning reared back and pitched the ball in a perfect line. It bounced off the cardboard around the target.

"These games are rigged," he muttered.

"Don't worry about it," I said.

"I *am* worried," he teased. At least, I thought he was kidding. He spoke lightly but also focused intensely on the target. Maybe something did have him worried.

Gearing up for his second throw, his t-shirt sleeve rode up his bicep. The skin there was whiter than the rest of his arm, smoother. His muscles strained the fabric.

Tiffany glanced over at us.

Manning missed. "God d—" His neck reddened and after a deep breath, he snatched the third baseball. He threw it so hard, everyone jumped when it smacked the target. Manning wiped his hairline with his sleeve and nodded. "There we go."

The attendant barely looked away from Tiffany. "Pick any from this side," he said, gesturing toward a wall with small stuffed animals and toys.

"What if I want a bigger one?" he asked.

"You have to hit the target twice."

"I don't want a bigger one," I said immediately, taking a step closer to Manning. I looked up at him, proud. I'd never seen anyone hit the target directly, not even my dad, and he'd played this game before.

"You sure?" he asked. "Because I'll—"

"I'm sure." I pointed to the first thing I saw, a white-and-blue pelican. "That one."

Manning leaned over the counter to wrestle the toy off the wall. "It needs a name," he said.

My cheeks flushed. "I don't name my stuffed animals."

He passed it to me. "I think you should."

I hugged it to my chest. Put on the spot, I couldn't think of anything clever. "Well, it's a bird, so . . . Birdy?"

"Birdy," he repeated, looking me in the eyes. He ran a thumb over the head of the stuffed toy, his knuckles brushing the neckline of my shirt, the top curve of my breast. He didn't seem to notice, but I shivered. "You cold, Birdy?"

It fit perfectly in my arms, the first thing a boy had ever given me—and not just a boy. Manning. "Birdy's warm." I nodded. "Birdy's perfect. Thank you."

"Welcome."

"Look what *I* won." Tiffany strutted over, her arms barely meeting around the middle of a giraffe as tall as her. She grinned. "And I didn't even have to throw a single ball."

"You going to carry that thing around the whole park?" Manning asked. "We'll have to buy it its own ticket."

She laughed. "Of course not. It's as big as me. *You* are." She shoved it at Manning, who tucked it under his arm, looking much less annoyed than I felt.

When I glanced over at the Ferris wheel, Manning noticed. "Still want me to take you?"

I curled my fingers into Birdy's soft, velvety fur. I couldn't have been happier. "No, it's okay."

Tiffany took Manning's free arm and guided him away, leaving me to follow behind them. "Thank you for taking care of her," she whispered loudly. "My dad will love you for it."

"*Dad?*" I asked. "You're going to introduce them?"

"*No.*" Tiffany looked back at me, and then up at Manning. "Well, maybe. Would you, Manning?"

SOMETHING IN THE WAY

"Meet my parents." She squeezed his elbow. "You could come over for dinner."

Manning, at the dinner table? With Dad? Tiffany had brought home two guys before—an older man who owned a tanning booth and a guy with dreadlocks. Neither had lasted a week past dinner. Dad didn't even like Tiffany's friends, much less her boyfriends. He went out of his way to make them feel small, and Tiffany knew it.

"I don't think he should," I said.

"Don't be rude," Tiffany said.

"But you know how Dad is."

"How?" Manning asked.

I recited my mom's excuse for Dad whenever he insulted someone. "People just don't get his sense of humor."

"Manning can handle it," Tiffany said, trailing her fingers over the giraffe's neck. "Can't you?"

Tiffany's words from the other night came back to me. The construction workers pissed Dad off, and she liked that. Maybe she even wanted it.

"Is it all right with you?" Manning asked me.

"Why should she care?" Tiffany asked.

"Because I'll be eating dinner with your family, and she's an entire quarter of it."

"You want to come?" I asked.

He looked back at me. "Might be a good idea to meet your parents."

He said it to me, not Tiffany. He wanted to meet *my* parents. And while I should've felt uneasy about it, the idea that Manning had any interest in my life had the opposite effect.

It made my heart soar.

7

LAKE

My dad rarely took days off, unless it was for something he deemed more important than work. Not much fell into that category, but USC always did.

That was why, at four o'clock on the Monday after I'd gone to the fair, my dad and I were finishing up our annual visit to the campus. My dad proudly called me a prospective student to the other parents on the tour, and I wore an old Trojans t-shirt that'd belonged to him before he'd shrunk it in the wash.

This year felt different than our past five visits. I really *was* a prospective student now, only two years out from starting here. As college sharpened on the horizon, the students around me no longer seemed ancient. They were just a couple years older than me. I'd even gone to school with kids who attended now.

Female students wore strapless tops, cut-off shorts, and bared their midriffs. A boy rode by our tour group on a skateboard. I'd never even been on a skateboard, and showing too much skin was a punishable offense at my school.

When the guide dismissed us for the afternoon, Dad pulled me away from the crowd. "You heard what she said about starting college classes now?" he asked. "Since USC is too far of a drive, we can sign you up at a community college to get some credits out of the way."

"My teacher said a college class might be too much at my age."

"Your teacher's an idiot. It'll be Disneyland compared to where you're headed. You should have no trouble keeping up."

If he believed I could do it, then I'd try. He'd pushed me to take advanced classes all my life, and although they were hard, I'd always earned A's.

The buildings were large and named after people. Students came in and out of every door, disappearing around corners or zipping by us. "How old were you when you came here?"

"Twenty. *I* couldn't afford anything other than community college, so that's where I started, but eventually I transferred to USC on a scholarship. I graduated at the top of my class and went on to complete my MBA. Imagine what you can do starting even earlier."

I thought back to my conversation with Manning about my interests and how he'd promised to get me books from the library. "I haven't decided on a major yet. Do you think I should do business?"

"You don't have to. You can be anything you want. Doctor, lawyer, accountant."

"Mona wants to be a teacher."

"The world needs teachers," he said as we headed down the concrete path. "But we also need leaders. If you like working with children, like you do at camp, you could be a pediatrician. Then you get to spend all day doing something valuable. Saving lives."

I couldn't remember much about doctor's offices, but my dentist was in a perpetually bad mood. "Wouldn't that be sad, dealing with sick kids? What if I can't make them better?"

"If you decide to go that route, there're different paths you can take. You could be an obstetrician. Try being sad while delivering a baby."

"How many years of school is that?"

"Probably eight, including undergrad, followed by a residency. I know it sounds like a lot, but you're young. And you're lucky, Lake. Your mom and I are willing to pay for all of it so you can come out debt-free at the end. College loans are a burden, and USC is at the top as far as tuition goes. You won't have to struggle for years like I did to pay them off."

Eight years and then some. I couldn't fathom it. I'd be twenty-six or older when I graduated, which meant I still had over ten years left as a student. I'd spent my whole life hearing about USC, and how great college was—I couldn't wait to be around other people who loved school and wanted to learn. But another decade sounded overwhelming.

"Look, there's the College of Commerce and Business Administration," Dad said, pointing as if I didn't already know the sandstone-colored brick building with majestic arches. "I spent many hours there becoming the man I am today. Let's go peek inside."

On the lawn out front, a small group of students had arranged rubber mats into rows. They were dressed casually in shorts and tanks. A couple of them sat picking blades of grass. One read a book. None of them spoke to each other.

My dad held open a door, and we walked down the hall. He tried some handles. "Maybe there's a summer school lecture we can sit in on."

"What was your favorite class?"

"I don't know if I had a favorite," he said. "I enjoyed learning about strategy and operations. How to minimize costs and maximize profits." He peered into a window on one of the doors before continuing on. "You know what I hated? Advanced statistics. It's an important class, don't get me wrong, but it was damn hard."

My jaw nearly hit the floor. "You hated a class?"

"Of course I did. You think I enjoyed learning to calculate standard deviation or worrying about variance and outliers?" He looked over his shoulder, saw my expression and said, "Oh, Lake. You *do* think that, don't you?"

The way he talked about college and what was ahead of me, I didn't think there was anything he didn't miss about it. "Kind of."

He laughed. "I know you think I'm fanatical about this stuff, but I just want to give you opportunities. Do you think I work as hard as I do for any other reason than to take care of you girls?"

The truth was, I never really thought about it. I just assumed he worked all the time because he loved it. "I'm sorry, Dad. I didn't realize . . . thank you."

He chuckled, took my face, and kissed my forehead. "I'm not asking for a thank you. I'm just trying to explain that if I'm hard on you, it's because I want the best for you. I'm proud of you, Lake. You have so much potential. I want to give you every chance to realize it."

My throat thickened. I knew he was proud, but it felt good to hear him say it once in a while. "I will," I said. I had no idea how, but I'd always been a good student, always put in the time to do better, and I didn't see that changing anytime soon. "I promise."

One of the locked doors opened, and a blonde woman who looked a little older than Tiffany leaned out. "Can I help you?"

Dad turned. "Oh. Sorry if we disturbed you. We were just checking things out." He put his arm around my shoulder. "My daughter's a prospective student."

She smiled at me. "Welcome. Will you be applying to business school?"

Dad had told me a few times that in business and in life, it was important to act confident, especially when you weren't. I straightened my shoulders. "Yes."

Dad squeezed my shoulder.

"Well, I'm an assistant professor in the Business Economics department. Maybe by the time you get here, I'll have my doctorate and you'll be in my class."

"How about that, Lake?" He winked at the woman. "You already know a professor."

She laughed. "Well, not *yet* . . ."

"Maybe I'll come with my daughter, sit in on your class," he said. "Who knows? I might learn something."

"And what do you do?"

"COO of a little company called Ainsley-Bushner Pharmaceuticals. Maybe you've heard of it?"

She gaped at him. "Of course I have. Forget sitting in on my class—I'll be shamelessly begging you for a guest lecture."

I might as well have left the room. My dad had a weird look on his face he didn't get around Mom, something I thought might border on flirtatious. Whatever he was doing, I didn't think I wanted to witness it. "I'm going to go outside and explore a little," I said.

"Don't go too far," Dad said, releasing me. "We have to leave soon to get home in time for dinner."

"So I know all about CEOs and CFOs," she said as I walked away, "but COO's are a bit more mysterious. What exactly do you do?"

Dad had a standard answer to that question, but his tone changed depending on who was asking. Sometimes it was meant to end a conversation. Other times, like this one, it was an invitation to ask more. "A little of this, a little of that."

I left them in the hallway and headed outside. The sun was beginning to sink into late afternoon, turning the sky orange. The students I'd seen earlier were lying on their backs on the lawn as a bearded man wove through the maze of mats. Each had one hand on their stomach and the other on their chest.

"We'll begin each session by consulting with our bodies," he said. "Breathe from your diaphragm. Don't know how? The hand on your stomach should rise higher than the one on your chest. Inhale. Keep your eyes closed." He looked at me. "Now, exhale for eight counts and expel everything from your body that doesn't belong in this class." He looked around, nodding. "Just breathe. Your life depends on it. So does your grade."

A few people laughed. I'd gotten closer than I'd meant, but they looked so at peace.

"Want to join?"

I blinked up at the man. "Sorry?"

"We have space."

It didn't look that way. They'd created two even rows. "There aren't any mats left."

"Do you need one?"

I hadn't thought of that. I could just sit in the grass. "No, but I'm waiting for my . . ." I stopped myself from saying *Dad*. These were college students. They'd left home already. "My ride."

"So lie down until then." He gestured to the end of one row.

It was tempting. It seemed as though my mind had been going since I'd met Manning, wondering about him, or about little things like what books I *really* wanted to read or how I could get to Tower Records to buy a Pink Floyd CD. I, too, wanted to sink into the lawn and turn my brain off, send my problems into the air like balloons. With no sign of my dad, I lay down on the ground.

"We'll stay in this position for sixty seconds. You have a lot of responsibilities as students, friends, children, siblings. Don't be afraid to think about nothing for a change. Clear your mind."

It was easier said than done. My mind wandered over to the business school, and then to how Manning had asked for a list of my interests. What were those, though? I did well in math, but did I want to do it for a living? I couldn't imagine anyone did. Making people feel better appealed to me, but things like blood and surgery and medical charts didn't. I liked reading and cooking for other people. I'd been a camp counselor last year and student council treasurer of my sophomore class. None of that really added up to a profession I could think of, though. Maybe Manning would know once he saw the list.

"You can sit up now," the man said.

I opened my eyes as a breeze rustled the leaves of nearby trees. Despite being on a busy college campus, our spot on the lawn was quiet. I got up slowly, blinking to adjust to the sun. I scratched my elbow, itchy from the grass. Everyone was smiling.

"Welcome to the summer session of Drama 101." He looked at me. "I'm Professor Bronstein, but you can call me Sal."

I checked over my shoulder. My dad was outside the building but still talking to the assistant professor.

"We'll meet out here before class from now on. Once we enter the classroom, you have two jobs. To become the part you're playing, and to support one another. At times, you'll feel foolish—I guarantee it. You'll also feel triumphant, and some other stuff in between. Trusting your classmates will go a long way when it comes to getting the most out of this experience."

"But we just met, and summer session only lasts a few weeks," someone pointed out.

"Precisely. We have a small amount of time to earn each other's trust, so let's begin with an exercise. Turn to face the person next to you."

Still deep in conversation, my dad didn't seem to notice I wasn't there. Since I was at the end of the row, I could only go one way. I sat cross-legged facing a dark-haired girl. "Hi," she said softly. "I'm Les."

"I'm not actually in this—"

"Now," Sal said, "close your eyes and touch your partner's face."

Les looked as surprised as I felt. I'd met her two seconds ago, and now I had to put my hands on her? It felt like an intrusion. Neither of us moved. She stifled a laugh.

"Where?" someone asked. "How?"

"You already have all the instructions I intend to give," the professor answered.

Les and I exchanged a sheepish look before I closed my eyes.

A cold finger landed on my cheek. Les giggled. "Sorry."

"Don't speak," Sal said.

It was even more uncomfortable not being able to laugh about it. I placed my palm on Les's face, and it warmed to her cheek. I had to stop myself from also apologizing.

"Good," the professor said. "Try to read your partner this way. Tune into their emotions."

"Lake?" I heard from somewhere behind me.

"You're nervous," Les said.

"What?"

"You just jumped."

"I-I have to go." We both opened our eyes. I stood, brushing grass off my legs, and announced, "My ride is here."

Sal nodded. "See you around, then."

I waved to get my dad's attention as I jogged toward him. The blonde was nowhere to be seen. "What were you doing?" he asked, picking a twig from my hair.

"They invited me to join a class." Maybe acting was something I could add to the list for Manning. I'd only been interested in it five minutes, but considering I had no clue what else to put on there, it was worth a try. "Maybe I'll sign up for it as a freshman."

"Which class?"

"Drama."

He snorted and turned for the parking area. I hurried to keep up. "I never understood why that department was so important here. It's silly, but I suppose not everyone can be gifted enough to do the things that really matter."

That was as good of an opening as I was going to get. I scratched my head. "Um, Dad, you know . . . if drama's a big deal here, they might like to see it on my application."

"Possibly."

"Maybe I could start looking into it now. Either at school or as, like, an extracurricular."

"Hmm." He put his hands in his pockets. "You *do* need to choose some electives next year. It could round out your schedule a bit."

I didn't know what to say other than "thanks." It was rare to get what I wanted if it wasn't his idea.

Tiffany and my mom, on the other hand, got what they wanted frequently. Maybe he was finally starting to see me as an adult.

It was a win in my book.

8
LAKE

Now *this* was what summer was all about.

At ten-thirty on the Thursday morning following our night at the fair, I lay on a beach towel on the south side of Huntington Pier with my friends. It was early, but beach real estate in August was valuable.

Normally, I applied a lot of sunscreen since I burned easily. Tanning was an art I had yet to perfect. Tiffany had my same complexion and she'd gotten it down to a science. She wanted to be tan three-hundred-and-sixty-five days a year. Tonight, though, Manning was coming over for dinner. He'd be at the house in about nine hours.

I applied sunscreen to my face and chest only. Vickie, on the towel next to mine, only used tanning oil. "Can I borrow some?" I asked when she'd finished with it.

She handed it over. "You missed a crazy party Saturday night."

"I was there," I said.

Mona, on the other side of Vickie, sat up on her elbows. She looked at me over her sunglasses. "You were not."

"I was outside for a minute." I squirted oil onto my legs, wedging my fingers under the elastic leg of my one-piece to even it out. "It didn't look like much fun."

"Are you kidding?" Vickie asked. "Everyone was there. We tried rum and played drinking games."

Not everyone, I wanted to say. Corbin Swenson popped into my mind. I scanned the surfers bobbing on their boards in the water, but they were too far for me to recognize faces. "I went to Balboa Park," I said. Since they looked up to my sister for some reason, I added, "With Tiffany. She says high school parties are lame."

"Of course they are—to *her*," Vickie said. "She's not in high school."

Mona drew her eyebrows together. "Maybe they are lame."

"Oh, did you hear?" Vickie asked excitedly. "Kim left the party with Jack Firestone, and I guess they were sitting outside in his car for, like, *ever*."

I gave Vickie back her oil, lay down on my towel, and picked up my book. I read two paragraphs before my mind wandered. Jack Firestone had graduated with Tiffany. Kim was my age. They'd probably had sex. I doubted nineteen-year-olds sat in parked cars with virgins.

As if the sun were a heat lamp directed at me, sweat beaded on my upper lip. I liked to think I was above sex, that I had more important things to worry about. That I'd have no trouble holding on to my virginity long after my friends had caved. But last night, I'd dreamed about Manning, about his big hands around my waist, and his dark, humorless eyes that sometimes weren't so humorless around me. I'd woken up in the middle of the night and masturbated. I'd never done it thinking about someone I knew.

All morning, the thought of Manning had come with a tightening in my belly. And it wasn't weird or bad or shameful. The opposite, actually. I liked it.

When water droplets fell onto my shins, I put down my book. Someone stood over me, silhouetted by the sun.

"Hey, girls." I recognized Corbin's voice. "What's up, Lake?"

Vickie and Mona stayed quiet. I doubted either of them had ever spoken to a Swenson. I lowered my sunglasses. Corbin held a surfboard under one arm. "Hi," I said.

"You see me out there?" he asked.

"I think so. I wasn't sure which one you were."

"The handsome one, obviously," he said, peeling down the sleeves of his wetsuit. He pushed it down to his waist. Between surfing and baseball, sports had done him well. He wasn't buff, but his muscles were cut, defined, and his skin golden-brown like his hair.

"What're you guys up to?" he asked.

"Just this." I waited for Vickie or Mona to jump in, but they just mutely stared at Corbin. "You?" I asked.

"It was a late surf today. Summer vacation and all."

He laid his short, cream surfboard upside down in the sand. The underside had a sticker of a frog smoking weed and 420 in graffiti. He shook out his hair, showering me in ocean droplets.

"How was it?" I asked.

"Decent." When he glanced at my chest, I realized my nipples were hard from the cold water. Turning to the other girls, he said, "I'm Corbin, by the way."

"Hi," Vickie said.

"Hi," Mona repeated.

I could see we weren't going to get much else, so I said, "These are my friends, Vickie and Mona."

"Cool." He nodded at me. "Wanna take my board out?"

Remembering my fib about my surfing experience, I hoped my sunglasses hid my blush. "I'm working on my tan."

"You got a hot date tonight?" he asked.

"No," I said, almost defensively.

"You want one?"

Mona gasped and Vickie giggled nervously, looking from Mona to me to Corbin and back again.

I studied Corbin, trying to tell if he was joking around. He grinned pretty hard but waited for an answer. If one of the most popular guys in school was asking me out, I'd be an idiot to say no, but I didn't feel that tightening in my stomach like I did for Manning.

Corbin squatted next to me. "Come over tonight. Watch a movie."

He really was as good-looking as everyone said and surprisingly nice, too. All last year, he and his circle of friends had seemed larger than life, but sitting right next to him, all I could think was how different he was from Manning. Corbin was golden, sunny. Manning was dark, shaded. Despite the fact that Corbin looked strong and healthy, Manning still dwarfed him, maybe because Manning's presence was even larger than his body. But even if Corbin were dark and large and sexy like Manning, I'd still say no. I wouldn't miss tonight's dinner for anyone. I never knew when I'd get time with Manning.

"I can't," I said. "Sorry."

He smiled crookedly. "Another time then."

"Sure."

"I'll give you a call. Cane has Tiffany's number." He stood, picked up his board, and flashed us a wave. "Nice to meet you, girls. Lake . . . I'll see you at camp, if not before."

"Later."

109

Once he'd walked away, Vickie pinched my elbow.

I yanked my arm away. "Ow. What was that for?"

"Since when do you know Corbin Swenson?"

"Since when do you *turn down* Corbin Swenson?" Mona added.

I rubbed my arm. "I met him the other night at the Fun Zone."

"But I saw him at the party."

"He must've done both," I said. "Not so dorky now, am I?"

"Um, yes," Vickie said. "You are. Because you said no to a date with a Swenson!"

The girls giggled, and I couldn't help from joining in. "They're just people, not gods."

"Did you not see him with his shirt off?" Mona asked. "You're mental."

"We're having a family dinner tonight." It was the truth, and it was better than the real reason I'd said no to Corbin: I'd rather spend my evening with an older construction worker.

"But you didn't just turn him down—you totally blew him off. You could've said you were free tomorrow or the next night."

Vickie rolled her eyes. "This is why you're single, Mona. Lake's playing hard to get."

"She doesn't know how to do that," Mona said. "She doesn't even wear makeup."

I rose onto my elbows. At some point, everyone I knew had started wearing makeup, as if they'd all gone and taken a course on it without me. I guessed that had to do with looking sexy. Up until now, I'd had little interest and even less knowledge in attracting boys at school. They tried to get away with dumb things like looking up our skirts or chewing gum in class. Most of them cared more about videogames or sports than learning anything of value. "What's that got to do with it?"

"Just that you don't care about these things," Vickie said. "You're what we call, a late bloomer."

Mona laughed like it was some kind of inside joke. "Maybe she's not so late if she's catching Corbin's eye. Or maybe she was just born with it. Like, it runs in her family."

It was ridiculous enough that I almost went back to my book, but then again, it wasn't entirely off base. My dad liked to brag about how he'd beaten out lots of other suitors for my mom's attention. I didn't doubt it. My mom was Miss Orange County when she was younger and had competed to be Miss California. I saw the way men looked at her in the supermarket, the way my male teachers paid attention when she came to parent night. Mom commanded nearly as much male attention as Tiffany did. If there were a gene for that, Tiffany definitely had it—and she'd gotten it from my mom. Maybe I had it, too—though it might be dormant.

It was late afternoon by the time I got home from the beach. I dropped my towel and bag by the base of the stairs. "Mom?" I called.

"In the kitchen."

I found her looking in the oven. "How's it going?"

"Right on schedule." She stood up and eased the door shut. "I might need an extra set of hands later, though."

She never asked Tiffany, who had no interest, for help in the kitchen. When I didn't have schoolwork to do, I usually enjoyed cooking with my mom, and tonight would be even more special. "I just need to shower."

"How was the beach?" she asked. "You got a tan."

"Did I?" I inspected my arm. It looked a little red to me. "It was fun. We got milkshakes at the end of the pier after."

She smiled. "Hope you left room for pie."

I hadn't forgotten. Last night, Mom had walked me through making a pie for tonight. I couldn't wait to see Manning's reaction. "I'll come help when I'm ready," I said.

I went up to the bathroom and turned on the shower. I pushed my regular products aside. Tiffany hid her expensive shampoo and conditioner on the back of the shelf, even though she warned me all the time not to use them, and I never once had . . . until today.

After carefully reading the instructions on the back, I washed my hair twice. Then, I saturated it with conditioner and shaved my legs slowly, carefully, from ankle to upper thigh. After rinsing and toweling off, I used one of Tiffany's lotions.

I'd never felt so soft and silky. I picked a sundress to show off my smooth skin. Tiffany said having a tan made you look thinner, and she was right.

After checking the hall to make sure Tiffany wasn't around, I went into her makeup drawer. I'd burned. Not badly, but my face and shoulders were pink. The sun had also darkened the smattering of freckles across my nose and cheeks. I didn't trust myself with makeup, so I kept it simple with just mascara and pink lip gloss. Despite the redness, or maybe because of it, my eyes seemed bluer. My teeth whiter. And for once, I saw what others did.

I looked like Tiffany.

———

After washing basil and slicing tomatoes and Mozzarella, I prepared five Caprese salads. Not knowing which would go to Manning, I took extra care to drizzle the olive oil and balsamic vinegar evenly.

"Where *is* Tiffany?" Mom asked.

I didn't look up. Didn't want to lose focus. "Maybe she changed her mind about him. She does that."

113

"I hope she would've told someone. At least him. Otherwise, we're in for an uncomfortable dinner."

I smiled. "Manning's easy to get along with. It won't be uncomfortable."

The front door opened, and Tiffany breezed into the house with paper shopping bags on each arm. "Manning will be here any minute. Is dinner ready?"

"We were afraid you might not make it." Mom pulled off her oven mitts. "Is that what you're wearing?"

"Of course not." Tiffany set the bags on the kitchen table, disrupting a pile of silverware. She pulled out a package. "I got the cutest outfit." She unwrapped white tissue and held up a short leopard print tube dress. "It's like what Drew Barrymore wears in the Guess? ad."

"Oh, that's darling." Mom always said stuff like that when Tiffany went shopping. The dress was too skimpy for Mom, but she and Tiffany shared clothes a lot. "It's not too dressy for tonight?"

Tiffany shoved it all back in the bag. "We'll probably go somewhere after."

"Well, wear something over it during dinner. Your dad won't like that it's so revealing."

"Duh. I'm not an amateur," she said.

"I know, honey," Mom said as she went to the sink to wash her hands. "Your sister and I have been working on dinner for an hour. Will you set the table?"

Tiffany grabbed her bags. "*Mom*. I have exactly five minutes to transform myself."

"Then why'd you wait until the last minute?" I pointed out.

Tiffany stuck out her tongue. "Did you get wine?" she asked Mom. "He might want some with dinner."

"I got wine." Mom wiped her hands on her apron. "He can have *one* glass. No more if he's taking you out afterward."

Tiffany flurried out of the kitchen the same way she'd come in, a tornado of crinkling paper bags and blonde hair. Would he really take her out tonight? If so, where would they go? It would be late when dinner ended. Too late for me to go with them, if I'd even be invited. Tiffany and her friends hung out until after midnight on the weekends. They had ways of getting alcohol. It was Thursday, but life was one big weekend to Tiffany. She had no job to get to in the morning, but Manning did. Didn't that mean anything?

I was straightening my tomatoes when the doorbell rang. My heart stopped.

Mom showed me her oven-mitted hands. "Can you get that, honey?"

I went through the house and stood at the front door, listening. Tiffany was still upstairs getting ready, and Dad was in his study. It was just me and Manning, and that wouldn't be the case for long. It seemed unfair that even though I'd seen him first, even though he was *my* friend, I had to savor my time with him before it was stolen.

I opened the door to Manning standing on the top step in jeans and a black, collared button-down he wore open over a white t-shirt. He'd shaved and gelled his hair back. I'd half expected him to show up in his work boots, but I thought he might even be wearing cologne.

I held onto the door handle until my hand began to sweat. Manning's dark eyes mostly stayed on my face, except for the second they flashed down, all the way to my ankles. Maybe men had some kind of radar for freshly shaven legs.

"Hi," I said. *Dumb.* I wanted to tell him how nice he looked.

A cricket chirped out front as Manning white-knuckled a bouquet of pink tulips. "You look different."

I straightened my shoulders a bit and tried not to smile. "So do you."

"Are you wearing makeup?"

"A little." I pointed my foot, showing him my leg. "I got a tan."

He didn't look. I moved aside so he could duck into the entryway. One of his tennis shoes could easily crush both my bare feet. I was nearly eye-level with the flowers. It was a good guess—my mom loved tulips.

"I hope you like steak? We should've checked with you first."

"I'll eat most anything. But yes, Tiffany already asked."

That meant they'd spoken since the fair on Saturday. When? It shouldn't have surprised me. Of course, she'd had to tell him when to be here, and maybe she'd also mentioned the tulips. It occurred to me that they might've even *seen* each other.

"She called," Manning said, catching my eye. "Just about dinner and timing and stuff. That's all."

"Oh." We both looked up when we heard footfalls upstairs. Finally, I closed the front door. "Come meet my mom. My dad'll be out in a second. He usually works in his office until dinner starts." I showed Manning into the kitchen.

Mom turned around, smiled widely, and came to us. "It's so nice to meet you, Manning."

"You too, Mrs. Kaplan." He held out the flowers, but she went past them for a hug. He bent down to make it easier but was otherwise stiff. "These are for you."

"You shouldn't have." She took the bouquet. Mom had twisted her hair back from her face, and as she inhaled, a few strands fell forward. "My favorite. Thank you."

"Thank you for having me. Dinner smells great."

"I've been in here all evening, so even if you don't like the steak, say you do." Mom laughed. Nobody ever disliked her food, but she said that a lot. "Lake helped," she said, and as an afterthought, added, "Tiffany, too. She's great in the kitchen."

117

"She is not," I said. "She wouldn't even set the table."

"Lake, honey." Mom chuckled and passed me the bouquet. "Put these in water and get our guest something to drink."

I frowned. I just wanted Manning to know I'd done my part of the cooking with him in mind. But when he nodded at me and patted his stomach, I understood—he did know.

"I put some wine out on the bar," Mom told me. "You like wine, don't you, Manning?"

He hesitated. "Sure."

It didn't sound convincing. "Dad has beer, too," I said.

"It's okay. Wine is great."

I put the flowers in a vase, then went to Dad's bar and carried two heavy bottles back into the kitchen. I'd never opened wine before, though I'd seen it done plenty of times. I set them on the island and went to find the screw-looking thing Mom used. I rifled through a couple drawers before picking out what I was pretty sure was the right utensil. I had no idea how it worked, though.

"Did you grow up here, Manning?" Mom asked.

"Pasadena."

I assessed the bottle of wine. The sharp part went into the top, but the top had a wrapper around it. Did that come off first?

Manning took the thingie—a *corkscrew*, that's what it was called!—out of my hand and peeled away the foil.

"I know how to do it," I said under my breath.

"You shouldn't. You're only sixteen."

I watched closely as he stuck the sharp, coiled end into the cork. Exactly what I would've done, but when he bore down to screw it in, I was pretty sure I would've messed it up somehow. "I don't know how to do it," I admitted.

That earned me his first smile of the night. His neck muscles strained and the cork slid out with a *pop*.

I turned around to find Mom watching us. She pulsed her eyebrows and mouthed, *So handsome.*

He was. It was like our first date, me bringing him home to meet my parents. Manning moved around me, looking for glasses. I couldn't bring myself to tell him where they were, because I couldn't speak. I just wanted to watch him. Manning was here, in my kitchen, where I'd made him steak, and it was going well.

As he pulled down two wineglasses, he glanced at me. "You okay?"

I nodded. Hard. "Yes."

"Got some sun today, huh?" He winked. "Were you outside?"

"I went to the—"

I heard Tiffany before I saw her. "I'm here, I'm here," she said. "Sorry I'm late."

119

My heart fell, my smile melting. Tiffany came around the corner in her short dress and a black cardigan. She'd ripped a synthetic daisy off an old hat and stuck it in her hair. She went directly to Manning. In her platforms, she had a few inches on me and came up to his shoulder. Mom wore heels. I was the only one without shoes on.

Tiffany leaned toward him, offering her cheek, but he kissed her forehead. "They kept me entertained."

She smiled. "You met my mom?"

"Yep. Just getting her some wine."

Tiffany moved aside so he could pull a third glass from the cupboard, but he only poured two drinks. He handed one to my Mom and kept the other for himself.

Tiffany put a hand on her hip. "What about me?"

"You're not twenty-one. Other one's for your dad."

"It's fine if she has one," Mom said. "We aren't stupid; we know Tiffany drinks. At least here, we can monitor it."

Manning had the bottle in his hand, looking unsure of what to do. He set it down, so Tiffany poured her own glass.

"So, Manning." Mom took a sip. "How long have you and Tiffany been dating?"

"We're friends," he said.

I looked at the ground to hide my grin.

Unlike me, neither Mom nor Tiffany liked that answer. "I'm sorry," Mom said. "I got the impression—"

"I told you he's a gentleman," Tiffany snapped, looking away. "He doesn't discuss stuff like that."

The timer beeped. "Well, we'll leave it at that then," Mom said. She slid the steaks from the oven and set them on the counter. "Lake, go get your father."

Like most other nights, I went and knocked on my dad's study, waiting until he said, "Yes?"

"Dinner's ready," I said.

"I'll be out soon," he said without looking up from his computer. "Start without me."

If it were up to him, he'd eat in here. One wall was a library of business and law books. His desk was topped with USC paraphernalia. Against another wall stood his regal glass case of guns. "We can't. He's here."

Dad glanced up wearing his default expression, heavy-browed annoyance. "Who?"

"Manning. Tiffany's friend."

"Christ. Come get me when dinner's on the table. I'm not interested in entertaining her flings."

I didn't want Dad at the table at all. At best, he wouldn't be nice to Manning. At worst, he'd try to cut him down in front of us. Manning didn't deserve to be embarrassed. I'd have been happy to let Dad stay in here with his toys, even though it'd surely kill Tiffany a little bit that she wouldn't get to rub

Manning in his face, but Mom would never let Dad skip dinner. As it was, they'd fought about it already. Mom thought Tiffany was better off with a boyfriend. Dad didn't want to deal with it. "It's on the table already," I said. "He's been here a while."

Dad stuck his elbows on the desk and massaged his temples. "I work all damn day. I should be able to enjoy a nice, quiet meal in my own goddamn home." He looked up at me as if he'd forgotten I was there. "Go on. I'll be right there."

He made it seem as if he was doing us some kind of favor, but his response sounded more like a threat than a concession.

9
LAKE

Mom, Tiffany, Manning and I were all seated in the dining room by the time Dad came out of his study. "Why are we eating in here instead of the kitchen?" he asked before he'd even pulled out his chair.

"Because we have company," Mom said.

Manning looked surprisingly relaxed in his chair, his plate served, food untouched like all of ours. He watched my Dad.

"Daddy, this is Manning," Tiffany said.

They locked eyes finally, holding each other's gazes, a silent conversation passing between them.

"Thank you for having me," Manning said.

"I'm not having you," Dad replied, scooting his chair into the table. "My wife is. Thank her."

"He already did," Mom said softly but firmly. "You're being rude, Charles."

He glanced at her and then Tiffany before picking up a serving bowl of broccoli. "Did you cook tonight, Lake?"

Even though everyone had started eating, my fingers were laced tightly in my lap. I was the tensest of everyone, and this didn't even involve me. I wanted it to go well for Manning. I didn't need to give him a reason to stop coming around. I wasn't sure what was developing between us, but if we couldn't find out until I turned eighteen, then he needed to stay in my life two more years. "I helped with the steak and dessert," I said.

"Good," Dad said. "I like when you cook."

"I was just asking Manning about home," Mom said. "He's from Los Angeles."

"Pasadena, specifically," Manning said.

"Aside from my time at USC, never been a big fan of L.A." Dad cut into his meat. "Too diverse. Even the neighborhood the campus is in is dangerous. Too much crime."

"Jesus, Charles." Mom said. "I've told you before, you can't say those things."

"The hell I can't. This is my home."

"Daddy, *please*," Tiffany said.

My dad made comments like that sometimes, but never in front of company, mostly because it upset my mom. It was the first I'd heard Tiffany speak up against it.

Mom turned to Manning. "He doesn't mean anything by that. I'm sure you come from a lovely home."

Manning chewed and swallowed. "It was all right." He glanced away as he said it. "Nothing like this."

"This," Dad said, gesturing around with his fork, "is the result of a lot of hard work and investment in education. Do you go to school?"

"Yes, sir. At night."

"For?"

Manning had a mouthful of steak, so the table sat quietly as he chewed and then sipped his water. "I'm going into law enforcement."

"A cop?"

"Yes."

"And after that? Want to be a lawyer?"

"No. I want to help people."

"If you want to help, go to the top," Dad said. "Officers don't have any clout. They just do what they're told."

Mom cleared her throat. "Charles—"

"What?" he asked. "What now? These kids need a dose of reality. I'm just trying to be helpful."

I'd figured this would happen, that my dad would try to make Manning feel small. Knowing how much Manning's future career meant to him, I opened my mouth to interject.

"Cops do help people," Manning said before I could speak. "I've seen it with my own eyes."

Dad shrugged. "Good, then. Do that. The world needs policemen."

"More than it needs lawyers," Mom added.

Manning turned to me, maybe looking for an out. "Did you make the salad, too?"

I hadn't even told him. I smiled. "Yes."

"You should try it then," he said, nodding at my full plate.

I'd been so wrapped up in a conversation that didn't involve me, I'd barely touched my food. I took a bite of a fresh, crisp tomato, and juice dribbled down my chin.

"Where are you on the reading list, Lake?" Dad asked.

I dabbed my mouth with a napkin. "The last book."

"Perfect. I've just picked up some more I think you'll love, including a non-fiction about perfecting the college essay."

"Maybe it's time for a break," Mom said. "Summer vacation's almost over."

"That's what I've been saying," Tiffany chimed in.

"Don't be fooled. USC looks as closely at summer vacation as they do the school year. They don't accept slacking off."

I'd heard the same speech every year since I'd entered middle school. Once it was clear Tiffany didn't have a shot at USC, my parents had turned all their attention on me. "I know."

"You want to go to USC?" Manning asked.

"University of Southern California," Dad said.

"I've heard of it." Manning was beginning to look irritated. "Private university in L.A., rival of UCLA."

"We're hoping to get her started in a pre-college program next year," Mom said.

"Already?" Manning asked.

Mom nodded. "These things start early. Years before college applications. And Lake wants this, so we'll do whatever we can to get her there."

Manning shifted his eyes to me. "Why USC?"

"It's where I went," Dad said.

I sensed by the fact that Manning ignored him that he was looking for an answer from me. Throughout my childhood, I remembered my dad happiest when relaying his years at USC, as if it were some kind of adult Disneyland. I hadn't ever considered anywhere else. One of the best schools in the country was practically in our backyard.

"USC has all kinds of great programs," I said.

Dad nodded, picking up his wineglass. "It's a top-tier school."

I smiled at Dad. I never felt closer to him than when we were on this subject. "They have a football team, a beautiful campus, and a great reputation." I wanted to make my dad proud. To call myself a Trojan with the same pride he did. "And, yes, my dad's an alumnus. I can't really think of a reason not to go there."

I looked back at Manning, and my world slowed. He wasn't listening. He watched Tiffany push food around her plate.

"Did you ever think about USC?" Manning asked her. She didn't even realize he was talking to her. "Tiff?"

"What?" She looked up and blinked. "Did *I* want to go there? Me?"

"Why not?"

"It takes hard work, dedication, and planning to get in to a top university," Dad said. "Tiffany spent her time in school doing God knows what, but it wasn't any of those."

"I knew a kid who started at community college and transferred to Berkeley," Manning said. "Tiffany could do that if she wanted."

"That's what Charles did," Mom said, raising her glass to Dad. "He couldn't afford private but he worked his way up through community college."

Tiffany crossed her arms, sitting back in her chair. "Believe me, I don't want to go to that dumb school. It's like a fucking cult."

Dad pointed his fork at her. "Watch your language. You'd be lucky to be at that school rather than wasting your time here watching TV and spending my money."

"That's not what I do all day." She glanced nervously at Manning. "I'm looking at schools. I just don't know where I want to go or what to major in yet."

"Business," Dad said. "Can't go wrong with that. Once you get your degree, maybe you could manage a clothing store. Since you love to shop."

She straightened her shoulders. "Maybe I'll open my own clothing store."

"Run your own business? Do you have any idea what that takes? Discipline. Hard work. Start-up capital. That's just the basics."

I could see where this conversation was going, and even though I didn't always agree with my sister, I didn't want to see her embarrassed. "How about a fashion designer?" I suggested. Managing people wouldn't be good for her. She was more creative than us and did better without confines or rules. That was how I'd heard Mom defend her to my dad, anyway. "You'd be good at that."

She ignored me. "You act like my life is over just because I don't know what I want to do," she said to Dad. "I could be a lot worse off right now, you know. I ran into Regina Lee at the mall today."

He frowned. "Who?"

"That girl in my class who got pregnant."

I remembered the name. The story of her relationship with a math teacher had been all over the news. Things like that didn't happen at our school. It was when I'd learned the term *statutory rape*.

"The worst I did in high school was get bad grades and maybe have a little too much fun," Tiffany said. "*Regina* has a baby. She was crying to me about how she's raising it alone."

"What'd she think was going to happen?" Dad asked. "She'd ride off into the sunset with a pedophile? How much time did he get? Three years?"

"I think so," Mom said. "Statutory rape."

"Goddamn ridiculous. They went too easy on him. I would've charged him with real rape."

"They were in love," Tiffany said.

"I don't care." Dad stabbed a piece of steak with his fork. "I have plenty of friends in the legal system. If that'd been Tiffany, that scumbag'd be away so long, he'd come back a different person."

"Oh, my," Mom said, glancing at Manning. "How'd we get on this subject?" She refilled Dad's wineglass. She knew when and how to steer the conversation, especially when Dad and Tiffany were at each other's throats. "You know, Lake's off to camp soon. Are you looking forward to it, honey?"

I was about to say yes. As a kid, I'd had fun, but I'd enjoyed last year even more as a junior counselor. Young Cubs was a week-long sleepaway camp in the woods with outdoor activities and nightly campfires. But a new thought occurred to me. What would happen with Manning when summer ended? I wouldn't be able to find him at the lot during the day. It wasn't as if I could get in a car and go see him, and that wasn't just because I didn't have my license. Summer ended in just over four weeks. If I spent one of those away at camp, that only left me three with Manning. "Do I have to go?" I asked.

"What do you mean?" Mom asked. "You had a great time last year."

"But yes, you have to," Dad said. "It looks good on your application."

Tiffany rolled her eyes. "Does *everything* have to be about college?"

Dad looked at her, then Mom. "Your daughter has more attitude than an entire sorority house." He chuckled.

Tiffany scoffed, but she was smiling. "And whose fault is that?" she asked. "It's genetics."

Dad, finishing his second glass of wine, muttered, "Attitude is not genetic. There—put *that* on a sticker and slap it on your bumper." Everyone but Manning laughed. Tiffany had stickers plastered on her school supplies, her desk, her walls, and even a couple on her car. They ranged from a pink, glittery one that read "Warning: I Have an Attitude and I Know How to Use it" to a black, round one with a red "A" scratched in the center. I'd asked why she had an anarchy sticker, and she'd given me a funny look and told me it was "punk, duh." Dad said it was to piss him off.

Manning had already cleared his plate and was going for seconds. "What's this camp thing about?"

"It's in Big Bear," I said.

He nodded his approval. "Love it up there."

"It's for kids," Tiffany added. "I would die of boredom."

"I'll be a junior counselor," I said, "which means I'm going to be paired with an adult counselor and we'll be in charge of a cabin for the week. We sleep there at night and do activities during the day."

"Like what?" Manning asked.

Everybody waited. For once, nobody was talking over me. I sat up a little. "All kinds of stuff. Archery, horseback riding, canoeing, arts and crafts, fishing. We spend practically the whole week outdoors."

Manning listened with his whole body, his eyebrows drawn. It almost looked as if he wanted to go to camp himself. "I haven't been fishing since I was a kid. You get paid for this?"

"I volunteer. It's just for my college apps. But the real counselors get paid."

"Are you interested?" Mom asked him.

Manning pulled back. "Am *I*?"

"Do you honestly think he wants to spend a week of his summer with a bunch of children?" Tiffany asked.

"Believe it or not," Manning said, "I like kids."

My heart nearly burst out of my chest at the idea of it. Manning. At camp. For a whole week. With me.

"What about your job?" Tiffany asked uneasily. She must've been thinking the same thing, except that she'd be spending a week away from him.

"We're breaking soon for a few weeks while we wait on some permits," Manning said. "I don't have anything solid lined up. I'm actually looking for work."

"What do you do?" Mom asked.

Manning stopped chewing at the same moment it occurred to me—Dad still didn't know the truth about how we'd met Manning. I looked to Tiffany for help, but as the realization hit her, too, her eyes sparkled.

Manning set down his fork. "I didn't realize Tiffany hadn't told you."

That got Dad's attention. He looked up. "Told us what?"

"I work construction right now. To put myself through school." He nodded behind Dad, toward the backyard. "I'm on the crew at that house next door."

"Excuse me?" Dad asked, looking at Tiffany. "What's he talking about?"

"I'm sorry I didn't mention it, Daddy." She looked contrite. "I didn't want you to get mad."

"I told you to stay away from there." Dad's voice rose. "What is the matter with you, Tiffany? Anything I tell you, you do the opposite."

"Charles." Mom touched his arm. "Stop."

He turned on her. "Did I not say this would be a problem? That transients in the neighborhood is never good?"

"What's a transient?" I asked.

"Someone who can't hold a job because they're not skilled enough to find work."

My mouth fell open. I'd known it was coming, some terrible insult meant to drive Manning away. So had Tiffany, yet she'd invited him over anyway.

Manning took his napkin from his lap and stood. "I should go. I honestly didn't realize this was an issue."

"No." My mom's voice cut like a knife through the tension. "Sit down, Manning. You're a guest in our home, and you've been nothing but polite."

Manning slowly lowered himself back into his chair.

"Polite?" Dad asked. "He didn't have the decency to mention he worked next door. It should've been the first thing he said when he came in."

"I agree," Manning said evenly. "I thought you knew."

"You have to excuse my husband," Mom said. "Charlie's been so upset about the construction."

"I understand." Manning shifted in his seat. "We try to keep it to a minimum outside work hours. We start early when it's cool, but we rarely go past five in the afternoon."

"That's a lie," Dad said. "I've heard you during dinner."

Tiffany played with her hair, and the daisy fell out. She tried forcing it back in.

"There's construction on the house behind yours, too," Manning said. "Maybe it's that."

"This is a safe neighborhood." Dad looked between us and him. "We don't like trouble."

Worried Manning might get up and try to leave again, I interjected. "There's no trouble. I've been over there."

Dad turned his head. "When?"

"Last week," Tiffany answered. She gave up on the daisy and put it on the table. "It wasn't a big deal. I was with her."

"Why does that not surprise me?" Dad asked. "I've repeatedly asked you not to bring your sister into your drama."

"I didn't." She balked. "She went over there first."

"Last week," Dad spoke over her, "Lake was in summer school. She should've been doing her reading, not—"

"Tiffany's right," I said. It was stupid of me to say I'd been there knowing how Dad would react. Quickly, I tried to come up with an excuse. "He didn't have a lunch, so I—"

"Don't interrupt me, goddamn it."

Manning sat forward. "With all due respect, sir—"

"Do you have daughters?" Dad asked him. "Are you responsible for a family? For keeping them safe?"

Manning held his stare, something dark passing over his face. "No."

"Then stay out of this. That lot is full of men who could be dangerous. Teenage girls don't need to be around that, bringing you lunch or anything else."

Manning took a deep breath and hesitated. "Lake didn't bring it to me. I came in the house."

"I beg your fucking pardon?"

"I invited him," Tiffany said.

I nodded, scared, but willing to take the rap so Manning wouldn't have to. "We both did."

"Are you hearing this, Cathy?" Dad asked, but kept his eyes on Manning. "I'm going to have a word with your foreman. You—"

"That's *enough*," Mom said. "Charles, you're overreacting. It's just lunch for Christ's sake, and Tiffany already told me about it."

Dad turned to her. "You knew he'd been in here?"

"Briefly. For a sandwich. It's not the end of the world." She picked up her wineglass. "Maybe you should go back to your study."

"That's fine," he said, tossing his napkin on the table as he stood. "Why should I sit at my own dining table and try to have a nice meal? I hope you're happy, Tiffany."

Once he'd left the room, we all turned to look at Manning. "I'm so sorry," Tiffany said.

"He doesn't dislike you," Mom added. "That's just how he is. He works hard and a lot, so he's grumpy when he gets home."

"It's okay. I'm just grateful to have a home-cooked meal." Manning had cleared his plate a second time. He pushed his chair back from the table.

"Thank you, Mrs. Kaplan, but I really think I should go."

"But the pie," I said. I'd wanted to make Manning as happy as he'd been when he'd eaten the Lake Special the other day. *I made it for you*, I wanted to tell him, but I knew I couldn't, so instead I just said, "I made it."

"Please stay," Mom said to Manning. "Lake was so nervous about getting the pie right for company. She made it with fresh blueberries just for tonight. Even the crust is from scratch."

Manning hesitated. "But what about Mr. Kaplan?"

"Don't worry about him," Tiffany said. "He's always like that, I swear."

I stood. "I'll go get the pie."

Manning got up, too, picking up his plate. "I'll help serve. It's the least I can do."

Together, we went into the kitchen. Suddenly, my palms were sweaty. I wiped them on my dress and opened a utensil drawer to find a pie server. With my back to him, I said, "I'm sorry about my family."

"What for?" Manning asked.

"All of it." I glanced at him over my shoulder. "If my dad offended you at any point, I'm sorry."

Manning smiled warmly. "Don't worry about that, all right? I can take care of myself."

"I know, but I—" *I want to take care of you.* I wanted to protect him. Comfort him. Feed him—as many servings as it took to fill him up. I couldn't think of anything more simultaneously appropriate and inappropriate to say. A sixteen-year-old girl taking care of a grown man? It felt completely natural, like I could slot myself into his life, but it wasn't. Not yet anyway.

"Your dad's strict," he said. "I'm glad he is. He cares about you."

"Why'd you tell him you were in here?"

"This is his home. I owe him that respect."

I didn't understand it. Maybe it was a man thing.

The pie sat on a cake plate on the island. I uncovered it while Manning looked for plates.

"Use the ones with the gold leaves," I told him. "Mom likes those for guests."

"When you grow up, will you be one of those women who has specific plates just for guests?"

I smiled to myself and cut the pie as he held out a dish. We were like a couple already. A couple who could get married one day, buy a home, own special china. Tiffany would get tired of him soon, and in a few years, when I was older, nobody would even remember that Manning had once come here to meet *Tiffany's* parents. The real obstacle would be keeping Manning close. I was too young for him, I knew it, and *he* obviously knew it, but I'd be eighteen in two years. USC was close to Orange County, too. Maybe he'd come with me, back to L.A.

Was Manning the type of man who'd keep special plates for guests? I couldn't see it, but then my dad wasn't, either, and he had them.

"I don't know," I said, gently sliding a slice from the server to a plate. "Maybe. It's not just the dishes, you know. There are guest towels and guest sheets. The guest bathroom has nicer toilet paper than Tiffany's and mine."

He held out the next empty plate. "I guess for some people, it's something to aspire to."

"Not for you?" I asked.

He shrugged. "I didn't say that. But I don't know if I'll be able to afford things like that on a cop's salary. Your dad doesn't seem to think it's anything great. I guess if my wife wanted all that stuff, I'd find a way."

I looked down, breathing a little harder. The word *wife* from his lips gave me goosebumps. What kind of girl would make him happy enough that he'd marry her?

"What'd I tell you?" Manning asked. "I can handle myself."

It took me a moment to realize he thought I was upset about what my dad had said about law enforcement. I was, but luckily, Manning didn't seem to be. "Are you really thinking of coming to camp? The first meeting is next week. I can find out if they're still hiring."

He avoided my eyes, looking at the pie. "It smells good. You like to bake?"

"When it's for someone special."

His smile looked almost sad. "Guest pie?"

I nodded. Manning was a good person. He took what my dad gave him, even though he didn't have to. He put up with Tiffany. He brought my mom flowers. I hoped a small part of the reason why, or a large part, was me.

He picked up two plates, and I took the others.

"Hey, Lake?"

I stopped on my way out of the kitchen and looked back at him. "Yes?"

"Get me more information. On the camp thing. I could use the work."

"Sure," I said, my voice calm, casual, but only to hide that I felt as though his words had just set off a battery of fireworks inside me.

10

MANNING

That blueberry pie. I took my time eating it to be polite, but I could've inhaled it in under two minutes. For one, it was delicious, but also, sitting at the Kaplan's dinner table after the fight I'd just seen was fucking awkward. It wasn't as if I'd expected Tiffany's dad to welcome me into their life after one dinner. Nor did I guess he'd be such a prick.

Lake didn't see it. Not yet. She'd been embarrassed, ashamed, and tried to take the fall for Tiffany. My sister had been like that, thinking she could help an argument by interfering when she should've just kept out of it. You don't stick your hand in a dogfight—I'd told her before, but a lot of good that'd done. I could tell by the way Lake looked at her dad, she still loved and respected him. I didn't understand that. Family shouldn't mean an automatic free pass to treat others like shit. At some point, you had to recognize people for what they were.

Charles stayed in his study. As the clock behind my head ticked on, Tiffany seemed to become more agitated. It was as if she wanted something, was waiting for something. I wanted something, too—a cigarette. I'd eaten a little too much, thankful for real, flavorful food. Between school and work, I didn't care about learning to cook. I just made what I could.

Unlike Lake, Tiffany knew her dad was an asshole. But I'd met plenty of girls who'd willingly tethered themselves to jerks. Maybe it was worse for Tiffany because it was her dad. I didn't have a good track record with dads. Hell, I hated my own. I thought I saw some of that in Tiffany's eyes tonight, but she'd also watched him a lot of the meal, more than anyone else.

Lake only ate half her slice. She hadn't finished her dinner, either, while I'd cleaned up a salad, two steaks, and dessert. Was she upset or just not hungry? As it was, I worried she was a little too thin. Then again, maybe it was a girl thing. Maddy'd rather have read or explored than come to the dinner table. Or bead. I'd forgotten about her jewelry phase until it'd hit me that day on the wall, when I'd fixed Lake's bracelet. Maddy'd stay in her room for hours beading stuff like necklaces and anklets. I didn't even know where those were. At my mom's, maybe.

"Thanks again for dinner," I said because they were looking at me. "I've never had better pie."

Cathy smiled. "The crust was a little soggy, but it was a good first effort."

Tiffany shrugged. "I didn't think it was soggy at all."

Cathy covered Tiffany's hand on the table. "I've been trying to tell Tiffany the way to a man's heart is through his stomach. That's why we're teaching her to cook."

I was more uncomfortable now than I'd been with their dad at the table. At least then, I'd known where I stood. Now, all eyes were on me. Why had I come here? Partly to see how Lake and Tiffany fit into this family. I figured the dynamic would help me understand them. Neither Lake nor her sister wanted for anything. I knew the property value of their home, the prestige of their neighborhood. They had a bar and expensive wine and special dishes. I suspected those things were important to Tiffany, but what about Lake?

I wasn't in the habit of wondering these things about anyone. I went about my life and did what was necessary to put food in my own stomach and a roof over my head. I didn't need much, not even to be happy or loved. Everyone I knew was killing himself somehow. Drugs, alcohol, work, shitty relationships, boredom. They pretended things mattered that didn't. They stopped asking questions because they didn't like the answers.

I'd seen too much and lost the goodness in my life young enough to understand nothing was fair. There were no guarantees. Lake didn't know that yet, and I wanted her to keep that innocence as long as possible. Maddy? I could've protected her better. I did my best as her older brother, but if I'd known what was to come for her, I would've done more. I would've done whatever it took.

And I wanted to do the same for Lake, except that men in their twenties didn't just hang around teenage girls they weren't related to. And that left me only two options, one of which was to walk away. The other was sitting across the table from me, smiling like she had me trapped in a corner.

"Let's get the dishes," Cathy said to Lake. "Give these two some privacy."

I didn't know what in the hell went through Lake's mind. Her eyes got huge and sad. At that moment, despite the makeup I was sure she'd stolen from Tiffany, Lake was a kid at the grown-up table. She reminded me of Maddy. Not physically, they were complete opposites, light and dark, but she looked up at me the same trusting way Maddy had. Like I could tell her anything and she'd believe it.

"Are you guys going out?" Lake asked.

"It's not your business," Tiffany said. "Mom told you to clear the table."

I stood. "I'll help."

Cathy put her hand on my shoulder. "Absolutely not. Please, sit."

"I really should take off," I said. "Maybe you can walk me out, Tiff."

"Sure." She got up, exchanging a look with her mom.

I took that moment to check on Lake. She wanted to come outside, I could tell, but Tiffany wouldn't invite her and I sure as hell wouldn't, either. Best she stayed away after the fight I'd just witnessed. I nodded goodnight, hoping she'd understand in her own way. Damn if the hurt in her expression didn't ease up.

Tiffany looped her arm in mine and walked me out front. "Was it awful?" she asked. "You were so good to put up with my dad."

"It was all right. Don't worry."

"My mom likes you a lot. I can tell. Plus, I'm sure she loved that you had a second helping, and complimented her cooking . . ."

I stopped listening. The food and a ten-hour work day and two glasses of wine hit me all at once. I just wanted to lie down. There was a small grassy hill down to the curb, and when we reached the bottom, I cut her off. "Thanks for inviting me."

"I'm glad you came."

She leaned back against the driver's side door. "You want to do something?"

"I worked all day, Tiffany. I'm exhausted."

"We don't have to go out. We can stay in."

"Where?" I nodded behind me. "Here? At your parents'?"

She wiggled her foot out of her shoe and ran her toes along the inside of my ankle. "No, silly. We can drive around a little. Or go back to your place."

Ah, fuck. I inhaled deeply to give myself a few seconds to think. I was tired, but the prospect of sex always gave me a second wind. It'd been a few months, which didn't bother me until it did. Like now. She tugged on my shirt a little, pulling me closer. Her breath smelled like blueberry, like the ones Lake had used to make a pie.

For someone special. For me.

"Your heart's racing," Tiffany whispered, her lips suddenly near my chin.

I felt like I was doing something wrong, and not in a good way. I didn't want to be thinking about Lake when I was this close to her sister. I took a step back.

"What's wrong?" Tiffany asked.

"Nothing."

She was quiet a moment. "I want this, Manning."

"It's not that."

"I'm not a virgin. If you're worried I'll get attached—"

"It's not that," I repeated.

"I'm on birth control."

My heartbeat hadn't calmed any, and that comment didn't help. It just reminded me of the terrifying conversation inside about the girl who got pregnant. "Who's Regina Lee?"

"A girl at my high school who had sex with a teacher. All the parents got worked up, but he was only like twenty-four or something."

"How old was she?"

"Seventeen. Regina says she'll wait for him to get out."

The way Charles had threatened to throw his power around scared me. Who knew if it was true what he'd said about bringing more charges against the teacher? But a man like that definitely had connections, and it was clear he didn't want me anywhere near Lake. He'd been angry enough that I hadn't mentioned my work next door, but it was Lake being over there, me being around *her*, that'd really set him off. I hoped we'd be done with this house soon and get out of his proximity. Anything in the neighborhood went wrong, and he'd surely find one of us to blame.

Tiffany cocked a hip. "So is that the problem?" she asked. "You're worried I'll get pregnant like Regina Lee?"

"No."

"What then? Not pretty enough? Too fat?"

Nobody in the Kaplan family could be considered fat. "Definitely not."

"You already told me you don't have a girlfriend. Were you lying?"

She asked it casually, as if it were nothing to lie about that. I urged myself to say yes. It'd be easier to be a cheater than admit I felt protective enough of

Lake that I wasn't ready to say goodbye to Tiffany yet. Then I could wash my hands of this and drive off. Tiffany would go inside and tell her dad. He'd be thrilled.

And Lake would think I'd lied to her.

"I don't have a girlfriend," I said.

Tiffany pushed off the truck. "Then you must be, like, gay. Or mentally unstable. I'm here offering you sex. If you're not just going to come out and tell me why you don't want it, then bye. Don't call me again."

She turned and walked up the grass. I couldn't breathe—it was an unwelcome and unfamiliar feeling. I didn't let shit like this get to me. Where girls were concerned, I'd generally not found them worth the trouble. But as Tiffany got farther away, so did Lake. I wouldn't be invited back. How would that look, a grown man trying to hang around her? If I saw it, I'd put a stop to it.

Without Tiffany, there was no Lake. No monster sandwiches, no blueberry pie. But what'd I done to deserve that sweetness in my life? Nothing. And who's to say I wouldn't spoil it? I might. So probably, I should just walk away.

But it wasn't just Lake I'd been watching tonight. Tiffany was right when she'd said she was a disappointment to her dad. He put her in a box, then got mad she was in it. Not that Tiffany didn't provoke him. She did. But she was just looking for someone to pay attention to her.

"Wait."

Tiffany turned around. "What?"

"It's none of that," I said. "I'm just old-fashioned."

"What do you mean?"

I climbed the grassy incline until I stood in front of her. I took her shoulders as if bracing us both. Maybe I didn't deserve sweetness, but Tiffany, yes. She was a decent match for me. She could use someone on her side. And she came with Lake. I leaned in and kissed Tiffany on the lips. "It means I like to take things slow," I said. "I'm old-fashioned."

Tiffany blinked up at me. "Well, that's a first."

Yeah, it was. "I gotta go. But I'll call you."

She nodded at the ground. For a minute, I wondered if she even wanted me to. "Okay," she said. "Goodnight."

She turned and went back inside. I would've expected any girl to swoon after that. Maybe Tiffany wasn't fast because she was desperate to be loved. Maybe she was fast because she liked it that way. She might actually leave me in the dust if I didn't make my move. I could lose my chance with her.

I wasn't entirely sure if I wanted to fight to hold onto Tiffany.

But I did know, that was the only way to remain a part of Lake's life.

11

LAKE

I didn't move away from the window until the front door slammed and Tiffany pounded up the staircase.

I couldn't be sure what I'd seen. If Manning had kissed her just now on the front lawn, it'd looked innocent enough, a peck on the lips. What did that mean? There was no connection between them. I knew that, but did Tiffany?

I went into our adjoining bathroom and made some noise, hoping Tiffany would invite me into her room. When she didn't, I knocked.

"What?" Tiffany asked.

"Can I come in?"

"What do you want?"

I opened the door. Tiffany sat on her bed with her address book open and the receiver of her see-through, touchtone phone in her hand. "I'm trying to find something to do tonight."

"I thought you were going out with Manning?"

"Does it look like I am?"

"What happened?"

At this point, the conversation could go two ways. Either she'd kick me out and accuse me of being nosy, or she'd spill her guts. I was hoping for the guts. Did Manning ask her the kinds of questions he asked me? About music, books, fancy dishware? I couldn't picture them talking about those things. When I had Manning's attention, there was no room for anyone else.

The dial tone began to beep. With a sigh, Tiffany hung up the phone and flopped backward onto the bed. "He wanted to hang out. We almost went back to his place, but he has to work early."

My face warmed. What I wouldn't give to see where he lived, what kinds of things he thought important enough to put on his shelves. What color were his sheets? What other books did he own? Did he keep photos on his nightstand? If Tiffany went there, she'd get to see all that before me. I walked a little more into the room. "Are you going to see him again?"

She reached up and flicked the corner of her Nirvana poster. "I don't know."

I stood taller. I wasn't surprised. I knew it was coming. I'd always assumed the two other guys Tiffany had brought home to dinner had broken up with her right after, but maybe it was the other way around. "Really?" I asked.

"Don't get me wrong. Manning's super-hot, and he's nice to me. But he's like an old man. He works and has classes and goes to bed early and takes things *slow*." She yawned, turning her head to me. "I thought college guys would be different, you know? Fun and cool."

I nodded as if I understood. In reality, Manning was the coolest person I knew because he didn't care one bit about being cool. "So you're going to dump him?" I asked, trying not to sound hopeful.

"No. If I don't want to see him anymore, I just won't pick up his calls." She sat up and fixed her hair in the reflection of her mirrored closet. "You saw Corbin today?"

I was still wondering what it'd be like to have Manning call me in the first place. "Who?"

"*Corbin*. Hello? Hottest guy in your school? You saw him at the beach?"

I blinked a few times. Had that only been this morning? "Um. Yeah. How'd you know?"

"I talked to him."

"When?"

"On the phone."

"He called?" I asked.

"Yep. While I was changing. I told him to call back because we were about to have dinner."

"Did he ask for me?"

"Why?" she asked. "Do you like him?"

"*No.*" It came out defensively, a reflex more than an answer. I'd spent the last couple years wanting nothing to do with the boys at my school. Now that I knew Manning, who wasn't anything like them, I was even less interested. But Corbin seemed different, too, like he was listening when I spoke instead of trying to see down my top. "I mean, I do like him," I said. "But just as a friend. You?"

"Do *I* like Corbin? He's only seventeen. Way too young for me." She flipped through her address book. "And it's not really sexy when a guy likes you too much. That's basically why I could never date someone like Corbin."

"I thought you said he had a small crush on you a while back."

"He did, but who knows if it was more? I just think it's weird that he's suddenly interested in you."

I had no idea what to say to that. Corbin hadn't brought up Tiffany at the beach, but maybe he did still have a thing for her. I didn't care either way. "I've never liked a guy who liked me back."

Her expression softened. "Don't worry, it'll happen. Especially when you get tits." She giggled. "Sorry. Don't use that word. It's gross. My friends always say it, but that doesn't mean you should."

Tiffany didn't get motherly often, but when she did, it was nice. Like she was looking out for me. "Okay. I won't. And thanks for saying the pie wasn't soggy earlier."

"It wasn't. I ate the whole piece and you know how I am about calories."

I smiled. Giving me her calories was a compliment. I had the sudden urge to hug my sister. It'd been a weird night. Some bad things had happened, like the fighting and the possible kiss, but it could never truly be bad because time spent with Manning was time getting to know him. It was true even when we didn't speak.

And now that Tiffany was losing interest, I'd have him back. At least until school started. After that, I wasn't sure.

I was about to embrace Tiffany when a loud, sudden knock on the door made us both jump.

"Tiffany?" Dad asked.

As when anyone came to her room, Tiffany snapped at him, as if it was her programmed response. "What?" she asked.

He came in, saw me, and pointed to the bathroom door. "Go to your room, Lake."

He was angry. Again. Normally, I wouldn't question him, but Tiffany had taken some of the heat tonight that should've been aimed at me. And I was feeling defensive of her. "Why?" I asked. "So you can be mean to her some more?"

My dad looked shocked. My first instinct was to apologize, but I didn't. I stayed where I was, my shoulders squared.

"It's okay, Lake," Tiffany said. "Just go."

I looked between the two of them. Clearly, they didn't think this involved me, but it did. It was about Manning. So I went into the bathroom and pressed my ear to the door.

"What was that tonight?" Dad asked.

Tiffany didn't answer for a few seconds. "What do you mean?"

"You brought a stranger into my home. Someone who could be dangerous. You made your mother and sister go through the charade of making dinner and buying expensive wine. Why? What are you trying to prove?"

"Nothing—"

"He's a lowlife, smug construction worker who jumps from job to job. Once he's done with that house, he doesn't have to show up for work the next day. What's to stop him from rounding up his friends to rob us in the middle of the night and leave town?"

I gritted my teeth so hard, my jaw ached. That was completely unfair. Manning had been nothing but respectful tonight. He'd even made an effort to look nice.

"He wouldn't do that, which you'd know if you'd given him a chance," Tiffany said. "But you didn't. You were so rude to him."

"Oh, *please*. You don't know anything about that guy. You just want to fool around. When are you going to grow up? Do your friends get away with this kind of behavior?"

"You're overreacting."

"I don't want you seeing him again."

"You can't tell me what to do. I'm an adult."

"Then start acting like one. Get a job. Or don't, but if you want to keep living under this roof, you'll do as I say."

"Maybe I don't *want* to live here anymore."

"No? And where are you going to go with no money? If what you want is to screw around all day and shop and party, then find a husband who can afford to take care of you. I guarantee you won't find him on a construction site."

"You don't even care what I want," she said, her voice rising. "You just want me to roll over and do everything you say without questioning it. Like Lake."

"You're nothing like Lake," he snapped.

They went silent. My heart raced, as if I were there, standing in the room, only it was worse because I couldn't see anything. It was true—I did do everything my dad asked. And Tiffany did nothing he asked. I wished, for once, she would just *try* with him instead of deliberately pushing his buttons, getting him to say things to hurt her.

Dad spoke first. "I'm sorry. I didn't mean—"

"I know what you meant," Tiffany said. "I'm not Lake and I never will be. If you don't like the choices I make, then kick me out. I'm not going to stop dating someone just because you tell me to."

"I will, Tiffany. Don't test me."

"You'd put your own daughter on the street?"

"If I did, it'd be for your own goddamn good. You need to learn—"

"Fine," she screamed so loud, I actually pulled away from the door. "I'll be gone in the morning."

After a few silent seconds, Dad's footsteps pounded the floor and a door slammed shut. My breath caught in my throat. Maybe Tiffany and I had our differences, but oh my God, I didn't want her to be *homeless*. I had no idea where she'd even go. Tiffany and I had grown up in this house, a bathroom apart. I stood there so long, listening to the silence, not breathing, I started to see stars.

I let myself into her room. "Tiff?"

She was still sitting where she was when I'd left, staring at her door. "What?"

"Are you okay?"

She blinked a few times and turned to me. "Are *you*? You look like you've seen a ghost."

My hands shook. Tiffany tried so hard to be tough, but I knew she wasn't. Maybe I was the only one who knew that besides my mom. I couldn't imagine how it'd feel to be on the receiving end of those things Dad had said to her. I crossed the room and she opened her arms right as I launched myself into them. *I* was the one who started to cry.

"Stop," Tiffany said. She laid us back on the bed, petting my hair. "They're not worth crying over."

"Who?"

"Men."

"Even dad?"

"Especially dad."

I drew my eyebrows together. I wasn't sure what she meant by that. I'd heard her crying enough times after their fights. "Are you leaving?" I asked. "I don't want you to go. Please, just go apologize to him."

"I'm not leaving."

"But you said . . ."

"I've said it before. I wasn't serious, and he knows that. He's not going to kick me out."

I couldn't remember any of their arguments ending that way. It was as if Tiffany wanted to see how far she could push him. I looked up at her. "Why didn't you just tell him you'd stop seeing Manning?"

"Because that's exactly what he wants. He's trying to control me and you and Mom."

"That's not true," I said. "He just wants what's best for all of us."

"For you and Mom, maybe. Me? He just wants to pretend I never happened. His life would be easier if I weren't around."

She said the words so simply, someone else might've thought they didn't affect her. That she didn't care. I knew she did, though. How could she not? He was her dad. Even after all the fights I'd witnessed, I couldn't believe she truly thought that. "He loves you," I said. "Things are just weird right now. When you find a job, he'll ease up."

"You don't know anything, Lake. You're too young to understand. I'll never get the kind of job he wants me to. *You* will. I'm not going to be a doctor or

159

a lawyer or any of those boring things. He can't stand that he's worked as hard as he has to give us opportunities just to have me waste mine."

Tiffany didn't even try. She'd barely studied, and she'd skipped a lot of classes, especially her senior year. I didn't know if I was smarter than my sister, but I definitely tried harder. "You could do whatever you want, Tiffany. If you apply yourself—"

"Shut up," she said without inflection. "You sound like dad. He says that all the time."

"But that fight could've been avoided," I pointed out. "You said you don't even like Manning."

Tiffany blinked up at the ceiling, tilting her head. Her hair tickled my neck, but I just watched her. Her eyes roamed until she finally said, "I thought I didn't . . . but maybe I do."

My heart dropped. She couldn't just change her mind back and forth like that. "Why?" I asked. "Just because it makes Dad mad?"

"I don't know. Maybe. It just made me rethink the whole thing, like maybe I didn't give Manning a real chance."

"That doesn't seem fair, using Manning to get back at Dad."

Tiffany tore her eyes from the ceiling to look at me. She pushed me off and we both sat up. I thought she'd kick me out, but instead she looked right at me. "I guarantee Manning has done worse than that to a girl. Men don't care about women. They use them. The sooner you understand that, the better."

My stomach churned. Not Manning. He wasn't that way. When I looked at him, spoke to him, we connected. He'd given me Birdy when I was sad. He'd returned my bracelet. He'd eat anything I made. In my gut, I knew—he was a good person. "I think it's the other way around," I said gently. "I've seen guys go crazy for you, and you just ignore them."

Tiffany smiled a little. "That's how you play the game. The truth is, men think they have power, but they don't. We do. Like tonight, with Manning. When he wouldn't do what I wanted, I told him not to call me again and walked away. And you know what he did?"

My heart thumped. I knew. I tried to pretend I didn't, but I did. I'd seen it with my own eyes.

"He kissed me. He puts on a good show—for a while there, I didn't think he liked me at all. But he's just like every other guy."

I knew in my heart that wasn't true, and maybe it made me a bad sister, but I didn't tell her so. I wanted Tiffany to believe Manning was just another guy, because then she'd treat him like one. She'd get what she wanted from him and move on.

12
LAKE

Monday afternoon, I was alone in the house for the first time since Manning had come over for dinner. I didn't have to look out the window to know the crew was working next door—I could hear them.

I went into Tiffany's room to borrow a pair of shorts. I wasn't brave enough to take her skimpiest pair, but everything she owned was shorter, tighter, or lower-cut than anything in my closet. I picked some from Tommy Hilfiger and held them up to my waist in the mirror.

Tiffany'd been right the other night about Dad. The morning after their fight, Mom had made bagels and coffee, Dad read his *Wall Street Journal*, and Tiffany had waltzed into the kitchen like nothing'd happened. She'd even mentioned going out to look for jobs that day and he'd kissed her on the forehead on his way to work.

I put on the shorts. In a tank top and Converse, I grabbed my Young Cubs flyer before heading out the door. The first time I'd met Manning, I didn't remember being nervous. Now, though, as I walked to the curb, I had butterflies in my stomach and sweat on my hairline.

There was lots going on, but I couldn't see Manning. I walked through the dirt, passing under scaffolding. A man in goggles glanced at me as I ducked into the frame of the house, but he didn't stop me.

I found Manning toward the back, his profile to me, arms raised, a drill in his hands and a screw between his teeth. Goggles, a hardhat, and a red bandana around his mouth hid his face, but I would've known him anywhere.

He drilled into a wooden beam. His navy shirt rode up, tan skin slivering over his waistband, bicep muscles bulging from the effort. I covered my stomach, unaccustomed to the violent way it flipped. Manning lowered the drill to inspect his work.

"Hi."

He jerked his head to me and ripped the bandana off his face. "What are you doing in here?"

Shit. He looked not only unhappy to see me, but kind of pissed. Maybe I shouldn't've barged in like this—I mean, I could've just waited for him at the wall until his break. "I—"

"Don't ever walk onto a construction site without the proper protection." He tossed the drill onto a worktable, his boots pounding the concrete as he came to me. "It's dangerous."

"I—I'm sorry. I hadn't really thought about it."

"Why do you think we're wearing all this?" He punctuated his question by removing his hardhat and dropping it on my head. It was hot, sweaty, and heavy—and it was Manning's. With a heavy hand on my shoulder, he pushed me out of the house, walking with me. His warm, rough palm on my bare shoulder gave me that tightening feeling again, only it started lower this time, not in my stomach like before.

"Watch your step." He grumbled his words. "There are nails, and—just . . . watch where you're going."

I inhaled men's sweat and sawdust. Outside in the dirt again, he pulled the hat off my head and tossed it on the ground. I looked up at him as he removed his goggles. His black hair stuck up everywhere. Despite the heat, he wore a dark, long-sleeved t-shirt with the construction company's logo printed across the pocket. A cigarette butt peeked out the top, and dust dirtied his collar.

"Is it time for your break?" I asked.

"I already took it," he said but led me over to the wall.

"How was your weekend?" I asked.

He leaned back against the brick and took out his pack. "You're not supposed to be over here."

It definitely wasn't the greeting I'd been hoping for. "I didn't know how else to get in contact with you."

He wiped his face with his shirt, flashing his flat, hard stomach. A tool belt weighed down his pants, and my heart nearly stopped. The dark hair I'd noticed before was actually a trail leading down to his waistband, where there was more of it. He dropped his shirt, but there was still dirt on his face. "Your sister, maybe?"

I swallowed, dumbstruck. "What?"

"She could've called me if you'd needed something."

But you're my friend, I wanted to say. "You're mad I came?"

He looked into his pack of cigarettes a while, and then set them on the wall. "Was everything all right at home?" he asked. "After I left?"

"It's fine." Sure, Dad had threatened to kick Tiffany out, but he didn't do it. I didn't want Manning to feel worse than he probably already did because of that night. "I brought you something."

He looked over at me. "What is it?"

I pulled the flyer out of my back pocket, unfolded it, and gave it to him.

He used his sleeve to dry his temples. "'Young Cubs Sleepaway Camp,'" he read.

"It has all the info for being a counselor," I told him.

He scanned the page. "Except what it pays."

"Eleven dollars an hour."

"Eleven?" He sounded surprised. "That's high."

"The days are eight hours long, even though you're kind of working the whole time. Even at night."

"But you get to do stuff outdoors, right?"

"All that stuff I said, like canoeing and fishing and more. There's also campfires. You even sleep in the cabins with the kids." I was rambling, but I couldn't stop. "The cut off to apply was last week, but she said you should try anyway because she thinks they're understaffed."

"She?"

"The receptionist at the Y," I explained.

He peered at the flyer more closely. "YMCA puts it on? My sister and I used to go to our local Y after school."

By the way his stance and expression eased, I guessed that was a good thing. The problem was that camp started soon. I didn't know much about construction, but our new neighbors' house didn't look quite finished. "The next two weeks we have training and meetings for the counselors. Then we leave. It doesn't look like you'll be done in time."

He folded up the flyer. "Can I keep this?"

I nodded. "The first meeting's tomorrow night at six-thirty."

He picked up his pack and slid out a cigarette.

"You probably can't smoke there," I said. "At least not where anyone can see."

"I'll manage."

"So you'll come?"

He studied me a moment. "You want me to?"

I squinted at the house. A flock of birds formed a "V" above us. Did a cloud want to float aimlessly? Did a sky want to be blue? I didn't know. I couldn't control my want for him. It just was. "Yes," I said.

"How come?"

"I feel safe when you're around."

His eyebrows lowered. "Is it dangerous up there?"

"No, not at all," I said quickly. "I mean, there might be bears."

The wrinkles between his eyes vanished. "You think I can protect you from bears?"

"I . . ." I couldn't tell if he was teasing me or not. If anyone could take on a bear, it'd be him. "No? Maybe?"

He laughed, a rare sound that made me relax.

"Why is that funny?" I asked. "You're as big as a bear."

"Maybe to you, Birdy."

I couldn't contain my smile, even if I wanted to. "The meeting's at six-thirty."

"You said that already."

"We could meet there ten minutes early, and I'll introduce you to the director. Or I was going to have my mom take me, but I could go with you instead?"

He leaned back against the wall and crossed his arms. "What do you think, Lake, that I can just pick you up in my truck and take you somewhere?"

Yes. Yes! A thousand times yes. I had never wanted anything more. "Why not?"

He shook his head, looking away. "Have you talked to Tiffany about this?"

Like a wet blanket, the mention of my sister's name ruined the moment. I stuck my hands in the back pockets of my jean shorts. "Can I ask you something?"

"Probably shouldn't."

"Do you like her?"

He paused. "That's something I should discuss with her, don't you think?"

My throat felt dry. I didn't care. I wanted to know. "She discussed it with me."

He studied me. "Oh yeah?"

"I'm not going to tell you what she said."

"I didn't ask you to. I'll talk to her about it."

I sighed up at the sky. Nobody ever told me anything. "But it's not fair. You and I were friends first."

"Friends?" he repeated. "Do you think that's appropriate?"

I frowned. "I thought we were."

"Your sister and I are friends. You and I—yeah, we are, too. But you have to think about how that looks. When you introduce me to the director of the camp, maybe say I'm your sister's friend. You know?"

"No, I don't know," I lied, just to hear what he'd say. "How does it look for us to be friends?"

Manning exhaled deeply. "I'm older and wiser. Just trust me."

Of course I understood why we had to keep our friendship to ourselves. It wasn't anything to be ashamed of, but not everybody would understand it. That meant that to other people, there was only one thing linking us: Tiffany. "Are you going to ask Tiffany to go to camp?"

"Yes."

"But why?" I asked. "She thinks camp is for losers."

"Because it would be good for her. Think about it. She's not working right now, maybe a little aimless."

"A little?"

"Maybe she'll end up liking it."

I looked over my shoulder at the house, surprised nobody at home had thought of it. It *was* a good way for Tiffany to make some extra cash and get some space from Dad. But it meant I'd be giving up a week alone with Manning. I turned back to him. "Is that really the reason you want her there? Or is it because it looks bad for you and me to be friends?"

Manning took out a cigarette. "I have to go back to work. I'll see you tomorrow."

"Fine." Frustrated, I walked back along the curb toward my house. I'd have to trust him. He'd been good to me so far. He'd won me a pelican. He made eye contact with me. He didn't talk over me like a lot of people did. Whatever his reason was for wanting Tiffany there, I'm sure he was looking out for all of us.

When I reached the front door, I turned and looked back. Manning still leaned against the wall, arms crossed, a lit cigarette hanging between his lips.

———

Tiffany parked her car with a sigh and stared out the windshield at the YMCA.

"You don't have to do this," I reminded her.

"Manning asked me to."

"So you like him again?"

She looked over at me. "I never stopped."

"After dinner last week, you acted like you weren't sure about him."

"And yesterday I hated overalls, but this afternoon, I went to the mall and bought two pairs because I saw them on Heather Locklear. It's not a crime to change my mind."

Thankfully for her. Tiffany changed her mind about a lot of things, like outfits and friends. She'd do the same with Manning, too.

I got out of the car and looked around the parking lot, half-expecting Manning not to show. But there he was, leaning against the side of his truck, smoking. I waved, but it was dusk, and I couldn't tell if he'd seen us, so I started over toward him.

When I was close, he put his cigarette out on the ground. "You're late," he said.

He didn't talk much, but when he did, my heart dropped into my stomach. All the time, when we were apart, I thought about his deep, rumbling voice and wondered when I'd hear it again. "I told you six-twenty," I said. "It's six-nineteen."

"Your clock's slow."

"No it's not," I said. Actually, I didn't know who set the clocks in my house, but I'd always been on time for school. "Is it?" I asked. "Are we really late?"

He lifted one corner of his mouth.

When he smiled, I smiled. "Are you teasing me?" I asked.

His expression changed when he looked behind me. "Hey, Tiffany."

"Hi." She brushed by me and opened her arms.

"What?" he asked.

"I'm trying to hug you."

He raised an eyebrow. "Do I look like a ten-year-old girl?"

"Please?"

With a sigh, he opened one arm. Tiffany snuggled into his side, wrapping herself around his torso.

My stomach soured like I'd eaten rotten seafood.

"I missed you," Tiffany said.

I turned away. If they were hugging, he might kiss her again—and I was certain I'd puke if he did. "We should go in," I said, walking off.

There was no time to introduce Manning to the director before the meeting. Gary was already standing at the front of the small, crowded room, trying to get everyone to settle down. There was a podium in the center, but Gary never used it. I'd know him anywhere just by his thick, black curly hair that would've been down past his ears if it didn't grow straight out. A beach bum his whole life, he had a perpetual tan and bloodshot eyes, and he was the only person I knew who'd rather have a conversation with kids than adults.

There was only one pair of seats left, and the rest were singles. Fine. Let Tiffany and Manning sit together. I took a seat near the front so I wouldn't have to see them *hug*.

"Welcome to the first Young Cubs counselor meeting," Gary said. He must've been at least thirty. He'd been running the program since I'd attended as a camper. "I'm happy to see familiar faces and some new ones."

Throughout the meeting, I refrained from looking back at Manning. He probably thought all this was childish, bored out of his mind. Being a counselor was fun, though. Last year, I'd been in charge of one of the younger cabins, and the girls had been endless in their love and affection. They'd thought the world revolved around my co-counselor and me. There was no feeling quite like a group of little girls all arguing over who got to be the one to hold your hand.

The meeting lasted a half hour and after, I found Manning and Tiffany seated at the back of the room. "What'd you think?" I asked them.

"Outdoors for up to eight hours a day?" Tiffany asked. "Sounds awful. And dirty."

I shrugged. "Don't bring nice things, and you'll be fine. Manning?"

He gave nothing away. "Let's find out if they have any openings first."

As if on cue, Gary wandered down the aisle between seats, a big smile crinkling the corners of his eyes. "Well, well. Lake Kaplan. We're lucky to have you for another year."

"Thanks. This is my sister and her friend." Manning didn't even look at me as he stood. I'd done what he'd asked by introducing him as *Tiffany's* friend, and that was my reward—nothing. At least if I'd called him *my* friend, I would've gotten a warning glance.

They shook hands. "Gary, right?" Manning asked. "Manning Sutter."

"Nice to meet you, Manning. You don't look like you're in high school."

"He's not," I said. "I was wondering if there were any paid counselor positions open for him."

"It's a little late for that. We've already done all the hiring." He twisted his lips. Gary was the kind of guy who liked to find solutions for everything. If he could help, he would. "We *did* discuss bringing on one more counselor due to a rise in campers this year."

"I'm interested," Manning said. "I work construction, and we'll have a break for a few weeks during that time."

"Construction? Think you could help out with some projects around the campgrounds?"

"Absolutely," Manning said.

"Great. Let me talk it over with the board and see if I can swing the budget. As for you—" He looked down at Tiffany. "I'm sorry. I didn't catch your name?"

"I'm Lake's sister." She paused. "Tiffany."

"Hi, Tiffany. I'm almost certain I wouldn't be able to convince them of a second position. We've got plenty of female hires. I'm sorry."

Tiffany opened her mouth. I'd seen that look on her face before. Dad had taken her car away for a week her senior year because she'd snuck out in the middle of the night to go to a party. She'd gotten it back two days later. "But I really want to go," she said, glancing at Manning. "And you just said you might need more help."

"We will." Gary smiled. "We'd love to have you as a volunteer."

Tiffany laughed nervously. "You mean for free?"

"For fun," Gary said, grinning some more. He turned back to Manning. "We'll need some information from you guys. Background checks and things like that since you'll be around a bunch of kids."

"No problem," Manning said.

"Good. Let me get your number, and if I can work it out, I'll give you a call."

Manning followed Gary to the front of the room, and I sat next to Tiffany. "This is so dumb," she said, pouting. "I don't even want to go."

"You said you did."

"If Manning's going, I want to. Obviously. A whole week away from Mom and Dad with him would be massive."

My entire plan dissolved before my eyes. "That's not really what camp is about," I told her. "Most of the time, you'll be so busy with kids, you won't have time for anything else. And like you said, it's dirty."

"They have showers, right?"

"Um, yeah. There are kids there. Personal hygiene is important."

"Well . . . I guess I don't really have any big plans that week." She flipped her hair over her shoulder and looked around the room. "I think I recognize some of these people."

"Almost all of them go to our high school," I said. "Some of them were in your class."

"Oh. What about hair dryers?"

"No."

"Makeup?"

"You'll just want to wear a lot of sunscreen."

"I didn't even think about that," she said. "I bet I'll get a killer tan being outside eight hours a day." She grabbed my hand. "Come on. Let's go tell that guy I'll do it."

I didn't have time to agree or protest. She pulled me up to the front. The year before, I'd asked Tiffany to come. She was fun, and I thought it might be good for her to be around kids. But now? All I could see was what I'd be missing. I wanted Tiffany to be happy, to find some direction. I just wished I could have Manning to myself again, like I had when we'd first met.

13
LAKE

I hoisted my overnight bag out of the trunk. With only two weeks left of summer, Dad had insisted I bring four books along for the week I'd be at camp, but he wasn't the one who had to carry them. Tiffany had no books—and somehow, more luggage than me, even though I'd tried to explain there'd be no occasion for a purse, let alone three.

Tiffany yanked her rolling suitcase from the car until it fell onto the street. "It's too early to be lifting heavy things."

"We'll be up almost this early every day of camp," I said.

"Are you serious? It's practically dark."

"It'll be good for you girls," Mom said. "I'm so glad you're doing this together. Who knows? Maybe

Tiffany will find that she—" She stopped and craned her neck, looking across the parking lot. "Is that Manning?"

"No," Tiffany said, but she couldn't hide her smile.

I followed Mom's gaze and took in a small breath. Manning stood next to a black truck, a big, army-green duffel bag slung over one shoulder, the sleeves of his heather-gray hoodie pushed up to his elbows. Gary got out of the driver's seat. Together, they walked over to the curb where kids and adults were congregating.

"You told your father he wouldn't be here."

Tiffany shrugged. "Manning must've changed his mind."

"Damn it, Tiffany. What am I supposed to do? Keep this from him?"

"It's *not* a big deal, but he'll make it into one."

They argued, and Manning looked over. I finally exhaled as our eyes met. He said something to Gary, dropped his things on the ground, and walked toward us. Even the gray clouds cast overhead couldn't soften the angles of his face or the purpose in his gait. "That looks about twice your weight," Manning said, reaching for my bag.

I readjusted it on my shoulder. "I've got it. Tiffany's the one who needs help."

"You're leaning so far to the right, I'm afraid you'll fall over." He gestured impatiently, so I transferred the bag over to him, and he put it under his arm.

"Don't you trust me?" Tiffany asked Mom.

"When have you ever given us reason to?" Mom replied.

"Excuse me," Manning said.

They turned to him. "I'm sorry, Manning," Mom said. "This might sound like it's about you, but it's really about—"

"It's fine, Mrs. Kaplan. I just wanted to say that I take this position seriously. There are kids around. I'll be on my best behavior. Also, we need all the counselors so we can start checking campers in."

"I appreciate that." Mom ran a hand over her hairline, smoothing some stray pieces back in place. "Tiffany'll be over in a moment. I just need to make a few things clear."

Manning signaled toward the grass with his head. I followed him over, staying quiet so he wouldn't hear the giddiness in my voice. Not only had he not taken Tiffany's bag, but he was going to be on his best behavior. No hugging, no kissing, no time alone with Tiffany. I trusted him to keep his word, unlike Tiffany. Mom would *make things clear*, but her lectures were harmless. Tiffany knew, had known coming here, that Mom would never rat her out to Dad.

When the buses pulled up, Manning raised his eyebrows. "This place doesn't spare any expense, huh?"

They wheezed as they rocked up over the inclined driveway into the parking lot. They were luxury liners, the kinds of buses that were always too hot or too cold with fabric seats that made you wonder who'd sat in them before you. "What do you mean?"

"I thought we'd be going on a school bus or something."

"This is Orange County. Even camping can be made glamorous."

"Okay then." He looked down at me. "You're not afraid of getting dirty, are you?"

"No way. I'll be in the mud with the kids."

"That's my girl."

I almost shivered with satisfaction. Manning's girl—I hoped someday I would be. In his presence, my body loosened. I'd been anxious about this trip. I'd seen Manning four times in two weeks during the counselors training sessions, but between Tiffany, Gary, and everyone else, we hadn't had more than a couple minutes alone. Did he notice? Did he care? He never gave any sign that he did, but I'd caught him staring at me during a meeting once . . . I'd tried to convince myself the longing in his face was my imagination, or that he was looking at Tiffany, who'd been next to me, but I didn't really believe that. Some invisible tether existed between us. Nobody could see it, not even us, but I felt it. I was sure Manning did, too. As long as we both knew it, that was enough for me. For now, at least.

Manning got a clipboard from Gary and flipped through the pages. "You're paired with Hannah Burke," he told me. "Do you know her?"

"She's new this year, but we talked a little at the meetings." I pointed to a short brunette in a polo shirt and knee-length shorts. Hannah's brown hair brushed as far down as her elbows as she gathered our girls and fielded questions from their parents. "I better get to work."

"I'll come with you," Manning said, tucking the clipboard under his arm and falling into step beside me.

"Why?"

"Make sure it's a good match."

"She seems pretty nice," I said, unsure what he was looking for.

He didn't respond.

Hannah had one hand on a girl's head as she spoke to a parent. She glanced over as we approached and smiled. "There's Lake now. She'll be my co-counselor for the week."

I recognized some girls who'd attended last year. They squealed, some jumping up and down and some running over to hug me. I had hoped to get this age group. Everyone knew the nine-year-old girls' cabin was easiest. They were old enough to know better and young enough that they still listened. Around age ten, one or two girls' priorities began to change. They'd talk back or sneak around, which the others in the cabin picked up on quickly. At sixteen, it wasn't as if I could really be in charge of twelve-year-olds like Tiffany could.

Katie, one of my girls from the year before, ran and hugged me, catapulting me backward into Manning.

He caught me by my upper arms. "Whoa there."

The warmth of his hands hit me first, then the firmness of his grip, his large body at my back. He was solid, his hold on me protective while I caught my footing and then for a couple seconds after. I could run at him full force, and I doubt he'd stumble when we collided.

As Hannah pulled Katie away, I caught her wide-eyed glance at Manning. I thought I noticed her blush before she turned around.

"I have to get back," he said, releasing me. "Will you be all right with Hannah?"

I looked up over my shoulder at him. "I'm pretty sure. Why?"

"I just want to make sure you're okay. She seems nice, though."

She was around Tiffany's age, but I'd found her easy to talk to so far. "She is."

"Okay, then. Just know you can come to me with anything you need, all right? Gary and I are cool."

"You like him?"

Manning nodded. "I like him."

Coming from Manning, that meant a lot. He didn't seem easy to please in the people department, but I'd introduced him to a new friend.

"So you'll come to me?" he asked, tapping the clipboard against his palm. "If something's not right?"

"Are you okay?"

"I'm fine. But we'll be away from home. From your parents. So you can come to me. Everyone should have someone looking out for them, and I am. For you."

"Who do you have?" I asked.

He swallowed audibly, his long neck rippling. "I said everyone should—not everyone does."

"I'll be that someone, Manning," I said.

He put his large hand on my head, making me feel about half his size. "You're going to protect me?"

I always wanted him to be safe. Cared for, fed, happy. Maybe it was naïve, but I felt I could do that for him, even if it had to be from afar for a while. "Maybe not physically. Protection comes in different forms."

"That means a lot to me," he said. "I'd rather you worry about yourself, though. And I'll worry about you, too." He took his hand back, and some of my hair went with it, falling over my face. He started to fix it but stopped himself. "Don't worry about your stuff. I'll get it on the bus."

I watched him return to Gary's side. He had no reason to worry about me. To keep me safe or happy. I didn't owe him that either, but I'd do my best to give it to him.

———

Hannah and I sat together on the way to Big Bear. I tried to listen to the conversation happening between Manning and Tiffany across the aisle, but Tiffany, turned inward toward Manning, did most of the talking and anyway, Hannah had other ideas.

"Should we talk about how we're going to do this?" Hannah asked.

"It's kind of hard to plan for." I leaned a little more into the aisle. Tiffany was listing her favorite music videos while Manning stared straight ahead. "Once we get there," I said, "it'll fall into place."

"But it's my first year," Hannah said. "I don't want to screw it up."

She'd soon discover the resilience of kids—and counselors. "You'll do fine."

"I graduated with your sister, you know," she said. "She doesn't know me."

I looked over at Hannah. "She's self-involved."

"She can probably hear you."

"Probably. But she won't." We exchanged a mischievous smile.

"Is that her boyfriend?" Hannah asked. "He's so fine."

"No." I sounded defensive so I added, "I'm not really sure. Maybe for the moment."

Tiffany stood and looked around the bus before her eyes lasered in on something behind us. "There are two kids with seats to themselves. Shouldn't counselors get that?"

"I don't think they *planned* it that way," I said.

"I'm exhausted. I need to sleep before we get there." She went down the aisle to a boy with headphones on. "Hey." She pointed to the other lone camper. "Go sit with that kid so I can have this seat."

The boy, eleven or so, didn't argue. He would've argued with me, but Tiffany had boobs and some kind of power over the male species. Apparently, no age group was immune.

"Wake me when we get there," she said to Manning, who remained facing forward through the whole thing. "Manning. Did you hear me?"

"I heard you." He winked at Hannah and me. "I'll do my best, but no promises."

We giggled. Tiffany must've gone to sleep, because she didn't speak again.

"So about our cabin," Hannah said. "I think we should be firm with them. Yes, we're here to have fun, but we're authority figures first, friends second."

I watched Manning as he looked out the window. Most riders who weren't talking to their seatmates had headphones on or played handheld videogames. "Sure," I murmured.

"I brought some stuff I think the girls'll love, like makeup and CDs."

I expected a week of rough-and-tumble sports and exploring, but I knew they'd love girl time as well. "We can sneak a boom box from the rec room," I said.

"And the campfire skits," Hannah said. "We have to come up with some ideas. Should we do that now?"

"Better to brainstorm with the girls," I said absentmindedly and stood. I had no idea what I wanted to do or say. With a sideways glance at Hannah, I said, "I'll be right back."

I crossed the aisle to Manning. It took him a moment to turn and look at me, but when he did, he gestured for me to sit. "Hey, Birdy."

Birdy. I wished I hadn't been so self-conscious about bringing a stuffed animal to camp, because I already missed it. It made me feel close to him when we were apart. I turned my shoulder into the seatback, angling away from Hannah and the rest of the bus. "Hi."

"What can I do for you?" he asked lightly.

"Nothing." I tucked some hair behind my ear. He smelled faintly of cigarette smoke mixed with aftershave. The bus driver turned the music up a little for Aerosmith's "Crazy." "What do you think so far?" I asked.

"Lots of things."

"Good things?"

"Good things." He glanced at my knees and then away. "Are you cold? You have goosebumps."

I did, but not because the air conditioning was too high. They were from being close to him, from having a secret nickname, from Steven Tyler's "*C'mere, baby*." I shook my head. "I'm fine."

He looked back out the window. Our beloved beach had been replaced with desertscape and rundown towns. Soon it'd be mountains, pine trees, curvy roads.

"Do you want to be alone?" I asked.

He didn't respond right away. He had a hard profile, darkened against the bright window. Always brooding, with his pitch-black hair and heavy eyebrows. Would he tell me what he was thinking about if I got up the courage to ask? I didn't think so. I'd never met anyone so private, and it only fueled my curiosity.

If he wanted me to go, I figured he was too polite to say so. I went to get up, but he said, "No."

He had a funny way of acting like he wanted me around since he didn't look at or speak to me. But I hadn't been alone with him in weeks, and I had questions—about nothing and everything.

I chose a safe topic. "Are you finished at the house?"

He turned to me. "Not yet. We're waiting for some permits to come through."

"Then what?"

"We'll be there another couple weeks or so."

Hearing he'd be around a little longer wasn't much of a relief because summer would be over in two weeks anyway—and I had no idea what would happen next. "Then what?" I pressed.

"I graduate in December, and I start training to be a police officer."

"Where?"

"Wherever there's a place for me."

My face flushed, my blood suddenly rushing. The idea of him leaving made my heart thump painfully hard. I was stuck in every sense of the word. I had two years left of high school. After that, I'd be in Los Angeles for at least four years for college. What if he didn't want to go back to L.A.? I couldn't even get in a car and drive anywhere until I got my license. Manning could leave at any moment without even telling me. No warning, no way for me to follow him.

I gripped the edge of his seat cushion in a fist, as if that'd keep him here. "You'd move?"

He must've heard the panic in my voice, because he studied me. His expression smoothed. "Only if I had to. I like Orange County, and I don't plan to leave. But I have to go where the work is."

"Will you tell me if you do?" I asked.

He wrinkled his nose. "Of course."

"Can I have your phone number just in case?"

He laughed a little and rested his head against the back of the seat. "You make me smile, Lake. Nobody else does. How could I walk away from you?" His joy, if you could call it that, eased as he stared up at the ceiling. He kept his voice down. "I'll promise you something better. Wherever I go, I won't abandon you."

"What does that mean? I can come with you?"

"It just means we'll always be friends. As long as you want that."

I held onto his seat even more tightly. I believed him, because it was the same for me. If I had to be away from him a few years, if I had to make long distance phone calls or write letters—no cost would be too high to keep him in my life. And maybe down the line, that would pay off. One day, he'd look at me and see a beautiful, sexy woman instead of the awkward, inexperienced teen I was now.

"Where would you go?" I asked.

"I honestly don't know."

"Home?"

He shook his head, still looking up. "I don't have a home."

I refrained from transferring my death grip from the cushion to his hand. I could give him whatever it was he was missing. I knew I could. "How is that possible?" I asked softly.

"Some people just don't. It's not always a bad thing."

"Tell me about your family."

"No."

"What about your sister? Is she with your parents?"

With his head back, his throat was exposed, so I could see and hear him swallow. "No. I don't talk about my family."

"Even with me? I won't tell anyone."

"It has nothing to do with you. I just don't."

I knew I shouldn't take it personally, but I did. Nobody made him smile like me—wasn't that worth something? Didn't he trust me? Feel close to me? I'd trusted him from the moment he'd held my bracelet in his palm and asked me to come get it. All this time, I'd thought he was asking me to read between the lines, to hear the things he couldn't say.

"We're friends, aren't we?" I asked.

"I already told you we were. I just said we'd always be."

"You don't know that. Are you embarrassed to have a friend my age?"

"No," he said flatly. He looked about to add something and thought better of it. He spoke slowly, as if choosing his words carefully. "You're not that much younger than your sister."

"But we're different."

"I know." He blinked. "How do you think you two are different?"

"She's pretty."

He shut his eyes and inhaled a deep breath. "She is."

It wasn't the reassurance I wanted. Maybe he thought I was fishing for a compliment, and I was, so why couldn't he just tell me I was pretty, too? Was that so bad? I wouldn't read anything into it. I was ninety-nine percent sure about that.

"Someday," Manning said, almost to himself, "when you're older and wiser, looking back on this, you'll understand."

"When?"

"I can't tell you that, because I'm not even sure I understand."

That wasn't fair. Maybe he didn't know exactly what he felt about me, but he had some idea, and he expected me not to wonder about it. I *would* wonder and think hard about it now—not 'someday' when it might be too late. When he was already gone. I wasn't convinced Manning wanted Tiffany, or even that she wanted him. So what was the link between them? When one didn't want the other, what had kept them together the past month?

"I said *someday*," Manning said, breaking the silence. "Not now."

"I can't wait that long."

He grinned at me. "There's no hidden prize or anything. Just understanding that comes with time and age." He looked at my bare legs and quickly away again, as if it were a habit he was trying to break. "You know our conversations—they stay between us. Right? You know that?"

I nodded. Our time together was precious and not to be shared. "I know."

"All right. Let's talk about something interesting." He sat up again and scratched his chin, thinking. "If you won a contest on the radio to go anywhere in the world and you had to leave tomorrow night, where would you go?"

"Big Bear," I said.

He laughed. "But you'll already be there."

So will you. I wasn't brave enough to say it. Instead I asked, "What was Tiffany's answer?"

"I didn't ask her."

A thrill ran up my spine. This was mine. "I have to think about it."

"That's fine." He turned to me, giving me his full attention. "We have time. I want to know."

"Why?" I asked.

"Because I care," he said. "I care very much."

14
LAKE

Something about a dining hall full of humans under fourteen amplified everything. Counselors shouted over kids excited to be away from home for a week. Trays banged against tables, silverware against plastic dishes. The camp's kitchen staff hurried kids down the buffet line. Cooked hamburger meat battled with body odor—I was glad not to eat near the boys.

Cabin nine sat in the middle of the hall with Manning in the center of the picnic-style table. The boys laughed at what he said, looked up at him between bites of sloppy joes, showed him stuff from their pockets.

Peals of giggles at my own table brought my attention back to where it should be. Hannah sat at the opposite end of a long wooden table, eight nine-year-old girls between us. "What's so funny?" I asked.

"Bettina likes Bobby Newman."

In the four hours we'd been here, it wasn't the first boy-talk I'd heard. "Which one's Bobby Newman?"

They all pointed at Manning's table and Bettina turned a bright shade of red. Luckily for her, the only "boy" who noticed was Manning. He sucked his teeth, holding back a grin, as if he knew exactly what we were talking about. Bettina's secret crush. Mine, too.

"What activity are you girls most looking forward to?" Hannah asked.

Reluctantly, I pulled my gaze away from Manning's. Was it fair to feel as if I knew him well enough to say he was happy? I hadn't seen him so relaxed, so quick to laugh and smile, as I had since we'd gotten to the parking lot this morning.

"Horses," one of the girls screamed.

I was the only one at the table who didn't agree. Climbing on a large, unpredictable animal sounded no safer than riding a hunk of unreliable metal into the sky. It was the only activity I'd sit out. Like last year, I planned to wait at the stable while Hannah and the instructors took the girls.

"We have arts and crafts next," I said.

Some of the girls groaned, some tittered. Katie tugged on my sleeve. "Can we make friendship bracelets?"

"Of course." We still had an afternoon full of things to do, so I did a drink check. "Did everyone have at least one full glass of water?"

"Yes," they all replied.

Hannah and I exchanged a look. We'd only gone through one pitcher between ten of us. I stood. "I'll get more."

As I waited for a refill from the kitchen staff, Manning came up next to me and set his tray on the buffet. He held his plate out to Bucky, who was packing up the chafing dishes. "Fill her up."

Bucky was a local I recognized from last year. He scrunched his mouth so hard, it almost touched his eyebrows. "No seconds."

"Come on, man. You got plenty left and I'm a growing boy."

Bucky'd just served food to over a hundred kids, but it didn't matter. He always looked that grumpy. "Please, Bucky?" I asked.

He snatched the plate and began shoveling food onto it.

"Do you always get seconds?" I asked.

"Are you calling me fat?"

"I wouldn't quit weightlifting just yet if I were you."

Manning laughed. "I'd ask if you want me to get you seconds, too, but it sounds like you can handle yourself."

I'd eaten everything off my plate but I wasn't satisfied. "There's dessert," I said.

"Yeah? You want some?"

"I'm always hungrier up here."

He took his plate back from Bucky and I got the water pitcher. Manning walked me over to the dessert section, picked out two chocolate puddings, and handed me one. "Are you having fun?" he asked on our way back to the tables.

"Yes, but I knew I would. Are you?"

"I am," he said. "A lot, actually. All the outdoor activities remind me of being a kid again. The boys' enthusiasm is infectious, and it's been a while since . . . I mean, they stink like hell, but they keep me on my toes."

I giggled. Manning's boys were nine, too. Same as last year, some of them hadn't discovered deodorant yet. "Do we have anything together today?" I asked since the same age groups were often paired for activities. "Just asking in case I should bring a face mask."

"I don't know." He nudged my arm with his elbow before stopping at his table. "Guess we'll see."

I went to turn away but stopped. I lowered my voice. "After lights-out, most of the counselors come back to the dining hall to hang out and play games and stuff."

"I heard."

"Will you come?" I asked.

He looked over my head a second. "Maybe."

When I returned to my girls, my smile must've been as bright as a light bulb. I was sure it took up half my face.

"I want dessert, too," one of the girls said. I handed over my pudding without protest.

"Have you seen Tiffany?" Hannah asked, nodding across the cafeteria. "You might want to go check on her."

I looked over. Tiffany had her finger in one of the girls' faces as though she were scolding her. She'd been assigned to a cabin nobody wanted—the twelve-year-old girls. They were vain, boy-crazy, and learning to test boundaries. Part of me thought it was fair payback for how snotty she'd acted at that age, and the other part worried only Tiffany or the girls would survive the week—not both.

I got back up, crossed the hall to cabin eleven, and plopped down next to Tiffany. "How's it going?"

I hadn't meant to sneak up on her, but she jumped a mile high, whirling on me. Dirt streaked her temple, and her normally perfect hair looked as though it hadn't been brushed in a week. "Jesus, Lake. Hell on earth. That's how it's going."

I had to laugh. "It's the first day. Things are always a little crazy."

"You have to get me out of here."

A couple of Tiffany's campers looked over. I shushed her. "They'll hear you."

"I don't care. They're a bunch of brats."

"*You're* a brat," said one girl.

"Shut up." Tiffany pointed at her. "I told you all to be quiet."

"Tiffany, stop. You can't say that to them."

She sighed, her upper body slumping. "I don't like this, Lake. My co-counselor is only two years older than them and she's not any help."

I bit my thumbnail. "Try to remember what it was like to be twelve. There's a balance between being their friend and commanding their respect."

"Can you help me? Please?"

"I have my own cabin to deal with," I said. Since I felt sorry for her, I added, "Once they're in bed, all the counselors come back here to hang out. We can vent then."

Tiffany grabbed my arm as I stood. "Don't go. Please."

"I have to. I'll see you tonight."

————

The girls were in their beds by eight and after some policing, including a lecture on gossip, they'd fallen asleep. Once I was sure they were out for the night, I grabbed Hannah to take her to the dining hall. It was a short walk, but we had to pass through woods to get there, guided only by the moonlight the trees let through.

"You're sure this is allowed?" Hannah asked.

"Yep. Once the kids are in bed, we all hang out, even Gary. Head counselors take turns throughout the week walking through camp to check on each cabin. You might have to at some point."

"By myself?"

"Are you afraid?" I teased. "You know I made up that story about the bear to get the girls to hand over their candy, right?"

"Really? So there aren't bears out here?"

One quick glance around the deadly silent dark made me shiver. "No, there are."

Hannah made a noise. I hurried her along—it actually was a little scary—but I also wanted to see if Manning would come tonight. I supposed I should talk Tiffany off the ledge, too.

In the cafeteria, the tables had been moved to the room's perimeter, clearing the area. A boom box sat on the fireplace mantel and a junior counselor rapped along to "Nuthin But A 'G' Thang." Some people stood off to the side talking, while others had brought cushions and blankets to sit on the floor in a circle.

Manning sat with Gary and some other counselors in plastic chairs they'd formed into a half circle. Hannah and I walked over, all eyes on us as we approached.

"What's up?" Gary said. "Grab a chair."

Manning stood. "I'll get some." He walked off to the side and lifted a seat in each hand. A girl I didn't recognize had her chair a little too close to Manning's. Now I not only had to worry about Tiffany, but other girls, too? "Move over," I said to her.

"Um." She glanced behind me at Manning.

"Please," I added.

She scooted aside as Manning added our chairs to the circle.

"When did you get so bossy?" Gary asked me as I sat. "Last year you were much more shy."

Even though my cheeks warmed, his teasing made everyone look at me, even Manning. "I said *please*."

"You should see her with the girls," Hannah said. "She's the boss."

"That so?" Manning asked.

I arched an eyebrow at him. "You look surprised."

"*I* didn't say you were shy."

Neither of us smiled, but the energy between us was light. Playful. Something about today had obviously softened Manning's outer layer and I couldn't help feeling responsible for that.

The song changed, and Hannah bobbed her head with the music. "God, I love LL Cool J."

Manning shifted his eyes to her. "Yeah? I would've guessed Mariah Carey or something."

She laughed. "I listen to both. LL is good to get in a certain kind of mood."

"Yeah," he said and laughed as if it were some kind of inside joke.

Maybe it was. I didn't know what an "around-the-way girl" was, but they seemed to. "What mood?" I asked.

Manning looked at something behind me. "Never mind."

"What are we talking about?" Tiffany asked a second before she fell into Manning's lap. He *ooph*ed, and she put an arm around his neck. "Oh, please. You're twice my size."

"Now I see where Lake gets it," Gary said.

Tiffany flipped her hair over her shoulder, sending a telling waft of Herbal Essences in my direction. There was no sign of the dirt I'd seen earlier, and she had on a full face of makeup. The girl had showered. "Gets what?"

"Playing the boss."

"I don't play. I'm bossy, and I make no apologies. How else would I get what I want?" Her eyes twinkled with everyone watching her. She looked up at Manning. "Right, babe?"

"Are you two dating?" Gary asked.

Tiffany looked at Manning, so we all did, too. "No."

"We're taking it *slow*," Tiffany said.

"It's cool," Gary said. "Just leave that stuff at home this week."

"You have my word, man." Manning patted Tiffany's outer thigh. "Up."

She kissed his cheek and stood, then motioned for me to let her sit. "Scooch."

I could barely function enough to slide over and share my seat. She just kissed him when she wanted. Hugged him. Sat on him. She didn't know how lucky she was. I didn't think I'd ever just reached out and touched him. I looked at my hands, at the dirt in my cuticles from planting trees earlier.

"How'd today go?" Manning asked her.

"Great."

Her smile was so fake, I couldn't believe Manning bought it, but he smiled back. "I'm glad. I was worried about you."

"Aw. Next time come check on me," she said. "I missed you, and I could've used some back up."

"Thought you said it was all right?"

"It was . . ." She shrugged. "But they're a little hard to handle."

"Too bad you aren't in charge of boys." Manning stretched his long arm along the back of our chair, his thumb ghosting over my far shoulder. "You'd have no trouble getting them to do what you say."

Tiffany actually blushed, which was rare. Meanwhile, my heart dropped a thousand miles. Why was he worried about her? Why did she miss him? They didn't even care about each other. She took a sip from a red Solo cup I hadn't noticed before.

"What is that?" I asked her.

"Special grapefruit punch."

I looked in at the pink drink. "With alcohol?"

"Yep. Want some?"

Manning had turned away to talk to Gary. I took the cup from her and sniffed the rim. It didn't smell like grapefruit. More than once, my dad had come home groaning that he needed a drink. I'd never really had the desire to get drunk, but Tiffany and her friends and mine all made it sound so glamorous. Like fun in a bottle. Much better than feeling like this, jealous of my own sister, invisible to the only man who'd ever seemed to *see* me.

Still, I wasn't brave enough to drink it. Camp was no place to be reckless. I wasn't sure where Tiffany had gotten the alcohol, but it definitely wasn't allowed.

I went to hand it back when Manning's arm flew over my head. He grabbed my wrist so fast, punch sloshed over the side onto my top. "Don't drink that," he said.

"I wasn't going to."

"Oh, come on," Tiffany whispered. "One sip won't kill her."

He turned on Tiffany, keeping my arm firmly in his hand. "What are you doing?"

"What?" she asked. "Our parents aren't around for once. I just want her to have some fun."

"That's your little sister. She looks up to you. If you tell her underage drinking is okay, she'll believe you."

My ears burned with embarrassment. I didn't feel this childish when my parents scolded me. "I'm right here," I said.

"If she gets caught drinking, you know what'll happen?" he asked Tiffany. "Did you even think about that?"

She shrunk down. "No."

Manning lowered his voice. "Gary will kick her out faster than she can apologize." He looked at me. "He'll call your parents to come get you. Tonight."

Going home was the last thing I wanted. I tried pulling my hand back, but I couldn't even move him. If he was trying to warn or scare me, his grip was having the opposite effect. My insides flurried as I realized the extent of his strength. I wondered if this was why Tiffany sometimes did things she wasn't supposed to. If she thought this kind of attention was better than none at all.

Tiffany took her drink back. "Sorry, Lake. I'd die if you left me up here by myself for the week."

Finally, Manning let me go to take the cup from Tiffany. "That goes for you, too. Where'd you even get this?"

"I have my ways." She pouted. "What about later, when it's just you and me?"

"No. And don't bring it up again."

I couldn't handle this. If they were making plans to be alone, I wasn't sure if it was better to know or pretend it wasn't happening.

Manning tensed in his seat. "Is that the guy from the fair?" he asked.

Tiffany and I followed his line of sight to Corbin Swenson, who looked as tall and swoony as ever in a sweatshirt, jeans, and skate shoes. Corbin walked toward us, his hood pulled over his head, hands shoved in the hoodie's front pocket.

"Corbin!" Gary said. "You made it."

Corbin opened his arms. "You wanted a baseball all-star, here I am."

"I didn't know you'd be here," Tiffany said. "You weren't at any of the meetings."

"Lake knew." Corbin winked at me, and Tiffany and Manning looked over.

"I asked him to drive up for a day to play some ball tomorrow," Gary said.

"Maybe teach these boys a few things," Corbin added.

"What's wrong with just throwing the ball around?" Manning asked.

"Nothing." Corbin shrugged as he and Manning locked eyes. "But when you have access to an all-star, might as well take advantage. I came here as a kid. Same as Lake."

It was a weird sensation to hear a Swenson say my name at all, but to have him do it in front of everyone made me giddy.

"So proud of you, man," Gary said. "Take a seat."

Corbin grabbed two chairs, and everyone but Manning scooted to open the circle for him. Maybe because of that, Corbin set both seats down on the other side of Manning. "Looks like you could use one of your own," he said to me, since Tiffany and I were sharing.

"I'm fine where I am," Tiffany replied, putting her hand on Manning's knee.

"I was talking to Lake," Corbin said.

With all eyes on me, including Manning's burning stare, I went to sit between Manning and Corbin.

Corbin took his hood down, ruffling a hand through his honey-colored hair. "How's your summer been?" he asked.

"Fine." Nobody spoke. I had the distinct feeling they were all listening to our conversation. "Keeping busy."

"'Course you are. Every time I see you, you're reading or with friends, or," he clucked his tongue, "eating cotton candy."

Oh, God. Corbin Swenson was flirting with me, and all I wanted to do was check to see if Manning was watching. Was he maybe just a little jealous? "You make it sound like I just screw around all day."

"Don't you?" he asked. "It's summer."

"No. My dad doesn't let me. That's why I was reading at the beach. For school."

"Ahh." He sat back in his seat, crossing an ankle over his knee. "Charles, right? That's your dad? My old man works with him."

"I know."

"So you're not screwing around here?"

"No. This is for my college apps. Just don't tell my dad I enjoy it."

We smiled at each other.

"I sense a love connection," Gary said, waggling his eyebrows at me. He sat forward. "But listen, you two—"

"Leave that stuff at home," everyone recited before erupting in laughter.

"All right, all right," Gary said. "I just expect you guys to set a good example for the kids. No alcohol, no sex."

"Unless you're the one having it?" Tiffany teased.

More giggling.

"You're all a bunch of degenerates," Gary said. He stood and stretched. "I need my beauty rest. Remember—Reflection is at seven tomorrow morning and not a minute later. Last cabin to show gets dining hall cleanup duty."

Hannah and I exchanged looks. "It won't be us."

Corbin got up, too, and gently touched my shoulder. "I'll be right back. I've got a few questions for Gary about tomorrow. Don't go."

I just nodded, watching him walk away.

"I'm bored," Tiffany said.

"There's a deck of cards," Manning said. "We could play a game."

"With alcohol?"

"Christ, Tiffany. I already told you no."

"I said I was bored, not fifty. I don't want to play cards."

"You don't have to." Manning nodded at a group of counselors across the hall. "You know any of them?"

"No."

"Why don't you go introduce yourself? Part of this experience is meeting new people."

"Because, I'd rather do other things, like . . ." Tiffany inched her chair closer to him and whispered in his ear.

Manning kept his eyes on the floor. "We can't."

"Why not?"

"You know why." His eyes shifted to my feet but stayed down as he stammered, "We're not . . . and I promised your mom."

"She isn't here." She tugged on his arm. "Can we go for a walk?"

He blew out a sigh. "I'll make you a deal. You go over and say hi, make some small talk, and then we can go for a walk."

She rolled her eyes but stood. "Okay, fine. Will you come with me?"

"Yeah. I'll be right there."

I couldn't look at Manning. My face burned just thinking of them out there alone doing things you could only whisper—now, later, the rest of the week. One minute, I swore he and I had some unearthly connection. And then there were moments like this one, where I questioned how well I really knew him.

He leaned his elbows onto his knees and spoke for my ears only. "We're just going outside for a cigarette. That's all."

"You said you weren't going to smoke at all."

"No, I said I'd figure it out." He cleared his throat. "You know how hard it is to go all day without one cigarette?"

"Would you quit if I asked you to?"

He blinked slowly, as if seeing me for the first time. "What?"

"If I asked you to quit, would you?"

"Why?"

"It's not healthy."

"I don't do it in front of you."

My mouth fell open. "Yes you do."

"When? Name one time."

I thought back to the day I'd met him and the night of the fair and the time I'd gone looking for him on the site. He'd held cigarettes, put them behind his ear, even stuck them between his lips. But he'd never lit one, or if he had, he'd put it out as soon as I'd gotten near. It hadn't occurred to me that was on purpose. I could recall the smell of smoke being near him, though. I could almost taste the bitterness on his mouth.

"You can't think of one because it didn't happen," he said.

I opened my eyes, not realizing I'd closed them. My mouth was watering. "You're right. But I'm not asking you to quit for me. It's because I care about you. I care enough that I want you to stop hurting yourself."

I'd never seen him look speechless. Quiet? Yes. Stoic? Definitely. But not speechless. "I will quit. One day. Soon." He swallowed. "I'm down to two or three a day." It wasn't good enough, so I didn't respond. "But if you want me to . . . I'll try harder."

I wanted him to not go outside with Tiffany. Truthfully, I'd come to like the smell of cigarettes because it reminded me of him, and I'd cherish the coarse taste on his tongue, the stink, if it meant one kiss, but more than that, I'd spent my youth learning about how cigarettes turned your lungs black and killed you over time. I didn't want that for him. "Try harder," I said.

He gave me a funny look. I hadn't said it rudely, but who was I to tell a grown man how to live?

"All right," he said. "I will."

Tiffany waved at us from the doorway.

"She's waiting for you," I said, turning away in my seat.

"Who?"

"Tiffany."

"Oh." He didn't get up right away. "I'll be back. Stay here."

Whatever. I always did what I was told, whether it came from my parents, teachers, Tiffany, or, now, Manning. And where had that gotten me? Here, watching him walk away with her. "Why should I?" I asked.

"Because I don't want you walking around in the woods by yourself at night. That's reasonable, isn't it?" He didn't wait for my answer, just stood and left.

What if I *did* walk alone through the woods at night? Would he put me in counselor time-out? He had no real power over me. Why should I listen to anything I said when he was outside with my sister?

"Are you all right?"

I looked up at Corbin, who towered over me. "Yes. I mean, no. I'm tired."

"Long day, huh? Can I walk you back to your cabin?"

Manning had told me to stay put. I knew it was because he cared, but in that moment, I questioned what that even meant. I stood. "That would be nice."

Corbin held the door open for me, and we passed into the night. As soon as we left the glow of the cafeteria, darkness was all around us. "Man, I love it here," Corbin said as we crossed through the woods. "So peaceful. I would've done the counselor thing, but I start baseball camp this week."

"Are you really on the all-star team?"

"Yep. I'm applying for scholarships, actually."

"Really? Where?"

"My dad wants me to go somewhere in California, like Stanford, but I've always wanted to move east."

I stopped to gape at him. "You're kidding. You're such a California guy."

He laughed. "I know. It's weird. But I love that the East Coast has history and that the city's like the center of the world. I want to do big things, Lake. Be someone. That's what New York's about."

"What about surfing? Skating? All that stuff?"

"You can surf in New York. There's this place called Montauk. It's bad-ass, or so I've heard. Haven't been yet."

We started walking again, his knuckles brushing my arm. "What about you? I know you're a year under me, but have you started thinking about college?"

"I'm going to USC."

He chuckled. "Just like that, huh?"

Just like that. Easy. Wasn't it? I hadn't really considered there might be other options. It'd only ever been 'SC. "Would you stay in California if your dad asked?"

"Only if I wanted to."

The east coast seemed so far away. Going to school there would be like moving to a new country. If I was honest, even Stanford in Northern California intimidated me. "My dad went to USC. We've been working on stuff for my college apps since middle school." We hadn't even discussed it. Dad and I had just started planning at some point.

"That's cool," he said. "I mean, it's a great school. They've got a baseball team, too."

I looked at the ground, unsure of how to respond to that. For a few silent seconds, the only sound was our feet crunching on the forest floor and the chirp of crickets. I smelled the cigarette smoke first. It made its way through me instantly, leaving me warm and cozy, because it usually meant I was close to Manning. With as strongly as I associated him with it, it still surprised me that he'd never actually smoked in front of me.

"I hear voices," Corbin said. "Who's smoking?"

"Who do you think?"

"Your sister?"

I nodded and called, "Tiff?"

"We're over here," she said.

Corbin and I cut through the trees until two shadowy figures came into sight.

"What're you doing out here, Lake?" Manning asked. "I told you to—" He stopped, and the four of us stood in silence a moment.

"Told her to what?" Tiffany asked.

"To stay where she was."

It was so quiet, I could hear Tiffany shift in her platforms. "Why?"

I was following his rules. He couldn't protest. And if he did, how would it look to Tiffany and Corbin? "He doesn't think it's safe to walk around in the dark alone," I said. "But, as you can see, I'm not alone. So, goodnight."

I felt his eyes on me. He wanted to say more. Now he knew how I felt, always having to keep things inside.

Finally, Manning took a drag of his cigarette and after a few seconds, he stepped back. "'Night."

What had I expected him to do? Ditch Tiffany to walk me back himself? He couldn't, but that didn't make me feel any better. It just frustrated me more.

"He's an intense dude," Corbin said as we walked away.

I couldn't answer, not without snapping at Corbin, who had nothing to do with this.

"You want to go check out the lake?" Corbin said. "It's a little bit of a walk, but it's amazing at night."

"No, thanks. I have to be up early."

"We both do." Corbin didn't speak again until we reached my cabin. He shoved his hands in his hoodie and backed away. "Later."

"Are you mad?"

He stopped. "I don't know, Lake. I've asked you out a couple times, and—"

"That was you asking me out?"

The corner of his mouth lifted. "Well. It was no big gesture, I admit, but you don't have to be mean about it."

Corbin had been nothing but gentlemanly tonight. Since I'd met him, actually. And he was right, I'd sort of blown him off both times. *Me*, blowing off a Swenson. It was so insane, I almost laughed. "I'm sorry," I said. "I'm not really . . . I don't date."

"Never?"

I shook my head. "For one, my dad says I'm too young."

"He's a real hard-ass, isn't he?"

"Kind of."

"And the second reason?"

"What?"

"You said for one. What's two?"

"Oh." I didn't have a second reason I could vocalize. There was crushing on a boy like him, and there was whatever I felt for Manning. They didn't compare in my eyes. "It's just an expression."

Corbin raised the zipper on his hoodie. The temperature had dropped once the sun had disappeared. He nodded behind him. "It doesn't have anything to do with that guy, does it?"

"Who? Manning?" Despite the chill, my scalp warmed. "No. Why?"

"No reason. Will you come to the baseball game tomorrow? Cheer me on?"

I'd pretty much been a jerk, turning him down, but he still wanted to see me. Corbin was sweet, fine, and by some odd turn of events, he might like me. I should just say yes. It was so much easier than this back-and-forth rollercoaster with Manning that left my stomach in knots. With Corbin, there were no knots. There wasn't anything, really. Maybe that wasn't a bad thing.

I nodded. "I'll come."

"Cool. See you in the morning."

"Corbin?" I said as he turned. "Thanks for walking me back."

He smiled. "Anytime."

15
LAKE

For morning Reflection, everyone gathered on the wooden bleachers to face the rising sun. Birds chirped, blue sky peeked through the treetops. While Gary spoke softly about positive intentions and what the day would bring, nine pairs of feet plus Tiffany's trudged in. At seven-ten, they were the final cabin to arrive, which meant Tiffany would spend her morning cleaning up half-eaten food and used napkins. I couldn't muster any sympathy. She knew the rules.

"Each morning, we'll sing a special song to begin the day," Gary said. "I discovered it earlier this year and thought—that song has a great message. You might've heard it on the radio. 'Shine' by Collective Soul is about the quest for guidance and acceptance. It has religious undertones, but you can sing it however it makes sense to you. But first, I want each cabin to come together and decide what they're grateful for on this beautiful morning. The counselors will share it with the group."

We huddled with the girls, who looked as energized and excited as they had getting on the bus the morning before.

"What are we grateful for?" Hannah asked.

"That we don't have to clean up our mess today," Bettina said.

"*You're* grateful for Bobby Newman," one of the girls teased.

Hannah and I looked at each other. "Let's try for something a little deeper," I said. "Any ideas, Hannah?"

"How about if we're grateful for each other?" Hannah asked. "Friendship."

"Three Musketeers," Katie added. "It's my favorite candy."

"Friendship it is," Hannah said.

Gary called everyone's attention back to the front. "Friendship" came up three times before Manning's turn. "We're grateful for a lot of things," he said, scanning the faces of the boys in his cabin. "But today, we'd like to say our thanks for the release of *Mortal Kombat II* last month. As a cabin, we agree that this is one of the best things to happen this year so far."

Everyone stayed silent until Gary burst into laughter. "All right. That's a new one. Videogames. I like it. Who wants to go next? Cabin four?"

I glanced at Hannah, who nodded and mouthed, *Candy*.

I sighed. "Cabin four is grateful for . . . Three Musketeers bars." The girls cheered. "And," I added when they'd calmed down, "having someone to share them with."

Gary clapped. "Good one, cabin four."

As it turned out, despite a morning of good intentions, large breakfasts, and lots of laughter, everything came crashing down when I checked our schedule for the day. Right off the bat, we were headed for danger—horseback riding. It wasn't even my fear that bothered me. It was that I'd miss out on sharing an activity with the girls.

As a group, we walked from the dining hall through dirt and dead grass toward the stables. "Look, there's Bobby Newman," Katie squealed, pointing. I spotted a couple more boys from Manning's cabin. Then his co-counselor Kirk. Like a trail of breadcrumbs, my eyes followed until they landed on Manning as he helped a camper up onto a saddle.

"We're paired with them today?" I asked Hannah.

"Looks like it."

Now, hanging back at the stable was even worse. I'd not only be missing out on quality time with the girls, but with Manning as well.

"Want me to stay behind with you?" Hannah asked. "I'm sure Manning and the instructors can handle it."

I turned and squinted at the stables. The horses were beautiful . . . and enormous. If possible, they seemed even bigger than the year before. A small part of me wanted to be brave just so I wouldn't miss this time with Manning.

"It's okay," I told Hannah. "The girls will want you there."

One of the handlers came out of the stable in cowboy boots. He waved at the girls. "Who wants to ride a horse?" They screamed and took off running toward him. For a moment, he looked terrified, but quickly recovered. "Okay, okay. Slow down. You don't want to spook the poor things."

"You or the horses?" Hannah teased.

Manning looked up at the commotion. Once he'd secured his camper, he came over to us. "I've never ridden a horse. Believe that?"

That he'd never climbed on the back of a wild animal and expected it do what he said? Yes, I believed that. What sane person would? I bit my thumbnail. "Me, neither."

"It'll be a first for us both, then. Come on."

Hannah followed, but I stayed where I was. Horses on the ground didn't frighten me—it was the thought of getting on and letting go. What stopped the horse from doing whatever the hell it wanted? What if it suddenly had some kind of psychotic break? I'd never broken a bone, and I didn't want to start today.

The handler came out with a shiny, black horse, scanned the crowd, and started toward me. "You're going to ride Betsy Junior," he said.

I looked around to make sure he wasn't talking to someone else. "Me?"

"She's a little on the wild side, but she's not as bad as her mom. Better if a counselor takes her."

I tried to back away, but my feet were suddenly made of lead. Betsy had black eyes and didn't blink, as if she were trying to send me a message—touch me and I'll buck you into a tree. Betsy Junior neighed, a sinister laugh. "I can't," I said. I was too young to die. I'd never even been kissed or learned how to drive. "I'm going to sit this one out."

"What's wrong?" Manning asked from behind me, and I jumped. Where had he come from?

"I can't do it."

"Why not?"

"She's scared," the handler said. "I see it in her eyes. Betsy gets the same look when I bring her around all these kids."

I gulped. "I'll stay here and wait for you guys."

"You sure?" the instructor asked. "You could ride with me."

I'd only just met the guy. He might do this for a living, but what did that even mean? He could've been hired yesterday. Maybe he'd been an insurance salesman who'd gotten laid off and had decided owning a pair of cowboy boots qualified him for this job. "I'm sure."

"Suit yourself. Looks like Betsy Junior's safe another day." He led Betsy back to the stable.

I turned and found Manning looking at me as if he were waiting for something. "What?" I asked.

"You know what."

"No I don't."

"You got out of the Ferris wheel, but not this one. I'm going to make you get on a horse."

"But—"

"Ride with me."

My breath caught in my throat. But that would mean being pressed up against him for an hour. An entire hour. I'd probably faint—and fall off the horse. And get trampled. "But you just said you've never done it."

"That guy gave me a quick lesson. I'm a natural sportsman." He smiled crookedly. "I've got this, Lake."

"It's okay. I really don't even want to."

With the sun high in the sky, his dark eyes were nearly black. "You told me you weren't afraid to get dirty."

"It's not that. What if the horse goes crazy and bucks me off?"

"Then you'll fall, and we'll get you up and dust you off."

"What if I break something?"

"What if? You tell me."

I opened my mouth. I'd expected him to tell me that wouldn't happen. That he'd protect me. If I fell off, I might hurt myself and have to go to the infirmary, maybe even the hospital. But that was true for all the girls and boys around me. Which meant now, it wasn't just about riding a horse. It was about proving what I could handle. How much hurt I could take and keep going. "Okay," I said without an ounce of confidence. "I'll ride with you."

"Today," he said. "And next time, you'll do it yourself."

I didn't believe I could, but he didn't need to know that. I nodded. "Which horse?"

"Betsy Senior. Come on."

My knees nearly gave out. *Of course* Manning's first time on a horse would be on the wildest one. I supposed if I was going to ride a Betsy at all, it might as well be with Manning. I followed him.

He tested the stirrup with his boot. "Put your foot in and get on."

I looked down and back up at him. "On the horse?"

"Trust me, Birdy." He gathered the reins. "I just did this with my own campers and a couple of yours."

My heart slowed a little hearing his nickname for me. As soon as I stuck my tennis shoe in the stirrup,

Manning lifted me onto the horse by my waist. "Christ, Lake," he said, adjusting my foot in the stirrup. His head came all the way to my shoulder. "You weigh the same as a ten-year-old."

It wasn't true, but it probably felt that way to Manning, who could lift a horse without a struggle.

Okay, maybe not a horse. But he was strong.

Manning turned to walk away, and panic gripped me. I reached out and grabbed the first thing I could, nearly toppling over as I latched onto his t-shirt. "Where are you going?"

He stopped in his tracks, mostly because I had him in a death grip. When he saw me lopsided in the saddle, he laughed. "You know animals can sense fear, right?"

He wasn't helping. "That's a myth."

"Is it?" He engulfed my fisted hand with his, but didn't pull me off. "I was just going to make sure everyone got on, but if you think you need me more . . ."

I did. I needed him. Why didn't I get to be selfish every now and then like everyone else? He would stay if I asked him to. Most of the girls had ridden horses before, some had even taken lessons. But I hadn't come here to be with Manning—I'd come for them. I loosened my fist, and he held my hand until I'd righted myself on the horse.

"Two minutes," he said. "If she moves, pull on the reins and say 'whoa.'"

Manning checked in with each of his boys and my girls, too. The way he made eye contact with each one and listened to whatever they said made me wonder why my dad wasn't like this with me when I got scared. He would've just told me to get on and quit whining. Did Manning get that from *his* dad? Where was Mr. Sutter? What did he do for a living? How often did Manning see him? After he'd shut down my questions about his sister, I wasn't sure I could ask. But if Manning had become the man he was because of his dad, I wanted to meet and thank him.

Betsy Senior neighed and took a few steps, jolting me back to reality. I tugged on the reins.

Manning looked over and mouthed, *Whoa.*

"Whoa," I said. Betsy stamped a hoof and settled.

It took longer than two minutes, but Manning returned once it was time to go. "You want to drive?"

"No. Will you? Please."

He scratched his chin. "I didn't think this through. You might need to get off so I can get on first. Can you do it?"

If it meant I wouldn't have to be in charge of this thing, then yes. He helped me down, hoisted himself onto the horse, and jerked his head for me to get on again. Tentatively, I put my foot in the stirrup again. I had no way of pulling myself up, so Manning offered his elbow. I used it to slide onto the saddle behind him.

"See?" he said. "You're a natural. "Ready?"

But now, what was I supposed to do with my hands? His nearness robbed me of everything from sense to speech. His camp t-shirt, still creased, smelled like plastic and a hint of sweat.

"You might want to hold on," he said.

There was only one way to hold on. He was asking me to put my arms around him—just like that? As if it wasn't something I'd dreamed of a hundred times? It was impossible that he wouldn't instantly know the depth of my feelings just by this simple hug. He'd feel the pounding of my heart against his back. My hairline began to sweat. I ached to do it, but I seriously couldn't bring myself to move an inch. I was scared stiff.

"I'm okay," I said.

"Suit yourself." Manning clucked his tongue, squeezed Betsy's sides with his feet, and she jolted forward. I seized onto his t-shirt to keep from falling. He pulled back on the reins, laughing. "Whoa, Betsy. Whoa," he said. She steadied into a walk. "It might take a few tries."

My hands might as well be on him now. I had the fabric of his shirt in two fists, and if I released it, I might fall. Probably. It was likely. I didn't want to fall. I didn't want to let go of Manning when I finally had him. I eased my grip and slowly, with appreciation for every detail, slid my arms around his middle. I clasped my hands together and scooted closer, my inner thighs pressing against his legs. My pulse beat everywhere, especially the places we touched. And I felt his, too. I couldn't tell if the fast, rhythmic *ba-boom* against my palms was just the robust heartbeat of a healthy man or if he was feeling as euphoric and turned on and nervous as I was.

As everyone started down the path, Manning and I pulled up the rear while one handler took the lead. Hannah and the other instructor rode alongside the kids.

Manning cleared his throat and asked over his shoulder, "Are you comfortable?"

My chest was mashed against him, my butt awkwardly pushed out to keep just a little distance between us so he wouldn't think I was trying to get too cozy. Worst of all, I couldn't see over him since he was so tall, and I didn't know where to put my face. It didn't matter. I sighed. "Yes."

"Did you fall off a horse as a kid or something?"

"No. I never even got on one."

"So this is like the Ferris wheel?" he asked. "It's not really a height thing."

"No. My friend had a treehouse growing up and I went in there sometimes. I get on the roof at home."

"The roof?"

"From my room. I can climb out the window."

"Hmm." His hum vibrated my body. "So it must be things that move. Not being able to control what could happen. Have you ever been on a plane?"

Those were worst of all. Talk about having no control. You could die a million different ways on a plane and most of it wouldn't be instant. If it started to fall out of the sky, you'd have to sit there, knowing you were going to die. Just waiting. I shuddered. "I had to as a kid when we took vacations. I didn't have a choice. I think I cried through my entire first flight and after that, my parents just gave me something."

"That surprises me," he said. "I know you're brave."

Me, brave? I wasn't so sure. "Why do you think that?"

"Just little things. Like when we went to that party before the fair, and Tiffany pressured you to go in. You said no when most teenagers would've done the opposite."

"That wasn't bravery," I said. "I just don't like those things—drinking, flirting, acting stupid because they think it's cute or funny."

"A lot of people don't like those things, but they do them anyway. Because people make them think it's cool. They back down. They're the cowards." Manning placed his hand over mine as I held onto his stomach. My throat went dry, my body tingling in places I didn't know could tingle. "Take the reins a minute," he said.

"I can't even see." That was a lie. I saw Manning, and Manning was all I saw.

"You don't need to, because I can." He removed my hand to place a rein in it, then did the same with the other. "There you go. You're a pro."

I wasn't doing a single thing but holding the reins. He could've been steering me into the lake, and I'd have no idea. For some reason, it was important to him that I do this on my own.

"Hey, Jake," Manning called out. "Mike. Stop screwing around. This isn't a videogame. These are real animals."

"Sorry, Manning," a couple boys said.

"You're good with them. I can tell they look up to you." My back started to ache from keeping some distance between us. "Do you want kids?"

He took the reins again. "Not really. No. Not right now."

I had nowhere to put my hands. "I do, one day."

"You're still a kid yourself."

"Just because I'm younger than you doesn't mean I'm a kid." I wrapped my arms around him again, this time pulling myself forward until we were snug, hardly any space left between us. "And I'm getting older every day."

He straightened up, and I rested my cheek against his back, closing my eyes, inhaling the scent of the pine trees around us. We rocked together with the steady bump-and-grind of the horse's hooves on the dirt path. The fresh morning air kept me cool, even while my body warmed where we touched. My jeans caught on his, but his t-shirt was soft under my bare arms. Based on what I'd heard from kids at school, this was the way I imagined it felt to be drunk or high, to reach a level of happiness and bliss that could only be achieved with help. Arms, chest, cheek. My entire self pressed against Manning's solid body—that was my drug of choice.

Was sixteen too young to fall in love? I might've thought so before Manning. Could he love me back, a man seven years older? I was sure if he did, he'd never admit it. But I would wait for him. Even I understood that for a while, ours ages mattered. There was no *right now* for us. Eighteen was a lifetime away. That was two more whole school years, another long summer. It was millions of breaths that would inevitably catch in my throat around him and thousands of pages read across so many books and hundreds of long, sun-soaked California days. But the wait would be, without a doubt, worth it.

The horse slowed. I opened my eyes but didn't lift my head. We were at the lake now. A couple cabins were canoeing. Because she was as familiar to me as my own reflection, but also because she was yelling across the water at some of her girls, my gaze went straight to Tiffany.

Her canoe rocked, and for a second, I thought she might fall in. She grabbed the edges, steadied herself, and sat. Her campers pointed at the parade of horses, waving to us. Tiffany shielded her eyes.

I turned my head away, resting my other cheek against Manning's back as I tightened my hold on him. Tiffany didn't know what she had, what she could have.

As much as it frustrated me, I was thankful for that.

16
MANNING

Lake carried a bucket of water that looked half her size. She put it down in front of Betsy and with a tentative hand, stroked the horse's nose. We were only halfway through the ride, and she was already overcoming her fear. It was what I wanted, except that when Betsy whinnied and Lake jumped back and looked at me, a part of me liked that. I craved that feeling of being needed again, of being held onto when she was scared. A hint of fear was good. It would keep her alert.

The air up here was crisp. I could practically feel it move through my lungs. I wished *my* fears were as easily overcome, but I was fucked any way I turned. Lake was important to me in a way she shouldn't be. Her naiveté about some things made me overprotective. Then, once in a while her girlish mannerisms or expressions reminded me of things Maddy did I'd forgotten about, like how she blinked a lot when processing something new. It drew me in. On a primal level, I wanted to keep bad things from happening to her. Was it more than that? I didn't want to know the answer. In some ways, she was still sweet and open. In others, Lake was more mature than people my own age. She wanted to understand things rather than accept them as they were. She took an interest in me nobody else had in a long time, grilling me about the smoking, asking why I wanted to be a cop. Trusting me when she had no reason to.

Lake returned to my side. She'd barely spent any time with Hannah or her girls since we'd left the stables. She was here to experience camp, not me. But I was greedy. When she looked up at me with her huge eyes, waiting for my direction, I knew peripherally that I was in too deep. I needed to pull back. But that look reminded me someone might depend on me again one day, and if things were different, Lake could've been that someone.

She was still standing there. Even if I pushed my heels into my eye sockets and forced her image away, she'd still be here. Looking up at me. Waiting.

"Why don't you go check on the girls?" I asked.

"I did. The boys, too. After I gave the horse water."

Time passed in a funny way around her. Maybe she *had* talked to the campers. Maybe she'd spent time with Hannah. I'd been the one standing in the same spot, watching her. Time could be slow like that with her, and then sometimes it went by in flashes. Sometimes I just wanted it to stop and others, I wished it'd go by faster.

"We should head back," she said. "There's a group after us."

I wasn't sure if it was the altitude or what. My head wasn't clear. All I could think was that I'd spent twenty-four hours on a lake, underneath clear, endless skies, and yet I'd still never seen a blue the shade of her eyes. I was sure the image of her looking up at me this way would be burned into my brain for as long as I walked this Earth.

"Manning?"

"Yeah." I tore my gaze away. "Get on."

"I want to drive."

Half an hour ago, she could barely bring herself to get near the horse. Maybe she didn't need me after all. "By yourself?"

"No, with you."

I nodded. "You get on first."

"Will you help?"

"You can do it," I said.

"I know. I want your help."

I ran a hand through my hair. The other instructors were helping campers on the horses. How was this different? I had no reason to feel weird. Lake was Tiffany's little sister.

She stuck her foot in the stirrup and looked back at me, waiting.

As I took Lake by the waist and put her in the saddle, I tried not to notice how her shirt rode up. "All set?" I asked one of the handlers.

"Got the back?" he replied.

"Yeah."

One by one, the group lined up to head back for the campsite. I grabbed the knob at the front of the saddle, right between Lake's legs, and pulled myself up behind her. She slid back into the "V" my thighs made, the two of us fitting together like puzzle pieces. I took the reins and waited until everyone had gone ahead of us. I could've rested my chin on Lake's head, or closed my arms around her and engulfed her completely. Her hair smelled like sweet summer strawberries, as if she washed it in the produce section of a fucking supermarket.

Distracted, I pulled on the reins without meaning to, and Betsy stopped.

"What's wrong?" Lake asked.

"Nothing." I squeezed Betsy's middle to get her to go again. I tried to remember how Tiffany smelled. Nothing came to mind except that she smoked cigarettes and chewed a lot of minty gum.

"I'm ready to try," Lake said.

My head was still foggy, my ears buzzing. I didn't want Lake to take over while I was out of sorts. Maddy had died around the same age as these girls surrounding me. I was responsible for them. Should I be doing more to keep them safe? Things I hadn't done for Madison? The day she'd died, it wasn't the first time my dad had gone into a rage. So why hadn't my mom or I had him locked up sooner? Why hadn't I been gentler, more understanding with Maddy?

"Manning?" Lake asked.

"In a minute."

"But we're falling behind."

The rest of the campers were yards ahead, so I tapped Betsy into a trot. Lake bounced underneath me, skidding backward in the saddle until she was right up against my crotch. Up until this point, as a grown man, I'd thought I could control myself. Even earlier, when she'd squeezed me as tightly as a predator would its prey, her hands dangerously low on my stomach, I'd kept it together. But now, my body reacted only as a man. I wanted to wrap my arms around her front, pull her closer, let her feel what she did to me. I was losing control.

"Take the reins, Lake." I slowed Betsy down and said, "Now. Come on."

She did, and I slid back to put some space between us.

"I'm not going to the dining hall tonight," I announced.

"What?" Her fine blonde hairs floated between us and stuck to my chest. "Why not?"

I guess I'd said it to put it out there. To put a different kind of distance between us. Because I knew, I *knew* she'd ask why. How much had she heard the night before in the woods? Tiffany and I had been arguing because I'd refused, yet again, to go on a "walk" with her. She didn't want to walk. She wanted to fool around.

"I came here for *you*," Tiffany had said once Lake'd gone off with that kid. "You think I *like* this?" she'd asked. "The girls hate me. I'm here for you, and you don't even care."

"I care," I'd said.

Tiffany had stamped out her cigarette in the woods without a thought for how dangerous that might be. "Then prove it," she'd said and walked off.

I'd needed to hear it. Being up here, rules changed. There wasn't anything wrong with hanging around a sixteen-year-old, and it was messing with my head. Tiffany was out of her element, and she needed my help. Lake could handle herself. Maybe it was the wakeup call Lake and I both needed.

"Tiffany and I have plans," I told Lake. "Alone."

Lake had the posture of a college professor. It made her reactions easy to read. I expected disappointment, and that's what I got. My instinct was to comfort her, but that'd probably be the worst thing I could do to a teenage girl I was pretty sure harbored a crush on me.

"What plans?" she asked. "You can't leave the grounds."

"I can if I want." I was a grown man, and I'd go where I liked. But I wouldn't. Where I wanted to be, one of the main reasons I'd come here, was where I could watch over Lake. I wasn't going to go off for a few hours and leave her behind. "Bucky's going to make us dinner after lights-out."

"Oh."

There was a fine line between hurting her and warning her off, and I could tell by her reaction I'd achieved the former. Knowing it was best didn't make me feel better. Not thirty minutes ago, she'd pulled her body close to mine, told me she was getting older every day. It wasn't news to me, and it tore me down the middle. I didn't want her to get older, to know what I knew, to do things Tiffany had done. But it would happen regardless. Someone else would be her first love. Some other man would be the first to cherish her. The first to ruin her. It couldn't be me. It wasn't so much the difference in our ages that scared me, but how much a person could change, could *be* changed, in only a couple years.

They were thoughts I didn't want to have, and they got louder as she sat quietly, guiding the horse. There wasn't a single blemish on her pink cheeks. I opened my mouth to ask if she'd put on sunscreen, but that wasn't what came out. "What about that guy?"

She sighed. "I don't want to do this anymore."

I'd gone too far, maybe. "Do what?"

"Drive." She held up the reins. "Will you?"

I took them back as discontent rolled off her. "Lake?"

"Were you with her last night?" she asked. "Is that why she was late this morning?"

I had no idea that was even on her mind. It really fucking shouldn't have been. She should be thinking about campfire skits and summer reading lists and whatever else young girls thought about. "That's between me and your sister."

"Oh. Okay. Then don't ask me about *that guy*. And his name is Corbin."

I knew his name, but I wasn't going to use it. I didn't like how he kept appearing out of nowhere, how he'd set his sights on Lake but also knew Tiffany through his brother. "Did he just take you back to your cabin or what?"

"I want to get off."

"And do what?" I asked. "Walk back?"

"It's not that far."

"I'm not prying, just making sure he was polite. That he didn't, you know, try anything."

Her breathing sped. Her heart had pounded against my back earlier. I was better than her at hiding it, but my reaction to her was the same. Physical. Powerful. Painful.

"I'm not going to let you down," I said.

She looked over the side of the horse, as if she were thinking of jumping off. I had no business asking her what I did, making her feel sad or bad for letting Corbin walk her back like any normal teen girl would've done. My hands sweat around the leather reins. "Hold on," I said.

"What?"

"Grab something. The saddle, my arms, whatever."

Once she had the horn, I applied pressure to Betsy's sides. She took off into a trot. "What are you doing?" Lake asked, grabbing my forearms instead.

I nudged the horse again, and she picked up her pace. "Relax."

"You don't even know how to ride," she cried. "Stop."

I steered the horse alongside the other campers, who hollered at us. One of the instructors cheered us on. He'd called Betsy wild, but he wouldn't put us on a horse that couldn't be controlled. We cantered to the front of the group.

Lake squirmed between my legs, her fingers digging into my skin. "Manning—please."

"Please what, Birdy? I've got you. Don't worry."

She didn't ease her hold on me, but she relaxed her back against my front as we pulled out ahead of the group. Instinctively, I put an arm around her, holding her to me, just us, just for a second. Some strands of her hair flew into my mouth, but she was laughing again. It came from a place of pure joy. I liked that laugh so much, that carefree sound in my ears.

My world had been so dark before Lake.

It worried me how far I'd go to keep that light in my life.

17
MANNING

Tiffany bounced in place, her eyes closed and her smile big. She'd pulled her hair back into a twisty-bun thing and kept everything simple with a loose sundress and little makeup. She was a natural beauty. "Where are you taking me?" she asked.

It wasn't as if I had the world at my fingertips, just a few places where there weren't any people. I led her away from the dining hall, where all the other counselors were hanging out, to a staff dining area off the kitchen. Gary and I had set it up earlier with a black tablecloth and a tall, white candle.

Tiffany opened her eyes when we stepped inside. "Oh my God," she said. "This is so romantic."

I pulled out a chair for her, then cupped my hand around the candle and lit the wick with my Zippo.

"You went through all this for me?" she asked.

I sat across from her. "You wanted me to prove it. I am."

She studied me. "You really are old-fashioned, aren't you? For a minute, I was worried you didn't like me."

"I like you." At least, I was coming to appreciate things about her. She was adventurous and bold. No girls I knew were as unapologetic about their sexuality. And, she was beautiful. I hated myself for thinking it, but it was true. All the counselors knew it. I'd shut down some of the guys talking about her, had heard some jealous snipes from the other girls.

"I like you, too," she said, sounding surprised. It occurred to me that she might also like other guys. I'd never had trouble getting women, but maybe I couldn't hang on to a girl like Tiffany as long as I wanted. And then what? I'd go back to being alone, trying to keep the past at bay. Drinking, smoking, using my hands to build things for other people. It wasn't a bad life. I slept with who I wanted. I didn't have to watch my mouth or not light my cigs.

"Are you seeing anyone else?" I asked.

She darted her eyes over the table. "Are you?"

"Nope. Are you?" I asked again.

"Well . . . not really. I didn't think you'd care if I did, though."

Bucky came strolling out and made no secret about looking Tiff over. "Dinner's about ready. I asked him what you like in your spaghetti but he didn't know. How's a man not know what his girl likes?"

Dick. I had a feeling he'd been waiting to call me out like that ever since I'd asked him for seconds the day before. I owed him for making us dinner, but if I didn't I'd have told him to fuck off.

"Meatballs, I guess?" Tiffany said with a smile to egg him on. "What else is there?"

"Anything you want, gorgeous. Mushrooms, eggplant, roasted pepper, chicken . . ."

"You mind calling her by her name?" I asked. "We're on a date here."

Tiffany's eyes twinkled. "I'll take some wine if you have it," she said to him. "Otherwise, whatever you made is fine."

"Yeah. Okay." Bucky sucked his teeth and returned to the kitchen.

"You're . . ." She shook her head. "Not like anyone I've dated."

"Same for you."

"Is that a good thing?" she asked.

"I don't know, Tiff. Most girls, I tell them something once and they listen, not three times. Even if Bucky flies to Italy and brings us back a bottle, I already told you, we're not drinking wine."

I prepared for her to argue, but instead she heaved a sigh. "I know. I'm just nervous."

"No you're not."

She smiled, looking up at me from under her lashes. "Yes I am. Usually when I'm alone with a guy, we're either drinking or smoking or there are people in the other room. It feels weird to just be out here in the middle of nowhere on a real date."

Huh. That was something we pretty much had in common. When I brought a girl home, it was probably after a drink or four at my local spot. "Bad weird?"

"No . . ." She picked at nothing on the tablecloth. "Just different. Why'd you ask if I was seeing anyone else?"

For a conversation like this, I needed a fucking cigarette. I guessed that's what Tiffany was talking about, getting too intense without something to take the edge off. "Maybe it's too early for that."

"Yeah." She unfolded her napkin into her lap. "Maybe."

"When I'm with a girl, she won't be sleeping with anyone else. Understand?"

"No. You don't want me for yourself, but you don't want me with anyone else?"

My stomach grumbled. "I guess. I mean . . . it sounds fucked up. What do you want?"

"I haven't been in a serious relationship since high school. And even then, it was . . ." She shrugged.

It wasn't really an answer, but she didn't say anything else, just twirled a saltshaker on the table.

Maybe she really was nervous. I put my hand over hers to stop her fidgeting, and I think it surprised us both a little. She flipped her palm up and flexed her fingers, lacing them with mine. Tiffany sat in front of me, but she wasn't quite the brazen girl I'd seen until now.

"Your hands are rough," she said. "Is that from work?"

"Pretty much. It's definitely not from baseball."

She giggled. "I guess not."

Corbin had left camp, but not before he'd beat my ass on the diamond. I'd had to sit through nine innings of baseball against him this evening. I'd played a little in high school, so I'd been picked to coach the opposing team. Corbin had been in and out of baseball camp all summer and obliterated us while Tiffany and Lake had watched from the grass. Smug satisfaction sat on Corbin's face as we shook hands after the game but disappeared completely as soon as Lake came around.

I released Tiffany's hand. "What's the deal with him?" I asked. "Corbin."

She folded her arms on the table. "He's a good guy, comes from a good family. Kind of a heartbreaker."

"So he's a little shit."

She laughed. "No. He doesn't do it on purpose. That's why I was worried about Lake. Like, if Corbin had a crush on me and thought he could get close to me through her or maybe that Lake was, like, a substitute for me, then I'd worry he might hurt her. But he wouldn't do it on purpose, you know? He's not like that. He's just a boy thinking with his . . . you know."

Brave, bold Tiffany couldn't come out and say what she wanted. It made me smile. Part of me wanted to hear it, just to tease her, but there was a bigger part of me that wanted to know about Corbin. "So do you think he's a problem?"

She cocked her head. "How?"

Did I *want* him to be a problem? Maybe a little. That way I'd have an excuse to keep him away. "I don't know. Will he try pressuring your sister into anything?"

"He's not like that." She rolled her eyes. "But maybe he should."

"*What?*"

"I'm *kidding*. Of course I don't want Lake to do anything before she's ready, and she won't. She's too uptight. I swear she's the youngest sixteen-year-old I know."

"Meaning?"

"When it comes to boys, she acts like she's twelve, but she isn't. When I was her age, I wasn't so naïve about these things. None of my friends were."

I shifted in my seat. It was just like on the horse earlier, Lake trying to convince me she was older while I wanted to keep her innocent. "Maybe you were like that and you just forgot what it's like to be that age."

She laughed. "My freshman year, my first boyfriend was quarterback of the varsity football team. A senior. You think he treated me like a kid? No. He taught me and my friends how to sneak out of the house. How to party. Before him, I'd had one beer in my life. By the end of the year, I took beer bongs as an appetizer."

I couldn't picture Tiffany at sixteen, which left me picturing Lake. They shared certain expressions that made me wonder if Tiffany had ever been as sweet and pure as her sister—or if Lake was bound to become like Tiffany. Lake was on the right track. USC would open up all sorts of doors for her. Nothing should get in her way, especially not someone like me who had no steady job, a murky past, and little more than what fit in a bedroom. Tiffany, though, she was going through something she probably couldn't recognize, not being motivated to find work or do anything of substance. She needed a hand out of it, and her dad was too busy with Lake. Even her mom hadn't seemed to want to help, more interested in getting me to date Tiffany.

There was a pretty good chance I could be good for Tiffany, and an even better one I'd be bad for Lake.

Bucky returned and set both plates down. "It took some bargaining, but I got your wine," he said to Tiffany. "It's in the back. Hope you like red."

"We don't want any wine," I said. "She's underage."

Tiffany nodded. "I changed my mind."

With a visible sneer, Bucky muttered something under his breath that sounded like *asshole*. I had no idea what the fuck his problem was, but I didn't ask him to repeat himself. I wouldn't be able to control my reaction if I was right.

"This is so good," Tiffany said when we were alone again.

The food smelled damn tempting, but our conversation still weighed on my mind. "You don't think she'll head down that path, right?"

Tiffany cut her meatballs into halves. "Who?"

"Lake." I was pretty sure I knew the answer, but I wasn't around much in the big scheme of things. "The parties and sneaking out and stuff."

"Oh. No."

I exhaled. Lake had a good head on her shoulders, and I had to trust that. I went to pick up my fork.

"She should," Tiffany added, "but she probably won't."

I paused. "What do you mean *should?*"

"It makes me a little sad how she just does what Dad says all the time. Like he's so perfect? He isn't, you know."

I had to agree there. "Still, it means she stays out of trouble."

"And has no fun. I'm not saying she needs to be like I was. I don't want her to be. I just don't want her to look back and wish she'd been more . . . I don't know. Balanced. Social. So *what* if she has a little too much to drink one night and embarrasses herself doing karaoke at a party? Or misses curfew because she lost track of time talking to a cute boy? Or ditches one class to go get ice cream at the mall?" She took a sip of water. "Big deal. She'll be eighteen in a couple years anyway."

I stared at her. I hadn't even taken a bite. Was she saying Lake was almost eighteen? The way I'd been looking at it, she still had two long years to go, to change, to become who she was meant to be.

"Why do you bring her up so much?" Tiffany asked.

That was simple. "I worry."

"But why?" Her tone was casual as she twirled noodles onto her fork. She lifted a shoulder. "You guys have a weird friendship."

A tremor of panic rose up my chest. Couldn't I have just kept my fucking mouth shut? No, because that was what Lake did to me. Truth was, I had good reason to be worried. A reason that would shut Tiffany right up. I just didn't want to share it. I sat back in my seat, staring at my food for a minute as I worked up the nerve.

"You're not eating," Tiffany said, blinking big, pretty eyes at me, seemingly concerned. "I told you you'd spoil your appetite if you ate dinner with the kids."

I glanced at my untouched food, my silverware, the melting candle. Then at Tiffany. She was right. The friendship was weird, and I didn't want her thinking too hard about that. "My sister died," I said.

Tiffany stopped chewing. "What?"

"I had a little sister. I can't . . . talk about it. I don't want to. But that's why I get so protective of Lake. I don't ever want you or your family to go through what mine did."

"Oh, God," she whispered, letting her fork clatter onto the plate. "I'm so sorry. I had no idea. When you mentioned your sister, I thought . . . I thought—"

"It's okay." I needed her to stop talking. "It's been years, so."

"What was her name?"

I swallowed. I didn't talk about Maddy. I would never say her name to a stranger, and that was how most people had felt to me since it'd happened. "Can't."

She took my hand. "Was she sick?"

My head began to swim. I nodded just to end the conversation, even if it was with a lie.

"Manning?" Tiffany stood up and came to me.

I tried to stop her. "You really don't need to—"

She moved the table, actually pushed it back a foot, so she could sit on my lap.

"Tiff," I said, but I put my arms around her. "I don't want to talk about it."

She touched my cheek, running her thumb over the corner of my mouth. "I'm sorry."

I wasn't sure how to feel. I didn't want to talk about it, period. But it felt nice to be touched. It was something I hadn't had in a long time, the soothing touch of a woman who cared. "Thanks."

She ran her long fingernails over my hairline, and my eyes drooped shut. "That's why you're so protective."

"Part of it."

She took my face in both hands and kissed my forehead. "I can't imagine if that happened to Lake. I'd die."

My throat thickened. Thinking that could happen to Lake, but also that Tiffany cared way more about her sister than she let on. I wished I could promise Tiffany it would never happen, but that was the thing about Maddy's death. I hadn't fathomed it was even a possibility until it'd already happened. If I had, I would've done anything to prevent it.

I patted Tiffany's ass. "Come on. Let's not ruin the date. It's going well."

She pulled back and looked me in the face. There was no minty breath, no cigarette reek stuck to her. Just the earthy tomato sauce and wood cabin. She got up and went back to her side of the table. "Will you finally eat something?"

I picked up my fork and took a bite. "You should know," I said, "that I eat a lot." I shoved noodles in my mouth, and my words came out muffled. "*A lot.*"

"Yuck." Tiffany giggled. "That's disgusting."

I washed down my bite with water. "You should see me with lasagna. Fucking massacre."

She laughed harder. Tiffany took a forkful, pursed her lips, and slurped up a noodle. Tomato sauce splattered over her mouth, and instead of wiping it off right away, she just smiled and chewed. She was all right when she dropped the show. Her attitude could even be cute. The highlights, pink nail polish, low-cut tops—they didn't attract me. Not more than any girl I might meet in a bar. This side of her, I could spend time with.

Dessert was store-bought chocolate cake with raspberry drizzle. Tiffany took two bites and slid her plate away. "I'm on a diet."

"You don't need to be on a diet."

"That's because I'm on one." She waggled her eyebrows as if she'd bested me. "If I weren't, I wouldn't look this good."

I wouldn't argue with that. She did look good, and I liked that she knew it. That was one difference between Tiffany and a lot of the girls I'd met over the last few years. I ate half her cake in one bite and swallowed. "You think *I* should go on a diet?"

She smiled. "No. You're a guy, and a big one. You can eat as much as you want. You work out, too. Don't you?"

"Construction kind of requires it."

She looked at her plate, which had become mine, and frowned. "I've been meaning to say . . . I'm sorry if my dad made you feel bad about what you do."

"I get it. He wants you to be taken care of." I liked construction but not that my next job was always up in the air. I saved every dime I could just in case. I didn't ever want to end up with nothing to offer. In that way, I understood Tiffany's dad. When the time came, nobody'd ever be able to accuse me of not taking care of my family.

"Well, it doesn't matter to me. Money's not important."

"You say that because you have it. Living without it sounds glamorous to you."

She waved me off. "I'd rather be in love than rich."

It was becoming clear Tiffany didn't expect much of me when it came to earning potential. And that she didn't know herself as well as she thought. A girl like her would always need money. "You're saying you're okay with spaghetti and meatballs in a small room with a shitty candle instead of a fancy restaurant?"

"I've been to lots of fancy restaurants. You can't do the slurp-y thing with your noodles."

She might believe she'd choose love over money, but I didn't. Not when it came down to it. "I get the feeling you aren't really enjoying all this. Roughing it."

She shrugged, her silliness dimming. "It's fine."

"That wasn't convincing." I sat back in my chair. "Is it the girls?"

"They hate me. I hate them. I can't even . . . I don't know how to handle them."

If I didn't think it'd hurt her feelings, I would've laughed. Surely Tiffany could see why she was having so much trouble. The girls were mini-versions of her. I leaned my elbows on the table. "Know what I think?"

"What?"

"There isn't a person here who could handle them better than you."

She rolled her eyes. "That's because you haven't spent any time with my cabin."

"Those kids, they're just starting to learn about makeup and boys and clothing. Who knows more about that girly shit than you?"

"Nobody," she stated.

"Exactly. People have different skills, Tiff. Use yours. It can't be easy to put that black shit on your eyelids."

She giggled. "Eyeliner? It's not. It's hard, actually."

Did I think twelve-year-olds away from home should be learning to apply makeup? Not really. But in the scheme of things, I guessed it wasn't so bad if it meant it'd change their experience here for the positive, and Tiffany's, too. "Give them a lesson."

"All right," she said. "I guess I could try that. Then I'll teach them how to be stylish, even in hiking boots."

"There you go." I finished off both desserts and stood. "I'll walk you back."

She also got up. "It's still early."

"Not in camp time. It's like I need twice the amount of sleep here."

As we walked outside, she grabbed my hand, but when I squeezed hers, she relaxed. My palm was probably clammy. The site was quiet, even more so as we headed into the woods. I could've used a cigarette, but I didn't want to stop. Best I got her to her cabin quickly.

She took it upon herself, though, not that it surprised me. She stopped, getting me to look back with a light tug on my hand. "I want to thank you for dinner."

"How?" I asked, but I knew.

She rose onto the balls of her feet and pressed her lips to mine. I stood still as a statue, as did she. This was the point where I was supposed to take over. I put my arm around her waist. For all her bravado, she melted against me quicker than I would've guessed, dissolving into our kiss. It didn't matter that I wasn't sure if I wanted it. It was happening. Any guy at this camp would've killed to be in my position.

I tried not to think of the horse earlier, of the defiant pout I'd left behind when I'd picked up Tiffany for our date tonight.

I didn't realize my hand was on the back of Tiffany's head until I pulled her hair, and she moaned, bringing me back to the moment. She pushed her tongue against my lips, and I opened my mouth. I owed her my attention, but she also demanded it. She wrapped her arms around my neck and kissed me harder. I followed her lead, going through the motions, trying not to give in to the wet, willing mouth attached to mine. She took my bottom lip between her teeth and nipped it. My dick woke up. *Fuck*, this girl knew what she was doing.

An owl hooted so loud, I jumped back as if we'd been caught. I held her at a distance by her waist.

"What?" she whispered.

"I . . . should get you back."

"Seriously?" She stepped into me and trailed soft fingers along the back of my neck, playing with the ends of my hair.

It'd been months since I'd kissed someone. Two seconds in, we'd stripped down to jump in bed. She'd told me her name, but I couldn't remember it now.

"I'm just getting started," Tiffany said.

"I know." Between being turned on and needing to keep our bodies apart, I was a little out of breath. "That's why I have to stop. You're getting me excited, and there's not really anything I can do about it until we get home. Know what I mean?"

"Who says we have to wait?" She removed an arm from around my neck, lowering it to my pants.

I caught her wrist. "I promised Gary we'd keep it PG."

She smiled. "How would he know? Unless he's watching with binoculars, the pervert."

"I told you." I had to force the words out while my angry cock throbbed. "I like to take it slow."

She sighed, softening against my chest. "I guess. But this is super slow."

"And what's wrong with that?" I asked with a grunt. Here was a girl who had what men wanted and actually knew it. Why give it up so fast? "You should be the one making me wait."

She moved away from me. "What do you mean?"

"You know what you're worth." The only sound was her breathing. "It'll happen," I said. "Just be patient."

She didn't respond right away. What she was thinking about, I had no idea. "Okay," she said finally. "We can stay slow for a while."

"Good." I took her hand again and led her to her cabin. "See you in the morning. Seven o'clock sharp, all right? I don't want to see you on cleaning duty again."

She wandered away, a little dazed, while I wondered why pointing out her worth had only seemed to confuse her.

18
LAKE

For the second night in a row, Manning didn't come to the dining hall after lights-out. Tiffany did—at least that meant she wasn't with him. With Manning away, boys had been approaching her all night like bees with honey or moths to a flame. That's what Tiffany was to them, whether they knew it or not. A honeyed-flame. One poor guy had been circling for an hour, working up the nerve to talk to her. Tiffany didn't even notice him.

Tiffany, Hannah, and I sat in a circle on the floor with a few other counselors. Tiffany crossed her legs under her. "I don't remember half these guys from high school. It's like they haven't seen a girl in months."

"They probably spent four years thinking they'd never get a chance to talk to you," Hannah said.

"Most of them are geeks." She scrunched her nose. "I guess that can be sexy."

I glanced around to make sure none of them were within hearing distance, then changed the subject. "How was last night?"

She checked her makeup in her compact. "Last night?"

"Your date."

"Oh." She snapped the mirror shut. "So good. So so good."

The hair on the back of my neck prickled. "Really?"

"Not even in a sexual way. Manning just made me realize I've been dating boys all this time when there are men out there."

"How?" It came out as a whisper, so I cleared my throat. "What did he do?"

"He arranged this dinner just for me. We had a great talk, where he opened up so much."

"About what?"

"Our relationship and stuff." She shook her head. "His sister died."

It came out fast, like an afterthought or an unwarranted slap across the face. I couldn't believe he'd shared that with her after I'd asked about his family and he'd said he didn't talk about it. With anyone. Not even me. He'd given Tiffany this intimate piece of himself and me nothing.

When the shock wore off, it hit me. He'd had a little sister. And she was gone. His gentleness with me, at times, could be almost brotherly, the way he didn't smoke or curse in my presence. I couldn't deny the attraction between us, but it made more sense, his sadness, his intensity, if he was a big brother without a little sister.

"Then he walked me back to my cabin," Tiffany continued. "He never acts like I owe him anything. He was a gentleman, you know?"

That sounded like Manning to me. A gentleman, someone who'd never push me to do anything I wasn't comfortable with. I wanted that for Tiffany, to be treated well, but not enough to give her Manning.

"Can you be more specific?" I asked.

"He was trying to be polite at first . . ."

At first. At *first*? "Then what?"

"Here's a lesson you're going to learn sooner or later, Lake, so it might as well be sooner. Men's brains turn to mush with a little physical contact."

My chest rattled with each breath, caving in on itself. I didn't even know enough about men to understand if getting physical could mean just a kiss or if it was always more. What I wouldn't give for a dinner date with Manning. And then to be alone with him afterward, to have our first kiss in the quiet dark under pine trees.

"I'm starting to like this place," she said. "It's romantic."

I didn't get a chance to ask for details. The boy who'd been pacing around like a predator finally pounced. "Tiffany, right?" he asked. "We went—"

"High school?" she asked.

His face lit up as he wrung his hands. He was definitely more prey than predator. "Yeah! You remember. Armando Diaz."

If Manning wasn't coming, I didn't want to be here. "You can sit here, Armando," I said, standing.

He took my spot without a glance in my direction. "Thanks."

After saying goodnight to Hannah, I left the hall. My tennis shoes barely made a sound on the forest floor on the way to my cabin. Bushes I couldn't even see rustled. There were no lights, just the sliver of a crescent moon, but even it was blocked by trees. Frogs burped a chorus by the lake.

I heard footsteps before I saw anyone. It unnerved me, not being able to see who was there, which direction they were coming from. I turned around. "Hello . . .?"

"You're not making a very good case for walking alone in the woods," Manning said.

It took a moment for my eyes to adjust to his big frame a few feet in front of me, shadowed, but undeniably his.

"Haven't you ever seen *Friday the 13th*?" he asked.

"No."

"Is everyone in your family this stubborn?"

I wanted to make some remark about *his* family and how he'd betrayed me by telling Tiffany something it would've made more sense to tell me, someone who cared. But if it was true about his sister, a snarky comment didn't seem right. "I'm not trying to be," I said. "I didn't want to stay in there by myself."

"You have your sister. Your friends are in there. You have Hannah."

I don't have you. Before him, I would've loved having Tiffany treat me like a friend instead of a pest. Now, I didn't care to be anywhere Manning wasn't. I glanced at the ground. "Why didn't you come tonight?"

"I'm on patrol. Supposed to be walking the site, checking on cabins."

I exhaled softly, quietly relieved. He hadn't purposely been avoiding me. "Can I walk with you?"

He hesitated. "It's not really a two-person job."

"I'm not ready to go to sleep. Please?"

Silhouetted against the trees, he ran a hand through his hair. "I'll walk you back to your bunk, but we can take the long way."

He passed me, and I turned to follow him in the opposite direction of my cabin. "Did you have a good day?"

"We have to be quiet. Don't want to wake up the kids."

"Did you have a good day?" I whispered.

His sigh ended in a light laugh. "It was hectic. Yours?"

"I got a bullseye during archery."

"Yeah?" He sounded impressed. "None of my boys managed that. Me, neither."

"I practiced a lot last year." I shrugged. "This was my first bullseye, though."

"Wish I'd seen it."

It was a pretty cool thing on its own, but knowing Manning thought so, too, made me proud.

We walked a little longer in silence, me sneaking glances at him. As my eyes adjusted, I noticed a paperback in his pocket. "Are you still reading that same book as before?"

"Nah. I grabbed something new from the cafeteria. You see they have a book exchange?"

"Yes, but I haven't had time to read at all."

"Started your dad's list yet?"

I'd imagined him asking me this a few times since my last visit to the library. I wasn't sure I'd be brave enough to say what I wanted, but it helped that he couldn't see me blushing. "Not yet. I decided to take your advice and check out a book not on the list. One about something that . . . interested me."

"Oh yeah? Which one?"

Despite the cool mountain air, my body warmed, because once I said what I'd chosen, it'd be obvious why. "*Lolita*."

Manning didn't respond.

My heart beat in my throat, getting louder as the silence stretched between us. "You know of it?"

"Yeah."

"It's about—"

"I know what it's about. And I don't want to talk about it."

I could almost understand why Manning shut down so many of our conversations when people were around, but we were alone now, away from everyone. I kicked a rock. Manning must've thought I tripped, because he reached out to take my arm. "What a surprise," I said, pulling away. "Something you don't want to talk about."

I felt his eyes on me, but I refused to look up. "I talk to you about a lot of things, Lake. More than anyone else."

"Liar."

"Excuse me?"

"Nothing," I muttered.

"You called me a liar," he said. "You can't say that's nothing." He waited, for what I wasn't sure. I wasn't going to apologize, because it was true. "I'm seeing a new side of you lately," he said.

"How was your date with Tiffany?"

"Ah. That's what this is about?"

"No. It's just a question."

"Date was good, thanks for asking."

"Did you kiss?" It wasn't my business, and I hadn't planned to ask because I wasn't sure what good it would do to know. But I had to. I wanted to hear it from him, not Tiffany, who exaggerated when it came to these things. At least, I was pretty sure she did.

"I told you yesterday," he said, "that's between your sister and me."

I wiped my clammy palms on my jeans. I was nervous he'd admit they'd kissed. I was nervous he wouldn't, leaving me to fill in the blanks. "So that's a yes. You kissed. Maybe you did other stuff, too."

"Lake," he warned, an edge to his voice.

"I know you told Tiffany about your sister," I blurted. "Why not me? She doesn't even care. I do."

He inhaled a loud breath. "That was private."

"Sisters tell each other everything."

"Do you talk to her about me? Does she know you and I spend time together like this?"

I closed my mouth, scolded. Of course I hadn't told Tiffany about us. She'd just ruin it by calling me childish or teasing me for having a crush. He'd made his point. "No."

"Good, and don't," he said. "That'd put an end to our friendship."

I looked up at him, panic tightening my chest. "You'd end our friendship if I told Tiffany?"

"Not me, no."

Somehow, I knew instinctively who he meant. Everyone who wasn't *us*. "You're not closer to Tiffany than you are to me."

"How do you know that?"

"I just do. You can't be. It's not possible."

"Tiffany and I are friends in a different way than you and me, Lake. Our *friendship*—it progresses differently. It means something else."

"That's not fair."

"Why not?" He waited, but I didn't respond. "Would you rather I broke up with her?"

I opened my mouth to scream *yes!* But *did* I want that? Tiffany wouldn't care too much—this was way more important to me than it was to her. That made it fair. "Would you?"

"Your sister's more than meets the eye, but I think you know that. Maybe people don't give her enough credit."

I had thought the same thing more and more lately. As I got older, I began to wonder if Tiffany was as aimless and flighty as Dad made her out to be, or if she was that way because my parents didn't understand how to push her. "I guess." If Manning could see that, then he was getting to know a different Tiffany than most people. I wasn't sure what to make of that. "Are you saying you like her?"

He scratched behind his neck and responded slowly, as if choosing his words. "I like Tiffany for a lot of reasons. But maybe there's one thing about her that brings it all together. Like glue."

"What thing?"

"It's not something I can really put into words . . ." He looked over my head and around. "Let's say it's because she makes me laugh. If I break up with her, then I'd miss laughing. You know?"

I frowned. "No. Surely she isn't the only person who makes you laugh."

"But let's say she was. Let's say, me laughing while Tiffany wasn't around would be . . . people wouldn't understand it."

"So you wouldn't laugh at all? Because of what other people thought?"

"Part of me doesn't think it's appropriate to laugh, either, Lake."

Appropriate—I'd heard that word from him before. Laughing wasn't appropriate the way our friendship wasn't. "I think I understand."

"I didn't tell you about my sister because I won't ever lie to you."

"What do you mean?"

He stopped walking when we reached a wooden fence running the perimeter of the camp pool. We weren't really by the cabins anymore, which made me wonder if he'd brought me here on purpose. He looked up, his feet apart, hands in his jean pockets, forearms tense. I could tell he was thinking, his eyes distant, but about what, I wasn't sure. Maybe I'd asked too many questions, and he was about to send me back to my cabin.

"Can you hop it?" he asked.

I realized he wasn't staring into the distance but at the pool. There were only two ways in—the gate on the other side, and through the locker room and showers. Both were locked at the end of each day. I had no idea if I could get over the enclosure, but I said, "Yes."

Leaves crunched under Manning's feet as he surveyed the area. He motioned me over to the fence and picked me up the way he'd hoisted me onto the wall the day we'd met. I straddled it, jumping over the side. Manning followed right after, landing heavily on the concrete deck. He brushed off his jeans. "No trees in here," he said. "It's one of the best places to see the stars."

I couldn't remember the last time I'd looked at the stars, really looked. There were too many to count, a paint-splatter of silver on indigo. At home, I barely noticed them anymore, but as kids, Mom had taught Tiffany and me the constellations. I pointed, drawing in the sky. "Little Dipper."

"That's the big one," he said, moving closer to me. He stenciled out his own square. "It's part of Ursa Major, which means Great Bear."

I looked over at Manning, a bear of a man. My great bear. "Ursa Major," I repeated.

He shifted his index finger over. "There's the little one. You can tell by the North Star. My sister used to make the same mistake. Until she knew more than I did, that is."

I could feel her there, a presence between us, and I understood that the reason we were here had to do with her. She was part of the side of him that lived in shadows—a secret, but not just any secret. One that belonged to Manning, one I wanted to keep for him. "You did this with her?"

"When our parents fought, I'd take Maddy—" He tripped on her name. As he recovered, I tried it out in my head. *Maddy*. "I'd take her out to the front lawn and make up stories about the constellations. I didn't know shit, but she started reading books about them." He swallowed. The emotion in his voice was new for me, and he'd cursed, which he never did in my presence. "Soon enough," he continued, "she was the one telling me stories."

"How old was she?"

"Only nine. When she died."

I audibly sucked in air. I wasn't sure what I'd expected him to say, but nine just sounded so young. It was the age of the girls in my cabin. I'd been nine seven years ago. Aside from a great aunt, I'd never known anyone who'd died. I couldn't imagine my life without my sister. My childhood would've been completely different without Tiffany, especially if she'd disappeared in the middle of it. *Poof.* I tried to think of some way to express my sympathy, to make this moment easier on him. I couldn't touch him, not that I'd know where or how. *I'm sorry for your loss* just felt like the worst thing I could possibly say.

Maybe talking about her life, instead of death, would help. "Will you tell me about the stars?" I asked.

I could feel his hurt from where I stood. I tugged on his arm and sat right there on the concrete. There was no grass in sight, just this and the pool. It seemed like a big deal for someone his size to sit on the ground, but he did. We both lay back, some distance between us.

"I don't remember them all." His voice was hushed. It could've been his grief, but I was pretty sure he kept his tone low in case anybody passed by. They wouldn't know we were here unless they heard us. "It's been a long time since I looked very hard at the sky," he said.

I could feel my elbows and shoulder blades on the concrete. I wanted to hear about the stars, but I couldn't stop trying to picture her. "What did she look like?"

"The opposite of you."

"You told me once I remind you of her."

"You do. She was smart and kind. Saw the best in people, always. She's the only person who loved me as I am."

Despite the balmy night, I got the chills. *Not the only one*, I wanted to say. *I* love you. But the thought of saying that aloud made my heart pound and shriveled my tongue. I wondered if I'd ever be able to admit it. Maybe he knew, though. Maybe that's how he thought I was like her.

I inched my hand along the warm concrete, toward him.

"She had black hair, like me," he said. "Dark eyes. We looked a lot alike, except you could tell there was a whole universe behind her eyes."

Manning could be that way. As if he were living in two different worlds, sometimes only half-present in this one. "How old would she be now?"

"Seventeen. I can't even picture it."

I did the math. "You were fifteen?"

"Yes."

Silence stretched between us. It didn't seem right to ask how it happened. I wanted him to want me to know, to just tell me. To give me something he hadn't given anyone else, especially not Tiffany. The longer we stared up at the sky, the more I realized he wouldn't. And what did that mean? Did he not trust me?

Eventually, he pointed at the sky again. "There it is. I was trying to find the three stars that make up the Summer Triangle."

I looked for the ones he was talking about. "Where?"

"It's not a constellation, but three stars from other constellations. That brightest one, it's the bottom. Altair. About a foot apart is Vega. Through the middle is the Milky Way. You see?"

I still couldn't find them, but he sounded so hopeful, I didn't want to ruin it. "I think so."

"I can't tell it the way Madison did, but it was her favorite story. There are different versions, but Altair and Vega represent lovers from different sides of a river—or the Milky Way. They married behind their parents' backs and her father punished them by keeping them apart."

"With the river?"

"Yes. They were only allowed to be together once a year, the seventh night of the seventh month. The Japanese have a whole festival in July. There was no bridge, so, as long as the night was clear and it wasn't raining, birds would carry Vega across the river to Altair for that one night."

Of all the stories Manning could've chosen, there must've been a reason he picked that one to tell me. I'd learned about star-crossed lovers in English class. Maybe that's where the term came from. People would try to keep me and Manning apart because of our age difference, but we had this—the stars, the lovers, the night.

"What about the third star?"

"What?"

"You said it was a triangle."

"Oh." His eyes roamed the sky. "I don't know."

"So the story is about Altair and Vega. It isn't really a triangle at all."

He reached up to make three points. "They're all there, Lake. Can't move the stars."

"But the other one, it has nothing to do with this, right?" He must've heard the panic in my voice. It was hard to miss. "It's about Altair and Vega. Just them."

He looked over at me. "Yes. It's about them."

My heart began to pound. Hope lived strongly in me, and I knew with just those words, the same was true for him. It was a promise. No matter what, the story would only ever be about us.

I brushed my knuckle against his to acknowledge what I couldn't say. Was holding hands physical? What would Manning do if I put my skin on his and asked for what I wanted? If, like Tiffany, I used touch to get it? I got up on my elbow and looked down at him. My hair fell forward, a curtain around us.

"Lake," he said—a plea? A warning? I couldn't tell.

I looked at his mouth. I had dreamed of it, the things it couldn't tell me, of his lips, which couldn't kiss me. We were alone, finally. He had told me in so many words, one day, we would cross the river to each other.

I leaned down.

He put a hand on my shoulder, stopping me. "We can't."

He was telling me no. Again. Like everyone else, he thought he knew better than me. Couldn't he see that wasn't true? That some things were bigger than right and wrong, bigger than *us*? Hot tears pierced the backs of my eyes. "Why not?"

"That's just the way it is." He touched his hand to my cheek, and I leaned into his palm. "This will have to be enough."

I shook my head. "I'm not a child, Manning."

"I know you aren't. But at your age, it can be hard to think past the moment. To consider consequences. The future."

"All I *do* is consider my future."

"And you're going to do and be great things. You'll fly far, Birdy. See places most of us never will." He moved my hair behind my ear. "I'm counting on it."

But I didn't want to fly without Manning. I was content to stay here on the ground with him, learning of the stars, but he sat up, forcing me to do the same. We got to our feet.

All at once, the dreaminess of the night wore off, leaving the shameful truth—I'd tried to kiss him, and he'd told me no. Yet he'd gotten "physical" with Tiffany. What did that mean? Could there possibly be anything bigger than my love for him, something big enough to swallow it?

My vision blurred with tears. I still hadn't figured out the Summer Triangle. There wasn't even a cloud in the sky—I just couldn't find the stars.

Manning turned away from me and walked back to the fence.

It wasn't fair. I'd seen him first. I'd *had* him first. But was I losing him?

Was I losing him to Tiffany?

19

MANNING

Sunny, dusty days outside passed too fast. Spending a
week in fresh air was exactly what I hadn't known I'd
needed. For the first time in years, I wasn't
surrounded by hardened men or straining my body so
my mind wouldn't wander too far down the wrong
path. I felt like I was part of the living. The kids'
enthusiasm was exhausting and infectious. Tiffany
had loosened up. Lake made me feel like a man again
just for having someone to look out for.

I didn't want it to end, but like all good things, it
had to. We were leaving in the morning. Tonight, the
counselors had thrown the campers a party at dinner,
then sent anyone under twenty-one to bed early.
Including Tiffany.

"But I'm practically twenty-one," she'd argued with Gary.

"Aren't you like nineteen?" he'd responded. "And even if you were twenty and three-hundred-and-sixty-four days, it wouldn't matter. You're underage."

I'd walked her to her cabin while Kirk had dealt with ours. Her girls'd asked for a bedtime story, and Tiffany had pulled out a surprisingly good one. She'd told me why afterward—she'd just summarized the first three seasons of *90210*.

After saying goodnight, I headed to the campfire Gary and the staff had made.

As I approached, Bucky dicked around on the guitar, plucking at random strings. Lexi, a lifeguard, passed me a Bud. All the chairs were taken, so I sat in the dirt by the fire.

"Welcome to the special adult party," Gary said to me. "We do it every year on the last night. Tiffany's not going to rat us out to her parents, is she?"

"Sutter don't call the shots in that relationship," Bucky said. "When you got a hot piece of ass like her, you just do what she says."

Fuck this guy. He'd been giving me shit all week. When I worked a job, I mostly kept to myself because there were always men like Bucky whose mouths were bigger than their muscles. My muscles were just big, a byproduct of being one of the younger guys in construction—the older ones were always making me do the toughest shit. I couldn't take the kinda bait Bucky was tossing in front of me. My dad had a temper that could flip at any moment and I knew, deep down, that switch existed in me. "Don't go there, man."

"Or what?" Bucky asked.

I opened my beer. "You're lucky there are kids around."

Lexi threw a bottle cap at Bucky. "Stop. Seriously. You're an ass."

Gary squinted at me over the fire. I wasn't so good at making friends, but he'd been good to me, giving me this job, making sure I was set all week. That was part of why I'd been on my best behavior. I planned to keep in touch, maybe even come back next year.

"Anybody know a good scary story?" Lexi asked.

"I got one," Bucky said. "Once upon a time, we ran out of beer."

"Bullshit," someone said.

"There's more back in the kitchen," Gary said.

"Nah, there ain't." Bucky strummed the guitar and sang, "This is the l-a-a-st of it."

Gary checked the cooler. "Fuck. Who the fuck's been sneaking it out?"

Everybody looked away. I hadn't drunk anything in a week, but if Tiffany had found herself some special punch our first night here, no doubt others had their ways of sniffing it out, too.

"Somebody's gotta go replenish the stash," Gary said. "The night just started. I've already had two, and with my job, if I get a DUI, I'm fucked."

"None of us are sober," Bucky pointed out, slowly turning his beady eyes on me. "Except Sutter."

I hadn't even taken a sip. Truth was, I didn't want to do much more than have a beer, two max, and head to bed. The days here were long, hot, and grueling. But everyone looked at me, which didn't leave me much choice. "I don't have a car."

"Take my truck." Vern, a gray-haired wiry man who worked full-time as a janitor for the campground, shifted around to shove his hand in his pocket. "It's about forty minutes to town and back."

He tossed me the keys. It was barely nine-thirty and didn't seem worth arguing about. Even if I wasn't going to drink, I was the new guy, and their only hope for refills. I passed my untouched beer to the guy next to me and stood. "All right."

"There's a liquor store on the main boulevard," Vern said. "If it's closed, just stop in any dive around there and slip 'em some cash. They'll sell you a bottle of something."

I nodded at them and headed for staff parking. Gary caught up with me after a few yards. "Forgot to get you cash," he said, passing me a couple twenties.

I thought about not accepting it, but I didn't have a dollar to spare on other people's alcohol, so I put it in my pocket. "Thanks."

"Also wanted to thank you," Gary said. "You did good this week."

"Yeah?"

We stopped at Vern's truck, a white, rusted Ford from the seventies that looked like it weighed as much as a whale and probably moved as fast. "I was a little worried about having Tiffany here," Gary said. "She seems like a rule breaker. But far's I know, you two kept it clean. That probably wasn't easy so I appreciate it." He ran a hand through the mop of curls on his head. "How long you two been dating?"

"Couples months I guess."

"Ah. Is it serious?"

I glanced back at the campfire. No, it wasn't, but it could get serious. If things kept up this way, Tiffany letting down her guard, Lake being off limits, it might. "Nah. Not yet."

"Good, good." Gary rocked on his heels. "You're too young to settle down, but I know how these girls can get. Don't let her push you in that direction if you aren't ready."

I wasn't sure what to say about it. Much as I liked Gary, I wasn't in the habit of talking about my personal shit with anyone.

He slapped me on the back. "See you in a few."

I climbed into the beat-up truck. The thing didn't look like it'd make it down the block, much less to town, but I figured Vern knew better than me. It growled to life, and I gave it a few minutes to warm up. Luckily, the heater worked. Walking away from the campfire had left me with a chill. I reversed out of the lot and headed for the trail toward the highway. I squinted through the pitch dark, the headlights showing only what was right in front of me.

At the mouth of the unpaved road, a movement caught my eye. Lake stepped out into the path, looking not even a little worried I might hit her. I slammed on the brakes. "Jesus Christ."

In denim short-shorts that looked a size too big and a t-shirt a size too small, she came around to the passenger's side and opened the door.

"What're you doing?" I asked.

"Looking for you. I waited at the pool, hoping you'd come since it's our last night."

I checked over my shoulder to make sure nobody was around. "Get in."

She hauled herself into the seat and pulled on the door. Using all her weight only moved it a few inches. The truck was hidden by trees, but we weren't even off the campsite yet. I leaned over to grab the handle, and the door creaked and groaned, closing heavily.

Her face was in mine. I smelled sweetness, watermelon or something, and chlorine. "You didn't get in the pool, did you?"

"Just my feet."

She kicked off her flip-flops. The fine, gold hair on her upper thigh shimmered under the dome light. I didn't know where to start. The skimpy outfit? Sneaking around in the dark? Swimming without supervision? "You can't be here, Lake."

"I know. But it's our last night."

We were on display. I started to drive to get the light to turn off. "It's everyone's last night."

I went slowly down the unpaved trail, but we jostled in our seats anyway. She didn't even bother looking out the windshield. "Where are you going?" she asked.

Hunched over the wheel, I glanced between her and the road. The seat was one long bench of three seats, Caribbean-turquoise vinyl. She pulled one bare foot up on it and faced me, like I was about to say something important. "On an errand."

"So you're coming right back?"

"Yeah."

"Then what's the big deal if I come?"

It was after dark, she was a minor, and I was responsible for her. All that said, she'd never be safer than when she was with me. I was sure of it. I adjusted the rearview mirror. "You promise to go straight to your cabin when we get back?"

"Yes."

"So what're you doing, swimming alone at night?" I made sure my tone conveyed my disapproval.

"I told you. Waiting for you. And I only put my feet in."

"Doesn't matter. It's dangerous. Water tricks you. It looks calm and inviting, but it can kill you. Fast."

She didn't respond. If I'd scared her, good. Nothing bad ever came of respecting the elements.

The final few yards of the road were bad enough to knock a pack of cigarettes out of Vern's visor. Lake picked them up. "How come you never smoke in front of me?"

"They're not mine." I pulled onto a main road, and the ride got about as smooth as it was going to get in this soon-to-be junkyard scrap metal. I relaxed back into my seat. "We talked about this. Secondhand smoke's bad for you."

"And not for you?"

Lake shouldn't be in the truck. I shouldn't've been noticing or still thinking about those soft-looking hairs on her leg. I should've sent her back. I didn't even want alcohol but somehow I'd ended up in a situation. I would've killed for a cigarette right then. "Gimme those."

She handed over the pack, and I stuffed it between the seats. "I thought about what you said the other night. I'll quit, it's just going to take some time."

"I can help," she said.

"How?"

"I don't know. There must be some way."

"It's not like AA where you get a sponsor."

I took the on-ramp to the highway. It was dead, not many cars around, just lots of black pavement flanked by shadowed trees. The sliver of a moon waxed from new to full.

"I could check in on you." Her voice barely carried over the grumble of the engine. "Or you could call me when you get the urge."

Seemed about right, replacing one impulse with another. Lake instead of nicotine. Only, I didn't think that was how she meant it. I glanced over in the dark. "What's going on?"

"What's going to happen? After camp?"

"I don't know. Guess I finish the job by your house. Then I find more work until I graduate. You go back to school."

"What about Tiffany?"

The way I saw it, I had two options. Stop seeing Tiffany and end my time with the Kaplans, or keep both girls in my life. "I don't know, Lake, but like I told you before, that's between me and your sister."

"Where do you live?"

"Lake . . ."

"You said you'd get me books about what to major in."

"I will."

"But when? I start school in a week. Next thing you know, it'll be time to fill out applications. I'll have homework, and my dad's making me take a college class. I won't have time for anything else."

I slid my hand down the wheel. "You freaking out a little?"

"No, but maybe I don't want to do all this anymore. I don't understand why everyone else gets to decide for me."

I only realized then, from the panic in her voice, what she was after, pestering me about the cigarettes, Tiffany, the future. She didn't know if we'd see each other after this. I didn't know, either. Maybe I wouldn't if I didn't keep things up with Tiff. The truth was, I had little control over the situation, and Lake had even less. "I'll get you your books," I promised.

"Forget the books. I don't care about them."

"You should," I said more harshly than I meant. "If you don't know your options, how're you going to know what to major in?" Truth was, her dad wasn't a big man, but he scared me. He had power over Lake. I had wondered more than once if she'd even ever considered a school aside from USC. This was too big a decision to let her dad make for her. "How're you going to stand up to your dad if he tries to force you into something you don't wanna do?"

"What if I don't want to go to school at all?"

I gripped the steering wheel, frustrated, even though I knew she didn't mean it. Neither of us had any control over this situation and she was looking for something to hold onto. "That's not what I meant. You know it isn't."

"It was just all laid out for me before I was even born."

"Then ask yourself what you really want, but don't say it isn't college. It is. The question is where you want to go and what you want to do when you get there."

"What do you mean 'where'?" she asked quietly.

"Doesn't have to be USC, Lake. Doesn't have to be what anyone else says."

She bit her thumbnail and sat quietly a while, obviously thinking. I hoped she was beginning to see she had options. She wasn't going to figure it out tonight, but it was a start.

We entered town suddenly, a building or two at first and then we were on the main boulevard passing fast food joints, log cabin inns, and souvenir shops.

"I live in Long Beach," I said, hoping it might calm her down a bit. "I've got a roommate and a kitchen that barely fits two people."

"I didn't know that," she said. "That's far."

"From where? You? About a forty-minute drive."

"Oh." The vinyl squawked as she adjusted her foot. "Are you happy there?"

I couldn't remember feeling much more than complacency since Maddy's death. Lake was the only thing recently that hadn't been some kind of job or obligation. "I guess. I'm not really one thing or another."

The first liquor store I passed was dark, so I pulled into a bar called Phil's a few stoplights down. It took me a minute to decide where to park. There were people out front, and I didn't want anyone to see Lake in the car. I chose a space off to the side, farthest from the building.

"Why are we here?" Lake asked.

"Picking up booze." A flyer on the window advertised line dancing. Three women stood by the door, smoking, and my mouth watered for a cigarette. "I'll only be a minute. You can't come in, so just lock the doors and wait, all right? Don't get out for any reason."

"What do you think'll happen in a minute?"

I guess she didn't know yet that one minute could change your life. That if I'd left baseball practice one minute earlier, things might've been different for Maddy. Lake was intuitive but too trusting. She hadn't hesitated to have me come into her parents' house that day, even though I was three times her size and carried tools that could kill a grown man with one swing. She should have someone looking out for her. I wanted to be that someone.

I got out of the car, slammed the door shut, and waited for the *thunk* of the locks. The girls were average-looking. Jeans, cowboy boots, tank tops spotted with sweat, hair stuck to their foreheads. "Hey there," one of them said. "Looking for a dance partner?"

I went into Phil's and took out the twenties. "Can I buy some beer off you?" I asked the bartender.

"How about Jack instead?"

"That's fine. Whatever you got for forty bucks."

He nodded and headed into the back.

"Got a cigarette I can bum?" One of the girls from outside sat on a barstool next to me. I had a pack in my shirt pocket, but cigarettes cost money, and money was finite. I only spent it on what I cared about. "No."

She took a swig from her beer. Her ring caught my eye, a big, bulky thing with a silver band that looked oddly familiar. The bulbous, dark stone covered everything below her knuckle. I looked closer. Maybe it was glass, and hunter green, not black stone.

"What is that?" I asked.

She showed me her hand. "A mood ring."

"Fuck. Yeah, I remember now." Maddy had one. My mom had bought it in the seventies and handed it down to her. Sometimes, when I was broody, Madison would force it on my finger and ask me to make it change colors, from dark to light. To make it happy. "What's the green mean?"

"I forget. I feel bored, though, so maybe that." She looked up. "Where you from?"

Words were like money, not worth wasting when it wouldn't get me anywhere. "Not here."

If I were at home, if Lake weren't in the truck, maybe things'd be different. Girls were a fine distraction. All but Lake. She was crystal clear to me, as was everything around her. Scenery was more beautiful. I felt blood pumping through my veins. Things sharpened that'd gone dull a while ago, even memories of Maddy. Over time, I'd forgotten some stuff about Maddy without realizing it, and around Lake, it was coming back. The way she read like

Maddy, or now, this ring I probably would've overlooked. Any memories of Maddy usually came with a blinding kind of pain I'd learned to accept, but seeing that ring again, it didn't make me want to drive off a cliff. It was okay.

But did that mean I was forgetting Madison? I couldn't even picture her as clearly anymore. Not as well as I could Lake.

"Where then?" the woman asked. "Never seen you here before."

"Can I buy that off you?" I asked. "The ring?"

She furrowed her brows, inspecting it. "It's not worth anything."

I didn't care. It wasn't as if I was going to drive up to my mom's and look for Maddy's, even though it might still be there. "How about I give you the change from the alcohol?"

She smiled. "Phil's not going to give you any change." She took off the ring and slid it across the bar. "Take it. I'll get another."

The bartender returned fisting two paper bags. He handed me them by their necks, and I gave him the money. I put the ring in my pocket and thanked the cowgirl. Maybe I owed her a little more time than I gave her, but I had none to waste.

I didn't want to be away from the truck another minute. From Lake.

20
MANNING

Lake was exactly as I'd left her. Foot up on the seat. Eyes following me. The way she sat, the leg of her shorts gaped. I wondered if she'd taken them from Tiffany. I couldn't see anything I shouldn't, but it made me feel like shit that I even looked.

I stuck the whiskey in the back and the key in the ignition. Lake turned on the radio. Janet Jackson lasted until the end of the parking lot before I switched the station to rock. "That's the Way Love Goes" was a little too breathy for the situation I was in.

"Can we drive a little?" Lake asked.

"We're gonna. It's another twenty minutes back to camp."

"I mean just drive. Without going anywhere."

There was hardly anyone on the street, but because the lot exited by a stoplight, I had to wait for a break to get across the lane and make a U-turn.

"Please?" she asked. "It's my last night of freedom."

"Technically, you're not free," I said. "You're working. And supposed to be asleep." I scratched my chin. I needed a decent shave. I'd started the week doing the best I could with what I had—a dull razor and cold water in a communal bathroom. Eventually I'd given up shaving every morning. It made me think of Lake's legs. I guessed she had hair at all because she never wore anything that short.

The fucking red light wouldn't change and a few more cars pulled up. Time was always slow when I needed it to be fast and vice versa.

Lake had only ever been sixteen to me. *Slow.*

I couldn't get out of this parking lot. *Slow.*

This rare moment alone with her would end before it began. *Fast.*

What was another few minutes when our time was up anyway? I could tell the counselors I'd had car trouble or something. I didn't care.

I gave up trying to cross the lane, reversed, and found another exit to a back street. It turned into a narrow alley, but with a few maneuvers, we got to a residential street.

Lake didn't make any comment about getting her way. She just used the truck's manual lever to roll down her window and shifted away from me. I turned up the music.

Lake looked over. "This is Pink Floyd."

I raised my eyebrows, impressed. "Thought you didn't know them."

"I do now. I bought some of their CDs from Tower Records," she said. "I like their album covers. *Dark Side of the Moon*. It's a good name."

Well, that was something. I'd introduced her to one of the greatest bands of all time, to "Wish You Were Here," one of the greatest songs of all time, and that could never be bad.

We didn't talk for a while. I put down my window, too, to cool down. The neighborhood was dark, not a streetlamp on any corner. Every few houses or so had a light on but that was it. It was a nice place. Fancy, two-story homes. Bright white garages, custom mailboxes, and neat, green lawns. I wondered what it'd be like to live here and be home. I felt a little bad taking this growler around so late, so I slowed down and shut off the headlights. My vision acclimated quickly, and it made it even more peaceful.

Lake had her window all the way down now. She stuck her head and part of her torso outside. Her long, blonde hair flew around her, and she had to push it out of her face. "You can see all the stars here, too," she said. "I'm looking for the Summer Triangle."

I smiled to myself and checked through the windshield. I couldn't see it, or maybe I didn't want to take my eyes off her long enough to find it. Carefree as she looked right now, the outfit and her confidence tonight reminded me that what Tiffany said was true. Lake wasn't a child. She'd be eighteen soon. Didn't mean anything for me, really. I'd never be the kind of man she deserved. But it did get my heart pounding a little, thinking of her body the way I thought of her mind—something belonging to a young adult rather than a teen girl.

We drove around that way for a while, miles under the speed limit. I told her we were going slow because I liked driving without the lights on, but the truth was, I wanted a few more minutes with her. No sneaking around. No checking over my shoulder. Finally, just her and me, not doing anything wrong, just being.

Eventually, the residential maze spit us out on to a main street, and I had to switch the headlights on again. Lake sat back in her seat, rolled up her window partway, and got the kind of quiet that made me wonder if she was upset.

I shifted gears on our way up the hill back to camp and looked over to check on her. Whatever had changed her mood, I suspected there wasn't anything I could really say to comfort her.

Lake gasped. I whipped my gaze back to the road as something darted in front of the car. Hitting the brakes, I reached for Lake, keeping her in her seat as I swerved to miss the animal. The truck shuddered, too much bulk to stop so fast, but I steered it off the highway.

"What was that?" she asked, sounding breathless.

I looked over at her. My hand was on her shoulder. "You all right?"

"I'm fine. It looked like a dog."

"Coyote. Must've been."

We sat there a moment, catching our breath. What the fuck was I doing out here anyway? What if we'd gotten into an accident and I'd had to explain why I had a sixteen-year-old girl and two pints in a truck that didn't belong to me.

"That was a rush," she said.

"A rush? No. No, it wasn't." I went to pull away, but she stopped me, spreading her fingers over the top of my hand. Hers was shades whiter than mine and probably half the size.

"Do we have to go back?" she asked.

The more I tried to ignore her soft palm on my skin, the harder it got. I needed to take my hand off. It wasn't as if she could hold me there against my will. "We've been gone long enough," I said.

"But I don't want to."

"I know you don't. That's why we went for a drive. But this—you're not supposed to be out here, and it isn't even about camp. Just in general, you shouldn't be here, now."

I only heard her breathing. She took her hand off, and so did I.

"Nobody even knows I'm gone." She unclicked her seatbelt. "Come on. I see water."

"Lake, no."

With what must've been a sudden burst of strength, she shouldered her door open and hopped out of the truck.

"Come on, Lake. Get back in."

"I just want to see. Maybe put my toes in."

Fuck. Barefoot, she headed into the dark. I fumbled with my seatbelt, barely remembering to shut off the engine before jumping out. "Lake?"

The trees were thick around the highway, and my voice echoed into the woods. I couldn't see shit. I strode down a soft-dirt hill, which opened up to a sprawling body of black water. The moon was just a sliver rippling over the lake. When I saw her near the shore, I exhaled a breath I'd been holding. She stripped off her shorts. My gut smarted, a warning. No way she'd get in there. You couldn't see your own foot in that lake.

With her back to me, in white panties and a t-shirt, she waded in like a water nymph, glowing against a black backdrop.

"Come on, Lake." My heart pounded. I'd warned her about the water. "I'm not messing around. You don't know what's in there."

"Fish?" She smiled at me over her shoulder. My gaze, the water, her hair, it all moved with her as she glided deeper. When the waterline touched her hips, she pulled one arm through a sleeve and then the other.

I stood paralyzed as she took off her top. It was clumsy, drawn out, long enough for me to tell her to stop. She threw it a few yards from my feet. I went and picked it up, a scrap of fabric that'd been a necessary barrier between us. She had this white, strappy bra thing on and, thankfully, enough long blonde hair to hide her breasts, not that there was much to cover.

I couldn't look away. I couldn't move.

I ran a hand through my hair, trying to decide what to do. I had a lot of self-control, but I didn't want to test it by taking off my pants. It wouldn't look good to show up back at camp in wet jeans, either.

Lake kept going. Her hair started to disappear under the surface, pieces of it plastering to her back. *The* memory scraped across my brain like nails on a chalkboard. Maddy—limp, soaked, sheet-white—her wet hair sticking to my forearms and knees as I'd pulled her from the water into my lap.

I tried to call Lake back. The words came out strangled. I took off my shoes and socks. Tossing her shirt with her shorts, I walked right in. The cold water bit, but she couldn't get any farther from my reach.

She skimmed her forearms back and forth over the surface as she blinked up at the sky, a small smile on her lips. "Show it to me again. Summer Triangle."

"No," I clipped. When either of us moved, the water echoed in the otherwise dead-quiet. "I know what you're doing. I don't . . . you think I want to go back?" I asked. "I don't, but we have to."

She turned on me, her euphoric expression replaced with frustration. "Why can't you just stop being an adult for a minute?"

"Because I *am* the adult. One of us has to be."

She closed her mouth, her jaw tight, and dove headfirst into the water.

The lake swallowed her without even a burp. She disappeared completely. I took a step. Then another. I couldn't see her. Couldn't see anything but a ripple here and then there, near and then far. I turned in circles, heat rising up my chest while my legs froze, my breath getting short. "Lake?" I raised my voice. "Stop it."

I tried to push Maddy out of my mind. This wasn't the same, Lake was just having fun. But Maddy'd been so alive when I'd last seen her and just minutes later, completely lifeless. The image had haunted me so long, was *always* waiting in the back of my mind, even during the best of times. I'd had to put my mouth on my sister's and feel nothing, breathe into nothing.

Seconds ticked by. My lungs wouldn't expand. I would've gone in after her if I'd had any clue where she was. She'd been under at least ten seconds and could've swum anywhere. "Lake," I yelled, angry. I thrust my hands under, grasping for anything.

Something slippery brushed against my leg. "Goddamn it. *Lake!*"

She popped up five feet from me, giggling, the slight moon turning her into a glittering, fluorescent mermaid.

"What's gotten into you?" I asked. Rage vibrated every bone in my body. "Do you have any idea how dangerous it is out here?"

She floated on her back, unapologetic, teeth chattering. "I know you wouldn't let anything happen to me."

It shook my confidence, hearing that. She thought I could save her. The truth was, if I wanted to or not, I couldn't protect her from everything. Especially not this. But to explain why, I'd have to bring her into a memory I never shared if I could help it. I'd already had to recount it enough times to the police and jury to break any man.

She spread her arms. Her tits poked through the surface, two white, wet, cotton peaks pointing to the stars. My hands shook, my body, too. Seeing how calm and open she was, my instinct was to go to her, to say *fuck it* for one night. Lake wasn't as confident as she pretended to be. Her inexperience showed in her every move. One touch, and she'd dissolve into a trembling mess. Wouldn't it be best if that first touch came from someone who cared? Who'd worship her? I knew what I was doing, when to be gentle and when to not, and I would do it at her pace.

I'd been trying not to see her since I'd returned her bracelet. As a child, I'd been warned by my mom against looking directly at an eclipse. I feared the same was true for Lake. How did I come off to others when I looked at her? As captivated as I felt? Adoring? Enamored? I didn't want to be looking at her that way. Someone could notice. People became suddenly more perceptive about these things—a grown man intently watching a young girl. Especially one like Lake, who was on the verge of beautiful.

But tonight, nobody was around.

Fuck. I turned around, shielding my eyes, even though it was too late for that. I couldn't look. It was killing me.

Hard as it was, I walked out of the water.

"You're just going to leave me here?" she asked.

Never.

But I had to. I put one foot in front of the other, fought every urge to turn back, just to make sure she didn't sink under. She'd given me no choice. I was going to make an even bigger mistake than I already had just by letting myself get into this situation. I passed her rumpled clothing, got as far as the trees, but, unable to breathe without keeping my eyes on her, I turned and looked back. I tensed when I couldn't find her but a few seconds later, my eyes adjusted. On shore, she put her clothes back on. Once I was certain she wouldn't be getting back in the lake, I went to the truck, found some greasy towels behind the seats, and wiped myself down. I sat and watched through the windshield. I couldn't even bring myself to turn on the heater or music.

After a few minutes, she trudged back up to the passenger's side door.

"What do you want me to do?" she asked when I looked over, her window still partly down. "I'm wet."

Her nipples were hard, so I averted my eyes and passed her a towel. It was dirty but better than being soaked. Once she'd dried herself a little, she climbed into the cab.

I put the key in the ignition, but the engine only turned over. "Great." I pounded my fist against the steering wheel. "That's just fucking great."

The whole bench shook with her shivering. "I'm sorry," she said.

Even though she faced me, her shoulder and half her back were pressed up against the door, as far away from me as she could get. She looked so small and breakable, tucked into the corner, the opposite of how she'd acted just a few minutes ago. In her lap, she wrung her hands around something. She breathed audibly, maybe trying not to cry. *In. Out. In. Out.* The t-shirt clung to her breasts, outlining them, the only two wet spots.

How could I stay pissed? All she wanted was more time. I wanted the same. "I'm not mad," I said. "I worry. I worry so goddamn much, Lake."

"Why? I don't understand." Her voice was tiny, frightened. "I've been swimming in the ocean since I could walk."

305

I gripped the steering wheel, even though we weren't going anywhere. The difference between Lake and every other person I'd come across the past eight years was that it felt as if her goodness could actually be enough to heal my ugliness. To fill the hole in me. I wanted to tell her. Knowing what I'd been through meant knowing me better than anyone since Maddy.

I turned the key to see if at least the heater would come on; it did, along with the radio. I lowered the volume and sat back in my seat. "My sister drowned while I was thirty feet away." The words were foreign. Saying it out loud was as hard as I thought it'd be. It changed the air around us. The molecules rearranged. The truth sat between us like a third person. In a way, it was. Madison was never far from my mind. I still carried her around, one long piggyback ride until the day I'd die. "I couldn't save her."

Lake didn't move an inch. She sat still so long, I looked over to make sure she was still conscious. "I'm so sorry," she whispered. "I didn't realize."

By the look on her face, I'd scared the shit outta her. I couldn't just leave it at that. "We had a pool, but that wasn't what killed her. It just sped up the process."

She pulled her knees up to her chest, wrapping her arms around them. "What do you mean?"

"I told you my parents used to fight. It was a war every time. They'd married young—for love."

"Isn't that a good thing?"

"Nah. Not when you're fundamentally different. My mom's family was middleclass, my dad came from the wrong side of the tracks. They didn't grow up the same or want the same things. That might be okay if you're not as passionate as you are different. Long story short, they fought as hard as they made up." I wasn't sure Lake'd understand what I was getting at, so I glossed over that. "Once in a while, something in my dad would flip, and he'd go too far. He'd hit her, apologize in tears at her feet, and that'd be it. He beat me up a few times, stupid shit like finding my dishes out after a particularly bad day at work. He hurt Madison only once as a kid. When I hit puberty and got bigger than him, never happened to either of us again, just my mom when I wasn't around."

Lake seemed farther away, her back glued against the door. Even in the dark, I could see her ashen face. Fine. She needed to hear this, and maybe it was best if it scared her off me. She'd grown up as sheltered as anyone I'd ever seen. Whatever schoolgirl crush she had on me, maybe this would cure it.

"He went after your sister, and you wouldn't let him."

I must've misheard Lake. "What?"

"Is that what happened?"

My chest constricted. There was no way she could've known that, which meant she'd figured it out on her own. Maybe she saw more than I gave her credit for. "Yeah. Pretty much. Maddy was trying to get in the middle of one of their fights. I came in the door from baseball practice right as he smacked her into a wall." The memory of the blank expression on my dad's face still made me sick to my stomach. I could count on one hand the number of times I'd seen that, the way his eyes turned to glass while he went some place none of us could name. "I knocked him on his ass. I didn't know what Dad would do, so I told Maddy to run, but she wouldn't. She didn't want to leave me. So I told her to get the fuck out or I'd kick her ass myself. I just wanted her gone. She looked terrified, which was how I felt, but it worked. She ran out the back."

"You did the right thing," Lake said.

Not really. I wasn't sure what the right thing would've been, but it wasn't that. "Mads had this friend next door, Beth. They had a secret, not-so-secret hole in the fence they'd use to get to each other's houses. That's where she was going." She'd run so fast out the back. Because of me. If I'd known it was the last time I'd see her, I wouldn't've threatened Madison that way. She'd surely been as afraid of me as she was of him in that moment. "My dad and I fought. Took down everything in the kitchen—the table, dishes, pots and pans." There'd been so much shit all over the kitchen. Noodles on the linoleum floor from an overturned pot. I couldn't remember getting scalded, but I'd had a burn from the water for a while after. Broken dining chairs. Blood on my knuckles. Everything falling away in a second . . .

"I swear, I would've taken my baseball bat to him if I hadn't heard the screaming."

"Maddy?" Lake whispered.

Hearing Maddy's name out loud, reliving the moments leading up to it, I needed to take a breath. I looked out my open window. "My mom. She found my sister floating face down in the pool. After the autopsy and all that, we figured she'd slipped while running, fallen in, hit her head on the way down. She was unconscious long enough—while we were all in the house . . ."

I didn't dream, but once in a while I had nightmares. Getting Maddy out of a pool red with her blood, the shock of pulling a cold body out of warm water. Trying to give life to a stiff mouth. Breathing so hard into her that I nearly passed out.

"When the cops showed, I was still trying to give Maddy CPR while Mom sobbed on the ground next to me. But my dad had cleaned himself up and calmed down. His anger was like that, quick to explode, quick to flame out. He knew they'd see the bruises on Maddy and my mom and the mess in the kitchen. He hadn't landed a punch on me, but he was bleeding from a busted nose. I was the only one unscathed. When the officers asked what'd happened, he'd explained that I'd snapped. Beat Maddy up and them, too."

"No." Lake covered her mouth. "He blamed you?"

It was fucked up, but my dad had always been a dick. Aside from the death, it wasn't the part I still wasn't over. "My mom couldn't speak to save her life, she was a wreck. But when the officers asked if it was true, she wouldn't say I didn't do it."

"She let you take the rap?"

"She was afraid if she said no, they'd take my dad away."

Lake readjusted her hold on her knees. "Did they arrest you?"

I sat forward and ran my hands over my face. Every time I thought about it, it renewed a sliver of my faith in humanity. "They took us both to the station. I told the cops what'd really happened, and they saw right through the bullshit. Figured out my mom and dad would rather send me to juvie than have Dad get in real trouble. Beth's parents vouched for me, too, said they'd heard our parents arguing a lot and that I'd been good with the girls." I shook my head. "I wasn't, though. Good. I should've had him locked up the first time it happened."

"But you must've been a kid. How long had it been going on?"

"All of their marriage, but it didn't happen that often. Something inside him that was just . . . off." And I had to wonder, how did I know I didn't have the same thing? I got angry like any man. I tried never to put myself in a situation where I might test the switch, though.

"What happened to him?"

"My dad? Prison. Hard as it was, I had to go up on the stand and convince them that he'd hurt us before, even though we'd never filed a report. My mom wouldn't do it. She tried to get me not to, didn't see what good it did if Maddy was gone anyway. I didn't see it that way, though. I wanted the max sentence."

Lake fidgeted with the bracelets on her wrist, kept twisting whatever was in her hand. "All this happened when you were fifteen?"

"You see why I get so worried? It's not just because of Maddy. I saw and did a lot of things a kid shouldn't. It changes you. Can't ever go back."

"I get it," she said softly. "Of course I do. I just can't believe . . . what about your mom?"

"Still in Pasadena. I guess."

"You don't know?"

"I went to live with Dad's sister. My mom was my mom—I loved her. I tried to protect her. But she picked a monster over me." I finally let go of the steering wheel, flexing my aching hand. "I couldn't go back after that. I realized once I moved out, I resented her anyway for staying with him all that time."

"I wouldn't go back, either," Lake said.

It was her way of showing support, but just thinking of Lake in a situation like that got under my skin. "My aunt was all right. She didn't forgive my dad like Mom did but she kinda checked out. She was torn up about Madison and felt bad she hadn't done anything sooner knowing my dad's temper. So we left each other alone. I couldn't give her anything. I had nothing."

"Do you still feel that way?"

"Do you?" I asked.

"No. You have something to give, I know it."

I nodded. "I'm going to help others. That's how I'm going to give."

"Because they believed you," she said, piecing it together. "That's why it means so much to you to become an officer."

"One of the cops who'd been there that night, he stopped by my aunt's to check in on me from time to time. Made sure I stayed on track and graduated high school. I never met anyone like him before that or since. Henry's a good man. That's why I want to be a cop. Help people like he does."

It wasn't exactly a happy ending, but it was something. It was all I had. Everything else was mistakes and broken relationships and loss.

"I never would've . . ." Lake's voice trembled. "If I'd known, I wouldn't have run off like that."

Without thinking, I put my hand on her knee, covering it and then some. She was far away, but I could still reach her. "I know. It just reminded me of everything, you disappearing like that." Her cheeks were wet. "Please don't. Don't cry."

"But I . . . I love. This. Our . . . you . . ."

I squeezed her leg. I understood Lake and her broken words. She didn't mean it like she was in love with me. She was trying to say she couldn't help her tears. Couldn't stop her heart from breaking for Madison. I loved her for it, too, for a tenderness so altruistic and pure, it overflowed outside her control. She released her legs and extended the one I was holding. I slid my hand down to her ankle, slower than I meant to, appreciating the smoothness of her calf. I wanted to say *come here* and wipe her tears. Hold her until she understood she was still safe, and I wasn't mad. My hand encompassed her ankle. I realized the thing clamped in her hand was her bra. She was still the young girl I wanted to protect. No toenail polish. No makeup. Wet hair. Wanting what she wanted, no price too high. But there was more to her tonight, there always had been. The look she gave me, as if she could sense me responding to her small tits and pink mouth. Those gaping shorts.

She was breathing hard again, but not out of fear. Her tears had dried. She dug her foot between the seats, where I'd shoved the cigarettes, and nudged the pack out. "You look like you need one."

I wondered if my face was as gray as hers had been a minute ago. She seemed warm now, loving, but now *my* hands shook, even the one holding her ankle. She sat forward without moving her legs and turned up the stereo.

I recognized the beginning chords of a song before the DJ even introduced it. ". . . slow things down with a little Sophie B. Hawkins," he was saying. "This request goes out from Naomi C. to John M., and I don't think I have to tell you what Naomi's trying to say. It's right there in the title."

Lake scooted closer, bending her leg between us. She picked up the pack and took out a cigarette, studying it. When she went to put it in her mouth, I caught her wrist.

"I just want to see what it's like."

I let go of her. It wasn't as if she had anything to light it with.

She put it between her lips, rolling them around the butt, then took it out and pretended to blow smoke. "Did I do it right?"

She held it in the "V" of her index and middle fingers like her sister—of course. She probably didn't know anyone who smoked besides us. She held it up to my mouth, and I was suddenly aware of my breath against her fingers. I took the butt between my lips. It tasted sweet. Sometime between the lake and the car, she'd made herself taste like watermelon candy.

I wanted it. The smoke, the girl. My vices. But here she was, trying to be something she thought I wanted. Something I was trying to protect her from. I took the cigarette, snapped it, tossed it out the window. "I told you. I'm quitting."

Before I even had the words out, she leaned in, stopping inches from my face. Her sugary breath became mine. It was so easy to forget everything else with her around. Being close to her didn't feel wrong. I could just sink into it, didn't have to be cautious like I did with other people, as if I knew on some level she'd protect me. She'd care for me. As a side effect of trying to restrain myself, I squeezed her ankle hard enough to make her gasp. She went for the corner of my mouth, pressing her lips to my skin soft and slow.

"I feel very protective of you, Lake," I murmured.

"I know."

"I don't want to change you."

"You already have. I want this. I can decide for myself."

"It's not that simple."

She smoothed her cheek against mine. To me, it was like nuzzling a peach but because I hadn't shaven, it must've been rough for her.

"I've never even kissed someone," she said close to my ear. "Never wanted to before."

It was more than I could handle. It made me happy she'd never been kissed, never wanted it with anyone else. She was maybe too young for that but I also wanted to be her first. I put my other hand on her shoulder, meaning to pull her off. She ducked her head, planting supplicant little pecks behind my ear that might as well have been her saying *please, Manning, please, please*. My head dropped back against the headrest. "Damn it, Lake."

With one leg still folded between us, she hooked the other over my knee and moved my hand to her thigh. She hummed along to the song, "Damn I Wish I Was Your Lover."

My heart pounded. I had to stop this, but she was heavenly. So soft, her lips and downy thigh, so inviting, her leg warming mine. Even her damp hair felt good in my palm. That's when I realized my fingers had tangled themselves in her hair, spanning the back of her scalp, holding her in place. While I was distracted trying to control my body parts, her kisses traveled up around my mouth. Her hand guided mine up her leg. All at once, I went from pleasantly warm to burning up. My neck, my face. My lap. The base of my cock constricted. She was bold but tentative, bringing us to the edge, but not brave enough to take the leap. Her balmy kisses made blood rush to my crotch, flooded out my guilt.

She took her hand off mine, but I didn't pull away. I slid it up into the hole of her jean shorts. She reciprocated with a hand on my zipper, right over my dick. Her panties were wet from the lake. From the water. That fucking dangerous, black water. I was no better than it, drowning her, taking what wasn't mine, turning beautiful things ugly.

"Lake."

"Please." Her breath fell on my lips. "One kiss. Then we can stop."

I wouldn't be able to stop. No fucking way. My hand got caught in her hair, and I yanked it by accident. She jerked back just long enough for me to take her shoulders and hold her at a distance. "We can't."

Her eyes shimmered with unshed tears. "Nobody has to know," she begged.

Headlights flashed in my side mirror. I immediately spotted the reflective red and blue top of a cop car, even though the lights weren't flashing.

"Fuck," I said, switching the song like it was porn I didn't want to get caught with.

Lake looked out the back window. "The police?"

"Yeah." He had no reason to pull over, but he might. We looked damn suspicious, sitting on the side of the road in the dark.

"Can we get in trouble?" she asked.

"I can."

She vaulted herself over the back of the bench, her long limbs nearly knocking me in the face. There was no backseat, just a narrow space behind the front one where I'd found the towels.

"What're you doing?" I asked.

"Hiding." She looked up at me, eyes wide with fear. She was still just a kid.

I had about ten seconds to make a decision. I respected law enforcement, but I wasn't naïve. I knew not all cops were good. But what kind of trouble could I get in just for sitting in the car with her? Would he believe we hadn't been doing anything?

"I think you should come back up here," I said.

The cop flashed his lights once, a shock of red and blue. He wasn't going to pass.

"I can't." Her voice broke. "I don't want you to get in trouble. He'll tell Gary. Maybe even my—my dad . . ."

If the cop wanted to see her ID and she didn't have one, he wouldn't just let that go. She didn't look eighteen, not yet. I was with a minor who'd taken off her bra. We were both wet from swimming. I really doubted he'd just let us go, which meant taking us back to camp, telling Gary. Gary and I were cool, but he'd never let me get away with this. These kids meant everything to him.

He'd tell Charles Kaplan. Lake's dad would obliterate me, no doubt, but what about her? He was her world. If he thought she'd snuck off with me in the middle of the night, how would that change their relationship?

"You're right, he might escort us back, probably will," I said, checking the rearview mirror. The officer had parked behind us. "But we'll get in worse trouble if he finds you."

"He won't. I can be quiet."

The black-and-white driver's side door opened. We were out of time. "I'll handle it," I promised her. What else could I do? "Just stay still. Don't make a sound." I wiped my upper lip on my sleeve. "I'll handle it."

He took his sweet time walking up to the window, checking my plates, looking over the truck. I turned off the heater and stereo. Crickets chirped. I'd been pulled over before. The window was already down, so I put my hands on the wheel where he could see them. My palms sweat around the leather. Thank fuck we'd been interrupted, not that I would've taken it any further. Would I have?

Boots shuffled in the dirt. A uniformed man not much older than me appeared at the window. He aimed his flashlight into the truck, barely skimming the back. "Evening," he said. "Car trouble?"

"Yes, sir. It won't start."

"Why'd you turn it off in the first place?" He looked around. "Not going to find much help in the middle of nowhere."

"I almost hit a coyote, pulled off, and the car just died on me."

"I see." He squinted at me. Or past me. I couldn't tell. If he were to lean in, really get inside the window, I doubted he'd miss Lake's blonde hair. "License and registration."

I considered arguing. He had no reason to suspect me of anything. It might've made things worse, though, and he was just doing his job. I pulled out my wallet and gave him my ID before leaning over to the glove compartment. "I'm sorry, Officer. It's a friend's truck." Fortunately, the paperwork was right where I needed it to be. "He was drinking, so I offered to do a beer run."

He read my license. "What about you, Mr. Sutter? Been drinking?"

"No, sir. That's why they sent me to get alcohol. I'm just on my way back."

"Oh, yeah? Where you headed?"

"Next exit. Young Cubs camp."

"You a counselor?"

"Yes, sir."

"Pretty sure you guys aren't supposed to be drinking, but . . . I would be if I were in your shoes. All those damn kids." He nodded at me. "Where's the alcohol then?"

Fuck. It was in the backseat. I blanched, a deer in cop lights. I had to come up with something. If I didn't, he'd have reason to doubt me and who knows where I'd end up. Probably at the station, a deer in the spotlight . . . of an interrogation room. I stuck an arm over the back of the seat. My hand brush against something soft. Lake. She pressed a bottle into my hand, and I handed it to him. He stuck his notepad under his arm and tried the top. "It's sealed, so there's no problem."

"Great," I said, trying not to sound too relieved as he gave it back.

The tension in my chest eased as the officer backed away from the window. "Step out of the vehicle, Mr. Sutter."

At first, I thought he was dismissing me. I almost answered him with "thanks." When his words registered, though, I was suddenly frozen to the spot. "Sorry?" I asked.

"Out of the vehicle."

I pulled sluggishly on the handle. The door stuck, so I had to ram my shoulder into it. The officer moved back as it popped open.

I wanted to ask why. I'd just had a little car trouble—there was no reason to make this into a thing. But I didn't. I *was* guilty. Not of what he thought, but I'd done a bad thing tonight. If I argued, he might get suspicious and look for more than what he had, which was nothing.

"What's this about?" I asked, stepping into the dirt. I sounded guilty even to my own ears.

The officer pointed to a spot in front of me. "Go ahead and walk in a straight line for me."

21
LAKE

Don't cry, don't cry, don't cry.

If I let out even a peep, the officer would find me in the back of the truck, take us back to camp, tell Gary and my dad, maybe even arrest Manning—and it'd all be my fault. I'd made Manning bring me along, go for a ride, get in the water.

My heartbeat filled my ears. I didn't know what was happening. Couldn't see anything, contorted in the small, dark space. The last I'd heard, Manning had asked why the cop wanted him out of the car.

Maybe everyone was right, and I *was* just a kid who didn't consider consequences. I always did the right thing, but tonight? Tonight, I'd sat on the edge of my bed, playing our night at the pool in my head. The good parts, like Manning opening up about his sister and then telling me the story of Altair and Vega. And then what I should've done differently when I'd stupidly tried to kiss him. I hadn't touched him, hadn't gotten physical enough. Tiffany did that, and I needed to also.

Tonight had been my last chance with Manning.

My last chance to touch him, to make him see me as something more than a girl.

To make him forget Tiffany.

And now we were here, about to get busted, because of me.

Minutes passed like hours. I strained to hear beyond the murmur of voices. I sat bent and twisted so long, my legs tingled. I recognized the bass of Manning's voice, the only thing that made my heart calm just a little. He wouldn't let the man find me. He wouldn't leave me here.

Finally, they got close enough to the window that I could hear. "Only if it won't inconvenience you," Manning said, opening the door.

"It's no trouble," the officer said. "If it doesn't work, I've got a pal I can wake up to take a look. Or I'll drive you back up to camp if you like, and you can handle it in the morning."

Unbidden tears filled my eyes. He wouldn't leave me. But what if he had to? What would I do—sleep here in the truck in wet clothes? Already I was doing everything in my power not to shiver.

"Let me just . . ." Manning leaned into the truck, and there was a loud, clunky pop out front. "There we go."

He glanced at me over the divider. I nodded to let him know I was okay, even though I was holding my sobs at bay. He left for a few more minutes, came back, and turned the key in the ignition. The truck tried to start and after a second, shuddered and came to life.

I'd never been so relieved in my life. My limbs went limp.

"Thank fuck," Manning said under his breath.

"Well, look at that," the officer said. "Your lucky night."

"Yes, sir."

They were both silent a few seconds. I could only see Manning's head turned away from me. I wanted to scream just to break the tension or look over the edge to see what was happening.

Finally, Manning pulled the door shut. "Thanks for your help," he said through the window.

"Hey, good luck with training. You get sick of the beach, consider Big Bear. We could always use good guys."

"Will do. Thanks again, sir." Manning stared into the rearview mirror. I was too afraid to speak, much less move. After a minute, he waved out the window and began to drive. We were a couple minutes up the road before either of us spoke.

With his one hand on the top of the wheel, he turned onto the unpaved road. I knew because I could barely sit still, the way it bumped and wobbled over potholes and rocks. "You all right?" he asked without looking back.

"Yes." My voice sounded foreign. "Is everything okay?"

He squinted out the windshield. I knew it wasn't okay, not really. I'd gone too far. Manning had been good to me the last five weeks. Protected me. Taught me. Confided in me. And I'd repaid him by almost getting him arrested.

"I'm sorry," I said.

I expected him to scold me, but instead he just said, "Me, too."

"You have nothing to be sorry for."

"I'm just glad we're okay." He stopped the truck, turned out the headlights, and looked back at me. "Nobody can know about tonight. Ever."

"I *know* that. I've told you a million times, I'm not a little girl. And we didn't even do anything, even though it was our last chance. I can't say goodbye to you tomorrow. I won't."

He pinched the bridge of his nose and inhaled. "Listen to me, Lake. You have your whole life ahead of you. You're going to one of the top schools in the country. You've worked hard to get where you are."

"But—"

"And so have your parents and sister."

I closed my mouth.

"Think of all they've done for you. They want nothing more than to see you succeed, and I feel the same."

"I want that, too, Manning. I can do all that. I can do *none* of it. It wouldn't matter. I'd still—"

"You're a smart girl, and I need you to understand."

I did to a point. Having sex with Manning could change things for both of us. If my dad found out, if he even knew I'd snuck off with Manning tonight, he'd never look at me the same. He'd see me like Tiffany. If Tiffany found out, she'd be embarrassed. And the reality was, Manning could've gotten into trouble tonight because of what I'd done. I was a minor. He wasn't. He'd be punished as an adult. He didn't have family on his side—in fact, maybe Tiffany and I were all he had right now. He would've lost that, and his job, too.

"I understand," I said. "I understand why we can't be together right now, but I can wait." I hadn't planned to say that or anything like it, but I'd been holding everything in too long. I'd watched Manning go off with my sister more than once. I'd fought to keep my hand from wandering over to his while he'd told me this was *our* story. I'd almost had him tonight, and I'd blown it. "Wait for me, too," I said.

"Don't ask that of me."

"No matter what happens, where you go, where I go, it won't change the fact—I'll be eighteen in two years."

"But *you'll* change in two years, Lake. So will I."

"My feelings won't."

"Get out of the car, Lake. I can't park until you do, and we've been sitting here too long." Manning leaned over and opened the passenger door. "Go straight to your cabin."

It was the last thing I wanted to hear, but he was right. I stood as best I could. My legs had fallen asleep. As I got myself over the seat, I became uncomfortably aware that I was wet, sticky, and tired. He waited as I crawled out of the car, grabbed my flip-flops, and eased the door shut. "Goodnight."

He kept his eyes forward. The window was still down, so as I walked away, I only just heard him respond, "'Night, Lake."

With my bra stuffed in my back pocket, I carried my shoes so I wouldn't make any noise. I passed Tiffany's cabin on the way to mine. For a moment, I was tempted to climb into her sleeping bag instead and hold onto her. I'd never felt so grown up and so childish. Tiffany would've understood, would've told me what to do . . . if only it hadn't been her boyfriend I'd been sneaking around with.

It'd all happened so fast, like a dream. We probably hadn't been gone more than two hours. I touched my cheek, where I could still feel the scrape of his stubble. My heart skipped as I remembered stripping off my clothes by the lake, knowing he was watching. And his enormous hands, in my hair, in my shorts. They could take over whole parts of me—the entire back of my head, half my thigh. By the time I reached my cabin, my heart was pounding but no longer out of fear.

Quietly, I set my sandals down and dug into my duffel bag for my pajamas. I changed limb by limb without making any noise. When I opened my sleeping bag, the zipper hissed.

"Lake?" Hannah asked. "That you?"

"I just went to the bathroom," I whispered. "Don't wake the girls."

She inhaled and turned over, toward the wall. Me, I stared at the top bunk for at least another hour, playing the night over and over in my head.

Manning's restrained but curious fingers, inching closer up my shorts.

His mouth so close I could almost convince myself we'd kissed.

I already felt myself changing. Inside the sleeping bag, I touched my outer thigh. My stomach. My breasts. I was more aware of my body than I'd ever been. Flannel was smooth over the top of my hand. The polyester sleeping bag crinkled. My heart beat steadily in my chest, but if I held still, I felt my pulse all over.

Was it wrong, what we hadn't even done? Manning would've said so, even if he didn't think it. He couldn't tell me we'd be together one day, but he had to know the truth.

You can't move the stars.

Manning and I were inevitable.

22
LAKE

I woke up before anyone else, even Hannah, and sat up in bed. My hair had dried but was tangled from my midnight swim. And from Manning's hands. The memory, only six hours fresh, made my stomach tighten. So this was what all the fuss was about. This was why Tiffany was always flirting with boys. Mouths. Hands. Hardness and softness. Adrenaline. We'd almost gotten caught. We'd almost gone too far. Getting wrapped up in Manning, belonging to him—I didn't see how it could ever be far enough.

Early morning light made shadows around the cabin, on the sleeping girls. It was our last morning, and I never wanted it to end, but still, I smiled.

"Hey," Hannah whispered, her eyes puffy as she grinned back at me. "Did you go somewhere last night?"

"No," I said immediately. "Why?"

"I woke up and you weren't here. At least, I thought you weren't." She laughed. "Maybe I was seeing things. Or not seeing things."

"I was here. I went to the bathroom, but that's it."

She sighed. "It's so peaceful right now. Do we have to wake them?"

"Only if we want to send them home with what they brought. Gary wants us to start packing before breakfast." Some of the girls stirred. "Then again, it's our last day. What's he going to do? Send us home?"

I threw open my sleeping bag. Hannah sat up, piling her mass of hair on top of her head, watching me move around the cabin. I put on the soundtrack to *The Bodyguard* and belted out "I'm Every Woman." Some of the girls giggled. They woke up confused but smiling, the way Hannah and I had.

Hannah got up, too. In just drawstring pants and t-shirts, we ran outside and started shaking our hips. "Are you guys seriously going to make us dance alone?" I called.

Girls crawled from their beds and hurried outside like ants from a hill. Someone turned up the music. Another cabin yelled at us to be quiet, but we went on dancing. It was a beautiful morning, and I was filled up by the memory of last night. Brimming with the possibilities of what was to come. For the first time since Manning and I had met, my feelings felt validated. Maybe Manning couldn't *say* how he felt, but it'd been there in his eyes, his touch.

Once we'd worn the girls out, Hannah and I walked them to Reflection. We hit the path to the clearing at the same time as cabin nine. Manning's hair stuck up in every direction. He had dark circles under eyes, like I probably did. We fell into step beside each other and slowed, lagging behind. "Your hair's a mess," he told me.

"I haven't washed it yet."

"Aren't you afraid something's growing in there?"

I giggled softly. "I wouldn't mind if it was. A souvenir."

Manning gave me a look I recognized. He was going to scold me. I mimed zipping my lips shut, and he seemed satisfied.

"Oh, before I forget." I dug into my pocket. "I made you something in arts and crafts."

"Me?" he asked.

I showed him a brown, orange, and forest green wax bracelet I'd woven earlier in the week.

He plucked it out of my palm, twisting it between his fingers. "What is it?"

"A friendship bracelet. But I gave it some thought this morning, and . . . I don't think it should be that for us."

Manning raised his eyes to mine slowly, looking at me from under his dark, long lashes. "Lake . . ."

"Every time you crave a cigarette, look at the bracelet."

"And?"

"And think of me. You seem to be really good at not smoking in front me, so just pretend I'm there. You still want to quit, right?"

Manning inspected the bracelet, swallowing. "Nobody ever gives me anything," he said. "Especially not jewelry."

"I tried to pick manly colors. They made me think of you." I smiled. "But you don't have to wear it. Just keep it in your pocket or something."

He scratched his jaw. "And when I feel like a smoke, I just pull it out and look at it?"

I nodded. "And think of me."

He seemed to consider it. "It looks small."

I stopped walking and took the bracelet. The clasp was adjustable, so I pulled it as wide as it would go. Manning held out his hand, and I put it on him.

As I did, he looked at the bracelets stacked all the way up my wrist. "You have lots of friends."

"But I only made one bracelet."

"Where's the gold one?" he asked.

"I left it at home." It was funny how these little wax ones could feel as valuable as the expensive one from my dad. "Didn't want it to fall off."

Our eyes met. We were close, unlike that first day, when I'd been hesitant to approach the gruff man who'd held my delicate chain coiled in his hand.

I could've lingered there all morning, grazing my fingers over his strong, tan forearm. He didn't exactly make a move to leave, either. But another cabin came into view behind us—Tiffany and her girls. Not only were they on time, but also in a straight line.

I tightened the bracelet on him and took my hand back. Manning shook his head. "After last night, I promised myself I'd never be alone with you again. Yet here we are, not even seven hours later."

"We're not alone," I pointed out. "Everyone's here."

"I've got something I want you to have, too," he told me, looking over at Tiffany. "But I'll give it to you later."

I smiled. The fact that I had no idea what it could even be made me extra giddy. "Later, then."

We all found our places in the bleachers and Gary waited at the front. Since it was the last morning, it took a little longer for the kids to settle down. "Good morning," Gary greeted the group. "You should know the drill by now, campers. Close your eyes. Breathe the morning in. Appreciate your existence. Let's all say thank you for such a beautiful day."

"Thank you," I murmured with everyone else.

"For a fun-filled and active week."

"Thank you."

I felt eyes on me, so I opened mine. It was him, finder of bracelets, hoarder of cigarettes, a Pink Floyd beast of a man. For the first time that I knew of, he'd looked over at me during Reflection.

"It's important to spend time outdoors," Gary said, "to take advantage of everything Mother Nature has afforded us."

Manning looked three times the size of anyone around him. He was significantly bigger than Kirk, his teenaged co-counselor. Gary, too, who had a big presence but was actually pretty wiry. Nobody could compare to Manning. He was a bear in the mountains. My great bear. One day he'd be mine; I already felt that he was, I just couldn't say it. But he knew. I knew.

We held each other's gazes until Gary cleared his throat. He was watching us, so I closed my eyes again, and he continued. "Sometimes we allow ourselves to be consumed by the television set or get caught up in problems that don't matter. Sometimes we let friends and family dictate our state of mind. When you wake up tomorrow, even though you'll be home, continue this practice of being grateful for what you have, and for the gift of the day to come. Be calm. Be grateful."

"I will be grateful," we all said in unison.

"This morning, we'll go around and say what our favorite part of this experience has been. Take a few moments to reflect on the week before you open your eyes."

Where to start? There were so many moments I wouldn't trade for the world. Last night, for one. Horseback riding with Manning. And maybe my favorite of all, our time under the stars as he showed me the constellations. But it wasn't as if I could say any of that.

Having the girls look up to me this week, I felt as if I'd grown up a little, unlike last year, when I'd still felt like one of them. I'd enjoyed getting to know Hannah and even spending time with my sister. It'd been thrilling to stand up in front of the crowd and perform skits at the nightly campfires.

A murmur made its way through the camp. When it got louder, I opened my eyes. Two policemen stood at the edge of the clearing, by the woods. One had his thumbs hooked in his belt, the other crossed his arms. My stomach dropped as I immediately thought of last night. I looked at Manning. He was talking to a kid but his eyes were on the officers.

Gary had his back to them, so he continued. "Counselors, discuss the week with your cabins and decide which moments you'd like to share with the camp. Then, we'll go around and—" When he noticed he'd lost our attention, Gary looked over his shoulder, but only briefly. "We'll go around and . . . share with the group. Lexi, take over a sec?"

I stopped breathing. A few moments earlier, I'd been inhaling the beauty of the day. Expelling the negativity, as Professor Sal had said. Now I couldn't even feel my mouth, my lungs, my hands. Just my heart pounding against my ribcage. The cops were here. Surely, it had nothing to do with me and Manning, but I couldn't ignore the coincidence. Last night was the first time I'd ever come close to getting in trouble with the police, and here they were again.

I looked to Manning for cues. He stood tall. Only his eyes moved as he watched Gary cross the dirt toward the policemen.

Lexi took Gary's spot, but everyone ignored her.

"What's going on?" one of my campers asked.

"Nothing." It came out as a whisper. Gary and the officers turned to look at us. All of us. Not me. Maybe me? Then they closed their circle, talking with their heads bent.

"Lake?"

"Hmm?" I blinked, looking at the sea of concerned faces below me.

Hannah rubbed one of girls' backs. "I'm sure it's nothing," she said, but to me, she whispered, "Why are they here?"

Manning wouldn't look at me, but I *needed* to him to look at me. I hadn't seen the officer last night, but he'd sounded younger than the two cops standing there. Bucky appeared out of nowhere, shuffling his feet as though he'd been literally dragged from his bed. Behind him came a couple other permanent staff members I recognized but couldn't name.

Manning finally turned to me and slowly, he shook his head. *No.* I could only guess what he meant. Don't look at him. Don't say anything. Don't act suspicious. To show him I was adult enough to handle this, I took a much-needed deep breath, tore my gaze from him, and turned to my girls.

"I think I know what happened," I said solemnly.

Eight pairs of eyes widened. "What?"

"Someone snuck candy into the cabin, even though Gary warned us not to."

Hannah clamped a hand over her mouth. "Are they going to arrest the culprit?"

"Maybe." I smiled. My face was stiff. I felt as though I could vomit any moment. "I tried to tell you guys . . ."

Some of the girls gasped. "We didn't do it. We swear."

"Then you have nothing to worry about," Hannah said.

"It was probably the boys' cabins," I said. "They're always pulling dumb pranks."

"Must've been Manning's," Hannah said.

I looked at her. "Why would you say that?"

She nodded over my shoulder. I turned. Gary made his way toward cabin nine as the cops retreated into the woods. I reached out to steady myself on something and Hannah was nearest.

"Are you okay?" she asked when I took her arm.

This was bad. They knew. Gary knew. Manning and I hadn't even really done anything, but would anyone believe us? What would they think, knowing Manning and I had spent a few hours off the

339

campground in the middle of the night? I wanted to go listen to whatever Gary had to say, but my feet felt like concrete, as if Manning's withering look before had glued me to the spot. And everyone in camp was watching.

Including Tiffany.

The girls tittered and giggled. They whispered to each other, excited by the distraction. "I have Skittles in my bag, but my brother said bears don't eat those."

Gary said something to Manning. The whole exchange only lasted a few seconds. Then he returned to relieve Lexi of the job she hadn't done. "All right, everyone. Calm down. It's no big deal." He smiled, but behind it, in his eyes, I sensed something was off. "Where were we?"

———

Manning wasn't in the cafeteria. Neither was Gary. I made myself a plate of food but didn't touch it. When breakfast was nearly over and it became apparent Manning wouldn't show, I asked Hannah to take over and went to look for them.

Camp was empty, one-hundred-plus kids crammed into the dining hall. I went directly to cabin nine and felt an ounce of relief to see Manning out front. He was talking to someone in the cabin.

I recognized Gary's voice. " . . . last night . . . alcohol. How come . . . what took so long?"

I crunched through a pile of leaves, and Manning turned around. He shook his head. "Give us a minute, Lake."

"Why are the police here?" I asked.

Gary came onto the front step. "We're handling it."

I ignored him. "Manning?"

He sighed, facing Gary again. "I need a second to talk to her."

"We don't have a second."

"She's Tiffany's sister, man."

Gary put his hands up. "Just saying, you probably don't want to make them wait."

Manning left him there, nodding for me to follow him.

When we were out of earshot, he stopped. His eyes darted around our immediate area, and when he seemed satisfied we were alone, he spoke under his breath. "Everything's fine. I just need you to promise me one thing."

Fine didn't sound fine. It sounded bad. I wanted to be strong, but my legs felt about to give out. "Why? What's going on?"

He went to put a hand on my shoulder but stopped himself. "Do you trust me?"

I nodded. No hesitation.

"Then believe me when I say, it's nothing." He looked over my head as he spoke. "The reason the cops are here has nothing to do with you."

"What about you?"

"I just need you to promise me . . ." He returned his eyes to mine. As if he had some kind of power over me, my heart rate calmed. I'd promise him anything, because Manning would protect me. I knew that. But who would protect him? "Don't mention last night to anyone. No matter what. If someone asks where you were, lie, and make it damn convincing."

"But—"

"Did Hannah hear you come in? Any of the girls?"

"No. Yes—Hannah. But I told her I was in the bathroom."

"Last night, after the party, you went straight to your cabin and fell asleep. Then you woke up this morning. If you feel the urge to tell the truth, don't do it without talking to me first."

"But why?" I begged. "Why would someone ask me where I was?"

"They won't. I won't let them. Your only job is to protect yourself. Mine is to protect us both. Now, go get your sister for me."

I reeled back as if I'd been slapped, face tingling. "My *sister*?"

"Send her here alone. Quick. I don't have a lot of time."

"No. You can't just tell me that and send me away. Where are you going?"

"They're taking me to the station. It's nothing, Lake, but if you open your mouth, it could become something. Understand?"

He wasn't in trouble. I had to trust in that. But he was right—no matter that nothing had happened last night, we were the only two who knew that for sure. I couldn't think of a coherent response so I just nodded.

"Go," he said. I wanted something. Anything. A kiss. A hug. I would've taken a pat on the back. All I got was a hard stare. "This is adult business," he said, his jaw ticking. "You're too young."

His words were as sharp as knives, and they cut deep. Even after last night, I was still a child to him. Immature. Not to be trusted with important things. I swallowed thickly to keep from crying like the baby he already thought I was. And then I went and got Tiffany.

23
MANNING

I sat in an interrogation room at Big Bear's sheriff station in shorts and a t-shirt. I rarely wore shorts, which was why they were the only clean thing I had left up here. My jeans from last night were in a soggy ball at the bottom of my duffel like buried evidence. I looked like a grown man who'd borrowed a camper's clothes.

My hands in my lap, I absentmindedly fidgeted with the bracelet Lake had made me. I wasn't used to having things on my hands or wrists. She played with hers when she was uneasy, but I had no reason to be nervous. From what Gary'd told me, whatever the hell the cops wanted had nothing to do with me. I took comfort in that, but it wasn't as if I were exactly innocent. And that made me sweat. I'd gotten carried away with Lake in the truck. I still tasted watermelon on my lips. Smelled the dampness of the truck's cab. Heard the drumbeat of the music. What if they sensed that fear on me?

Two men entered the small room, an older man with a gut that hung over his belt, and a tall thin one in a suit. Neither was the cop from last night, and I wasn't sure if that was good or bad. He'd turned out to be all right. He'd made me walk in a straight line, and when it was apparent I was sober, we'd talked about my plans to join the force while he'd jumped the truck's battery.

"Morning, Mr. Sutter," said the burly man in uniform. "I'm Officer Vermont, and this is my colleague, Detective Krout."

I shook both their hands. "I'll be honest," I said, "I don't know why I'm here."

"We'll get to that," he said. "Need anything before we start? Water? Coffee?"

"Sure." What I wanted most was a cigarette. My head hurt all over from lack of sleep and now this. The bracelet felt like no more than a hair on my wrist, but I hadn't forgotten it was there. This was a special circumstance, though. I'd quit tomorrow. "Any chance of me getting a smoke?"

Vermont laughed as Krout stood at a table against the wall, separating paper cups by a coffee urn. "This isn't a TV show, son. But nice try."

The gray, concrete room, lit by a single lamp, did look a little like a set. Not to mention short-and-fat and tall-and-skinny would've made a fine pair for a primetime courtroom comedy. I kept it to myself. I respected the police. They might have the wrong guy, but they were just doing their jobs.

Krout set three waters and coffees on the table. My mouth had gone tacky from my cravings, so I went for water.

"Do you have any guesses?" Krout asked. It was the first thing he'd said.

I swallowed my water in one gulp and set the cup down. "About?"

"Why you're here."

"Gary relayed what you told him." Gary had convinced the cops to wait at the gate for me, their presence upsetting the kids. "There was some kind of robbery last night?"

"A house in town, nice, upstanding folks," Vermont said. "We just have a few routine questions for you, but it's our duty to go over your rights."

I sipped coffee as he read my Miranda rights. I had nothing to worry about, and the longer the process went on, the more this became a thing. I wiped my mouth with my sleeve. "I'm good. We can continue."

"For the record, please state your name, age, and occupation."

"Manning Raymond Sutter. Age twenty-three. Camp counselor, construction worker, and anything else that pays the bills."

"Where are you based?"

"Long Beach, California."

The detective made notes in his folder. "Did you grow up there?"

"No. Pasadena."

"Have any family in California?"

"My mom's still in Pasadena I think."

"What about your dad?"

I wiped my temple, my hairline getting hot. "I'm not sure. Last I heard, he was in Pelican Bay, but that was a while ago."

Krout looked up at that. "Penitentiary? What for?"

Having a dad in prison probably didn't look so good. Fucking me over from afar, no surprise there. "Assault."

"I see." Detective Krout's pen continued to scrawl across the page. "Tell us about your evening."

I blew out a breath. It was simple, really. At least, what they'd know of it. "I was at camp most of the night. We ran out of alcohol, so since I was the only sober one, I was volunteered to do a run. I went into town, got some, and went back to the campsite."

"What time did you leave?"

"I'd say just before ten."

"And you went right back after you got the alcohol?" Krout asked. "Because that's not what we heard."

That caught me off guard, that they'd heard anything. I swallowed to buy myself a second, then remembered the officer from last night. Of course they knew I didn't go straight back. I'd been with one of their own. "Yeah. No. I had some car trouble so it took a little longer."

"Nobody seems to know what time you returned. According to one source, you said you'd be right back, but by the time your peers went to sleep at one in the morning, you still hadn't returned. We figure, being generous, it's half an hour into town and half an hour back. If you left just after ten, you should've been back well before midnight."

"Like I said, I had car trouble. It wasn't my truck, believe me, that hunk of metal had its problems. You can go take a look. Better yet, ask your officer."

Both men's eyebrows dropped. "What officer?"

Were they fucking with me? There was no way they didn't already know. How else had they pegged me as a suspect? "I forget his last name. He found me on the side of the road, made sure I wasn't drinking and driving, then gave me a jump."

Krout sat back in his seat with a sigh. "I didn't see any record of it."

I shrugged. "Maybe because there was nothing to say. I wasn't doing anything wrong." I had the urge to swallow again, but I worried they'd read into that. I resisted and ended up coughing. "Can I get some water?"

Vermont and Krout exchanged a look. "Was Anderson on duty last night?" Krout asked him.

"Don't know off the top of my head, but he's most likely sleeping right now." He turned to me. "We'll be sure to talk to Officer Anderson. What was the truck you were driving?"

"Ford clunker. Seventy-nine, I think. It belongs to—Vern. You know him? He works at the camp."

Vermont ignored me. "Color?"

"White."

"And where'd you stop for alcohol?"

"The liquor store was closed so I tried a bar. The bartender, or maybe it was the owner—he sold me something from the back."

"And that's it? From there, you headed back and the truck broke down?"

"Yes, sir."

"Where was that?"

"About a mile from camp."

Vermont tapped the end of his pen on his notepad, nodding. Nobody spoke for a few moments. Krout checked his watch and got me a refill that I immediately downed.

"Thing is, Mr. Sutter," Vermont said, "we have two witnesses placing your vehicle in the neighborhood where the crime occurred, at the time it occurred. Not too far from Phil's bar. But I can't think of no reason you should've been near that residence. It's not on the way back to camp."

Fuck. It'd been such a blip in time, I hadn't even really thought about our drive through the neighborhood. Lake popped into my head first. She'd hung out the window, and I'd let her, like a fucking idiot. I'd been too caught up in her, in our last night together. Did they know about her? As long as they didn't, I was fine. I hadn't done anything wrong. I shifted in the plastic chair, suddenly aware of how hard it was. "I went for a drive. Never been to the area, so I was curious."

The men just stared at me. It was about the truth, though. "Why didn't you mention it?" Vermont asked.

"Guess I forgot."

Vermont blew out a sigh, looking over his notepad. "Two different neighbors say they spotted a loud, white truck outside their houses. Same plates as yours. Couldn'ta been driving more than ten miles an hour. With the headlights out. To me, that sounds like someone casing the neighborhood."

The lamp over our heads got brighter. I willed my heart rate to slow down; I needed my wits about me. Sitting up a little straighter, I said, "I don't really have a good explanation for that. I just like that time of night. The peace. Stars."

"Not peaceful up at camp, smack in the middle of the woods?" Krout asked, his voice a little harder, wryer. "Can't see the stars up there where it's dark? Had to go looking for it in town?"

I massaged my face. "It looks bad, I agree, but it's not like that. I just—there are kids everywhere up there, I needed some time to myself. I work construction. I'm not—not used to being around all those kids." The officers let me ramble, probably hoping I'd trip myself up. I took a breath. "They say anything else?"

"Like what?"

I shook my head. I just needed to know about Lake. If anyone'd seen her. "Just trying to figure out—I mean, I didn't do anything wrong. I didn't. You can search the truck. My cabin. All I brought up here with me was a bag, not like I could fit any stolen goods in it. What'd the robber take?"

Vermont looked at Krout. "Nothing. He was interrupted. The woman who caught him described him as tall with dark hair and clothes."

"So then it wasn't actually a crime?"

"Of course it was," Krout said. "Someone came into a family's home and confronted the wife. Her kids were there. What we have to figure out is who and why."

I knew from my criminal justice class that first-degree robbery was a felony, and a felony charge could fuck me long after I served time. "Was anyone hurt?"

"Fortunately not. The woman wrestled her wallet from him and he ran. She's all right. He knew enough to pick a lock. No major damage done. You know how to pick a lock?"

"No." Of course I did, for fuck's sake. My breathing shallowed. I needed more water, but it didn't look like I was getting a refill. "Can I get an aspirin or something?"

"In a minute." Krout looked over his notes. "Vermont's niece was at Phil's, that bar you visited last night. She ID'ed a tall, dark-haired man and your vehicle, so we know you were there."

I waited for the bomb to drop. *Who was the girl in your car?* I'd fucked up huge. Lake was innocent. Last night, I'd made some mistakes. I hadn't been thinking straight. Now, in the light of day, I saw how bad it was. Fooling around with her could have lasting effects on her. If they brought her in, it would traumatize her. People would talk. Her bright future could be tarnished. Her dad, fuck, he would fucking *murder* me, and who knew what kind of emotional punishment he'd put Lake through.

"We haven't spoken to Phil over at the bar yet," Krout continued, "but we'll get to that. I assume he'll remember you. Tall. Dark hair."

I nodded mindlessly. *Just say it. Just ask me who she was.* I didn't know how I'd answer, but the anticipation was killing me.

Krout straightened his file on the table. "That's all I got for the moment. We'll have to keep you here, though. We're vetting some other suspects, then we'll need you for a line-up."

I didn't know what to feel. There were other suspects—that was good. Lake hadn't been mentioned. Also good. But I was too apprehensive to feel relieved; it didn't seem like they believed me.

"We go home today," I said. "They're packing up the buses as we speak."

"Not much we can do about it, Mr. Sutter," Vermont said.

It's Manning, I wanted to say. Mr. Sutter was my piece-of-shit dad who was in prison for a real, actual crime, and whom I wanted nothing to do with. "I didn't do this," I said. "I swear."

"If that's true, then it'll work itself out," Vermont replied automatically, as if he'd heard it a thousand times before. "In the meantime, we'll confirm your story with the officer on duty last night. Is there anyone else we should talk to? Anyone who saw you come or go? Maybe vouch for your whereabouts?"

Lake. She was the only one who knew where I was last night. That I was innocent—at least of what they were accusing. But there was no way in hell, none, I'd be bringing her into this. I couldn't put her through it, and I was pretty sure it'd do more harm than good anyway.

I swallowed for what felt like the millionth time in an hour. My throat was raw. "I think I'd like to speak to a lawyer."

24
LAKE

Everybody went about his or her business as if nothing had changed.

As if Manning hadn't been gone almost two hours.

As if taking away an innocent man in a police car was normal.

I helped every girl in the cabin pack her things, leaving mine for last. The cabin was messier than I realized. Hannah and I worked in silence to pick up, strip beds, empty the trash. The girls sat outside in the sun on their packs.

"Can we turn on the radio again?" one asked.

"No."

They were quiet after that, and even though I wanted them to be, it didn't help. My hands were busy, but my mind wandered. Manning had said I wasn't involved with why they'd taken him, but I couldn't see how that was possible. I'd been there every step of the way. The officer had to have seen something and gone back to the station with it. Would they come for me next?

I hoped so, that way I could explain everything. The sneaking off, the driving, the swimming, the almost-kissing—if the alternative was Manning getting in trouble for being with a minor, I'd tell them the truth: it was all me. I was responsible for all of it. I'd make sure they knew that, even if it meant being grounded for life. Even if the result was ruining myself in my dad's eyes.

When the cabin was clean and all the girls had their bags in hand, Hannah looked at my bunk. "We're supposed to take them over now."

I wiped sweat from my brow. I wished I'd showered, because I was sure after all that labor, I smelled like a swamp. "It'll only take me a second to pack. Let's get them situated."

Kids were everywhere, bees buzzing around a hive, as we walked the girls to the buses. I searched the area for anyone who might have news. Manning wasn't back yet; I could sense his absence.

I spotted Gary before he saw me. "Start loading your things," I said to the girls, and to Hannah, "I'll be right back."

Gary looked up, waving his clipboard at me. "Hey, Lake. You girls ready to go?"

"Yes. What happened?"

He made a note. "What?"

"With Manning? Where is he?"

Gary glanced around the immediate area. "He's still at the station."

"Why? What happened?"

"I can't tell you that."

"Did Tiffany go?"

"No." He looked back at his list. "In fact, go check on her for me. She isn't here yet, and we have to stay on schedule."

My mouth dropped open. "We can't leave him here."

"We have no choice."

"But he's by himself with no way of getting home."

Gary dropped the clipboard to his side. "What am I supposed to do? Keep the campers here all weekend while we wait to hear if one of our counselors is getting arrested? How do you think the parents would feel about that?"

Arrested. The word hit hard enough to make me step back. "But we can't just—"

"I think you ought to get your sister. I need her girls here, and . . . she's probably more upset than you, don't you think? He's her boyfriend after all."

Anger rose in me like a wave. Tiffany only cared about Manning when it was convenient for her. *I* was the one who cared. She had no right to be upset. *I* did.

I wanted to explain all that to Gary, but my frustration must've been written on my face. Gary put a hand on my shoulder. "You have to calm down, Lake."

"I need to see Manning."

"You can't."

"Then I want to talk to his lawyer."

"Why?"

"I can't say."

Gary frowned. "I'm starting to get concerned."

"About what?"

"I don't know." We stared at each other. "Should I be concerned?"

It probably looked as though I were overreacting. Gary didn't get why this was so important to me, but making him understand could get Manning and me in more trouble. I'd promised Manning I'd keep my mouth shut. "No," I said with a deep breath. "He's just been a good friend to—us. Our family. And Tiffany."

"Okay. So you'll go check on her?"

There was nothing left to do. It wasn't as if I could go into town and talk to Manning myself. At least Tiffany could drive. Once again, she was my only link to Manning.

———

Tiffany was frazzled. She'd thrown her hair up in a messy bun, and her bangs stuck to her forehead. "Kimmy, why are you taking everything *out* of the bag we just packed?" she asked.

"I can't find my Walkman." As Kimmy dug around, her dirty socks jumped onto the floor like fugitives on the run. "I need it for the bus."

"But you guys wouldn't shut up on the way here!" Tiffany began shoving Kimmy's things back into the duffel. "You didn't even listen to music."

I put my hands on Kimmy's shoulders. "We have games planned for the bus. You won't need your Walkman. Right now, I need you to do a job for us."

Kimmy pouted. "What job?"

"Go around to every bed that doesn't have a sleeping bag, yank the sheets off the mattresses, and pile them in the middle of the cabin. Sounds fun, right?"

I'd given her permission to cause mayhem. She sprinted the two feet to the nearest bed. "You make it too hard on yourself," I told Tiffany.

"If I ever, ever mention having babies, remind me of this experience," Tiffany muttered. "I'm just glad Manning isn't here to see me like this."

That's because he's with the police, I wanted to snap at her. But that wasn't the way to get through to Tiffany. "What'd he want?" I asked. "When I sent you to talk to him."

"*Iris!*" Tiffany gaped behind me. "Are you kidding me?"

I looked back to find Iris grinning in red lipstick. She made kissing noises. "Oh, Manning. I lo-o-o-ve you."

I recognized that lip color—it was Chanel. This wouldn't go well. I was about to intervene when Tiffany stood up. "Come here," she said to Iris.

Iris took a step back.

"You did it wrong. I taught you guys the other night how to use lip liner. You should've put that on first because now the lipstick is bleeding. You look like a hooker."

"Tiffany," I said through my teeth.

"What?" she asked me. "Do you want her to look like a hooker?"

Iris narrowed her eyes and then went to Tiffany, digging the lipstick from her pocket. She handed it over. "Sorry."

"It's okay." Tiffany popped off the cap, inspected the lipstick, and muttered under her breath, "This would cost you a month's allowance, but it's okay."

If I hadn't been so concerned about Manning, I might've fainted with shock. Somehow, at some point, Tiffany had been struck with an ounce of patience. Though it made me happy to see her try, I needed her to focus. "Tiff? What'd he say?"

Tiffany capped the lipstick, sat on the ground, and put it in the mesh pocket of her luggage. "Who?"

"Manning."

She blinked up to me. For the way she'd just screeched at Iris, her voice was eerily even. "He's in trouble because he left camp last night."

I scratched my elbow. I shouldn't feel guilty about lying. How many times had Tiffany lied to me or omitted information to get her way? "Do you know why?" I asked.

"Don't you? You talked to him."

My palms sweat. I didn't know what she was talking about. "When?"

"This morning. You were the one who told me to go to his cabin. Didn't he tell you all this?"

"No. He said it was . . . adult business."

Tiffany arched an eyebrow and laughed. "You're an adult, aren't you? You've been trying to act like one lately. To be like me."

My face reddened. "What do you mean?"

She looked away. "Manning doesn't think it's a big deal, whatever the police want. But he wasn't sure how long they'd keep him, so he might need me to come pick him up later."

"That's a long drive to get back here."

"Who else is going to do it? You? His family? He wants me there." She sat on her overstuffed suitcase and tried to pull the zipper closed. "All I know is it has to do with something that happened last night. He wouldn't tell me more."

I knew it. Either he'd lied by saying it didn't involve me, or there was something else going on. Manning wanted to protect me, he'd made that clear since we'd met, but at what point was he making things worse? I didn't exactly feel safe with him in custody, unable to talk me through our next move.

"Can I come with you to pick him up?" I asked.

Tiffany yanked on the zipper so hard, her fingers slipped, and she flew backward. "*Fuck.*" She shook out her hand. "God, that hurt. And I broke a goddamn nail."

"Tiff?"

"I'm so sick of this place," she said. "It's dirty and loud. I only came for him, and now he's . . ."

"What?" I asked, every hair on my body prickling.

"Never mind—"

"What else did he say?"

"Nothing, I already told you."

"But if there's anything else, *anything*—I need to know."

"What do you want from me, Lake?" she said, pounding her fist on the suitcase. Surprised, I stepped back. "I have no idea what's going on. He wouldn't tell me shit. I don't know what to do or if I should do anything or just . . ."

Her body shook with the threat of a sob. I was so shocked by her tears that I got on the floor next to her. She rarely cried if it wasn't to get something out of my dad. I pulled her hands from her face to put my arms around her. "It's okay."

She pulled away. "Don't."

"Why?"

She narrowed her eyes on me. "You're the reason we're in this mess."

It seemed to me Tiffany and Manning were adult enough to decide whether or not they wanted to be here, but when had Tiffany ever taken responsibility for her decisions? "Whatever, Tiffany. I came here to check on you and Manning, not fight."

"What if he gets in real trouble?" she asked. "How will you feel then?"

"He won't."

"How do you know?" she asked.

"Innocent people don't go to jail."

She looked at me hard. "What if he's not innocent?"

"He is," Gary said from the doorway. "Manning's a good guy. Whatever happened, I'm sure it was just a misunderstanding."

"Take us to the station, Gary," I said. "Please."

"I can't. Not only would it not help, but Manning specifically asked me to keep you two out of it."

"But I'm his girlfriend," Tiffany said.

"He's trying to protect you." He sniffed at us, his eyes roaming over our faces. We must've looked as bad as we felt, because he conceded, but not without an eye-roll. "If it'll make you feel better, I'll come back as soon as I can and check things out. Once everything at home is sorted, I'll drive back up here on my own and make sure Manning's all right."

It wasn't exactly what I wanted, but I could see it was all we were going to get. It was better than Manning being alone. "Thanks," we said.

"But I have one condition—relax. You girls are too young to worry about this sort of stuff. Actually, I have two conditions. Pack up your shit and get over to the buses *now*." With a poor attempt at an angry-face, he turned and walked off.

Tiffany looked exhausted. I could tell she was thinking about leaving her stuff behind just so she could stop packing. Considering there were designer purses in there, she must've been desperate.

"I'll sit on the bag, and you zip," I said. "I'm heavier than you." I might've been, if I'd had the boobs and butt she did, but it was exactly what she needed to hear. She inhaled a breath and stood so I could take her place. After wrestling with the zipper, she got the bag closed. Her face and eyes were red, her hairline sticky with sweat. I couldn't help wondering what'd happened just now, before Gary'd interrupted us. Tiffany was clearly distraught. Was it possible she actually cared about Manning?

With that realization, a new fear settled over me. Not for Manning or even myself. If Tiffany found out I'd snuck off with her boyfriend, she'd be furious. Embarrassed. *Hurt.* What I'd done, I'd done without considering how it might affect my own sister. It'd been easy to convince myself it wouldn't matter to her because she didn't have real feelings for Manning. But did she?

"I'm sorry this week was so bad," I said sincerely. "I'll go to the mall with you when we get home and buy you something."

She wiped her nose. "With what?"

"I have some allowance saved. Probably more than you."

She turned around and climbed onto her bed to remove pictures of her and her friends she'd taped to the wall. "You know I can have almost anyone. Manning's lucky I'm still around."

I wasn't sure where that was coming from, but there was only one way to answer that if I wanted to get out of here alive. "I know." I waited for her to continue, but she just picked tape off the corners of the photographs. "Did something happen with him?" I asked.

"I don't know."

"Are you thinking of breaking up with him?"

"Maybe."

So many things ran through my mind at once. If they broke up, Manning would be out of her life. But would he then be out of mine, too? No. He and I had to find a way. We knew it'd come to this. It wasn't as if I'd expected her to stay with Manning for two whole years until I turned eighteen.

"We'll see how it goes if I pick him up," she said.

I didn't know which way to encourage her. It was a very real possibility that without Tiffany, Manning and I would be separated until I turned eighteen. That was two excruciating years away from him. But the thought of them together felt like having a piece of glass lodged in my chest—I couldn't go very long without being reminded it was there.

Manning and I needed Tiffany, but at the same time, there was no denying—she was also in the way.

25
LAKE

By Tuesday morning, three long days since they'd taken Manning away, I could no longer handle doing nothing. This time next week, I'd be back in school, even more helpless than I already was.

I went through the bathroom, knocked on Tiffany's door, and entered.

"Rude much?" she asked. Tiffany lay on her stomach, reading *Cosmopolitan*, blowing on her nails. A bottle of purple polish sat precariously on her white comforter. "I could've been naked."

"I've seen you naked."

"What do you want?"

Tiffany's room was the personification of a rundown childhood. In elementary school, Mom had redecorated it with white wicker furniture, ruffled bedding, and pastel walls. She'd helped Tiffany and me paint tulips along the bottom. But as Tiffany had gotten older, she'd tacked concert posters around her bed. Paint chipped off the wicker desk where she'd thrown her phone at it. She'd glued pictures of celebrities to her vanity mirror. One tulip head had been covered with a glittery sticker that said "Goddess" and another with Daria's face. Her shoe collection had overflown from the closet, floral Doc Martens sprouting from her plush, white carpet.

I turned the stereo volume down. "Did you get ahold of Gary?"

"Hey. That was Alice in Chains."

"Did you?"

She sighed. "He called last night. Manning robbed someone. That's why he's there."

But that made no sense at all. "Are you sure?"

"Yup."

There were so many ways to tell her Manning couldn't have committed any crime that night, but how? I'd have to admit I was with him, and I'd promised I wouldn't tell. "What . . . who do they think he stole from?"

She looked up at me. "Guess."

"How would I know?" Her eyes stayed on me so long, it was as if she actually expected me to respond. "Another counselor?" I asked.

"No." She returned to her magazine. "He didn't take anything. Just broke into some house in the suburbs during an alcohol run. Nobody, not even Gary, knows what happened between when he left and morning. At least, nobody has come forward."

My throat went dry. There was no robbery. There was no house. Just a truck, a lake, and infinite stars. Manning was innocent. "Does Gary think he did it?"

"No. Neither do I, obviously."

I tried to feel relieved. Gary and Tiffany were adults—they knew better. They'd handle this. "What else did he say?"

"Manning meets with his lawyer this week, and they'll go before a judge. I forget what it's called, but Gary says that's when he pleads 'not guilty.' We'll know more after that."

"But what happens until then? Is Manning coming back?" Either my chest was caving in or my heart had begun to swell. I couldn't picture him held at the station for days, just waiting, thinking of all the things he would've done differently that night. Maybe, even, regretting our time together. "Or is he already back?"

Tiffany carefully flipped a page and checked her polish. "I don't know. I guess he's in jail."

On her desk next to her phone sat a pink, lined notepad with hearts doodled in the margin—and notes in her handwriting. "Did Gary give you the name of the lawyer?"

369

Tiffany tilted her head at the magazine. She didn't respond for so long, I assumed she'd forgotten I was here. Upside down, I read the title of the article she found so engrossing: "Best Autumn Makeup."

I was fed up. Either it was her narcissism that got under my skin, or the fact that autumn was practically here, pressing down on us when summer could so clearly not end this way. "Tiffany, you have to take this seriously. If you don't want him anymore, fine, but he's still a friend of ours."

"What makes you think I don't want him?"

"You said that at camp."

"And he's *my* boyfriend, not *your* friend. Why do you want his lawyer's name?"

"Because I have to talk to him. I think I—I might've seen something that night."

Tiffany closed her magazine and sat up, catching the bottle of nail polish just as it started to tip over. "Okay, so tell me, and I'll call him."

We stared at each other. I felt as if I were taking a quiz without knowing the topic. Tiffany was being weird and cryptic and I had zero time for that. I went over to her desk and grabbed the notepad.

"Stop," she said, swiping for it.

I jumped back and read her handwriting. "Tuesday arraignment. One o'clock." I looked up at her. "That's *today*."

"So?"

Manning was going to court for something he hadn't done, and I still hadn't told anybody my side of the story. For all the times he'd protected me, I owed him the same. I didn't know much about the law, but I'd heard of attorney-client privilege on TV. I was almost positive Manning's lawyer would need to know the truth, whether or not it could hurt Manning.

I returned to my room and carried my phone to the bed.

Making calls in this house was a dangerous business. At any moment, someone could pick up the line. Sometimes, you wouldn't even hear the click, you'd just go on talking about stuff parents and older sisters could later tease you about. Vickie had once raved over Luke Harold's hair, the ways in which it was better than even Jonathan Taylor Thomas's. My dad had heard ten seconds of it and still hadn't let me live that down.

Tiffany was the only person home, but she of all people couldn't hear this call. She'd have every right to demand answers if she found out I had sensitive information about the night her boyfriend was arrested.

I read over her notes again—*Arainment Tuesday. 1pm. Dexter Grimes public defender (lawyer).*

Once Tiffany had turned her music back up, I dialed four-one-one, got Dexter's office number, and made the call. As I waited for him to pick up, I glanced around my room. It needed a makeover. My CD collection was a quarter the size of Tiffany's. Like her, I also collected stickers, but they were confined to my school binders and a bookshelf crammed with paperbacks. *Sweet Valley High* and *Goosebumps* had to go. I hadn't even picked one of those up since sixth grade.

Were *they* the last books I'd read for fun?

The line clicked over to voicemail. "You've reached Dexter Grimes of the public defender's office—"

Shit, shit, shit. This wasn't good. The arraignment was in less than three hours. The recording beeped, and I realized I had no idea what I wanted to say. "Hello, Mr. Grimes," I started.

Tiffany pounded on my door, and I jumped a mile high. "What are you doing?" she asked.

I put my hand over the receiver. "Go away." I lowered my voice. "Sorry, Mr. Grimes. I'm calling about a client of yours, M—Mr. Manning Sutter. I have information about the night he got in trouble." I paused. How much should I tell him? I needed to see what he already knew, figure out if I could trust him. "I can't say it in a message, but it might help him. Please, please call me back when you get this." I hung up and immediately realized I hadn't left a number. Or a name. My hand sweat around the receiver. I wasn't thinking straight, and I needed to. For Manning. I hit redial, stood, and paced the room, back and forth, as far as the cord would allow. "Hi, Mr. Grimes. I just left a message but I forgot to give you my information. I'm Lake. Like the body of water." I cringed. I hadn't introduced myself that way since I was a kid. "Lake Kaplan. When you call back, if I don't answer, please don't mention what this is about. I live with my family, and they can't know I'm calling. But it's really important what I have to tell you." I relayed my phone number twice and my name again.

I dropped the receiver into its cradle, flopped onto my bed, and looked up at the ceiling. I practiced breathing with my diaphragm as if I were back on the lawn at USC. I tried forcing myself to appreciate what I had around me like Gary had taught us to do. But Manning only grew bigger in my mind.

I had no idea about arraignments. My dad would, but I couldn't ask him. It'd only been three days. Maybe that was good—I wanted Manning out of there—but it almost seemed *too* soon. Was an arraignment the same as a trial, like the ones I'd seen on TV shows? In class, we'd watched *To Kill a Mockingbird* last year. Some of my classmates had fallen asleep, the movie black-and-white, slow-moving, but if the trial scene had been happening in front of my eyes, it would've felt fast, with words meant to confuse. Overwhelming. My heart began to race just thinking of Manning in there all alone. Did *he* even know what to do in an arraignment? How could he, in only three days? If I had information that could help, shouldn't I be there just in case he needed me?

I sat up quickly, went downstairs, and found Tiffany in the kitchen. "We have to go to Big Bear," I said.

She pulled her head out of the refrigerator. "What?"

"We need to drive there for the arraignment. Now."

She took out a carton of orange juice. "Are you kidding? Dad would kill us."

"Then we won't tell him."

She raised a manicured eyebrow as she put the OJ on the counter. "Wow. Since when do you lie to dad?" she asked, unscrewing the cap. "Must really be important to you."

"You said it yourself—Manning's all alone. He has no family. You told me," I swallowed, "you said his sister died. So who's there with him?"

She took a glass from the cupboard, set it on the counter, and looked back at me. "Nobody, I guess. But he . . ."

"What?" I asked. "Why are you acting so flippant about this? What has he ever done to you besides be nice? You said he was a gentleman."

"He was."

"So? That's not good enough for you?"

"He's innocent," she said, staring at the empty glass. "Why does it matter if we go? They're just going to release him."

I didn't have time for this. I had to make a choice. Nothing would happen to Manning; he hadn't done anything. I had to believe that. But if there was even the slightest chance he might turn and look for me . . . if he needed me to speak up, and I wasn't there . . .

"Fine." I turned to leave the kitchen. "But I'm taking your car."

"*What?*" She followed me upstairs. "You don't even know how to drive."

"I know enough," I said on my way into my room.

"You're such a brat," she said through the door.

I ignored her and changed into the nicest sweater and slacks I owned. I found a pair of pumps in my mom's closet. They were a size too big, but I put them in my purse. By the time I'd brushed out my hair and attempted a little makeup, Tiffany was downstairs waiting by the front door.

"You'll come?" I asked.

"He's going to need a ride back anyway. Like I'd ever let you drive my car," she said, opening the front door.

She acted annoyed, but I knew my sister well enough to recognize the look in her eyes. She was just as nervous as I was.

26

MANNING

Forty minutes before my arraignment, a brown-haired man in his early forties entered the courthouse interview room and slapped a briefcase on the table between us. "Manning Sutter?"

"That's me."

I stood to shake his hand, but he stopped me. "No time for formalities. I'm Dexter Grimes, your public defender." He pulled out a handful of manila file folders, put on his glasses, and rifled through them. "Richards, Rosenblatt, Stephenson," he muttered, reading them off. "Here we are—Sutter." He opened my file and frowned. "No, this is wrong." Fanning them out on the table, he picked one labeled

Sweeney and swapped the contents of our files. "There we go. Sweeney was in Sutter, and Sutter was in Sweeney. It happens."

I'd had my personal effects taken, been fingerprinted, photographed and stood in a line-up, then held in a cell—all within seventy-two hours. All as an innocent man. I'd been told I'd meet my lawyer before my arraignment. This was the one I'd been assigned. Upon closer inspection, I decided he was mid-thirties with deep lines around his eyes. He looked as if he'd been through the grinder. There was a mayonnaise stain on his lapel, or at least I hoped that's what it was.

I stared at him until he cleared his throat. "We're a little overloaded," he said.

"No shit."

"But don't worry." His glasses slid down his nose. "I've done this a thousand times."

In my experience, having done something a lot didn't necessarily mean you were good at it. But he was all I had, and at least when he talked to me, he looked me in the eye. I placed my forearms on the table. "I'm innocent."

"Of course." He sat back in his seat, looking over my slim paperwork. "Do you know how arraignments work?"

"Not really."

"It's going to be fast. The judge'll read the charges, you'll plead 'not guilty,' and they'll set bail. You have anyone to post your bail?"

I had nobody, period. Even if my mom had the money, I'd rather sit in jail than crawl back to her. My aunt and Henry, the officer who'd looked out for me as a teen, had done enough for me in one lifetime. "No."

"Depending on the amount, a bondsman can front you the money and take a percentage."

The money I'd saved over the years was a small sum by most standards, but it was all I had. I'd worked hard for it. "I'm not paying anyone anything for a crime I didn't commit."

"Okay." He made a couple notes. "So Friday night, you were pulled over."

"No. My truck stalled, so *I* pulled it over. The cop stopped to check on me."

"Says here he suspected you were drinking."

"No. I walked in a straight line for him and then we had a nice, friendly chat."

Grimes looked up. "Did he administer a Breathalyzer test on you?"

"I wasn't drinking."

"That wasn't my question."

"No, he didn't."

"Then that's irrelevant. It's your word against his."

The officer and I had hit it off; there was no reason for him not to believe me. I opened my mouth to explain.

Grimes checked his watch. "Your charge is attempted robbery. A felony."

"It doesn't much matter what it is, because I didn't do it."

"It *does* matter."

"I didn't go in anyone's house. I don't even know which house it *was*. Look, all you need to do is tell whoever needs to know that there's some kind of mix-up so I can go home. I work under contract. Every hour I'm in here is lost wages."

"I understand, Mr. Sutter. I'm moving as quickly as possible." He darted his eyes over the page in front of him. "This officer says he saw you just before one."

"I guess."

"Witnesses have you leaving Phil's around ten-thirty. Neighbors spot you driving in the dark around eleven. What happened between eleven and one?"

"I went for a drive. Then when I got close to camp, my car stalled."

"So for almost two hours, you sat on the side of the road, waiting for a jump?"

"Yeah, so fucking what? I drove around a while before that."

Grimes closed the file with a sigh. "Look, Mr.—"

"Manning," I said. "I'm not mister anything."

"Manning, I'm on your side. Anything you tell me is confidential. I can't win this if you don't work with me."

I ran my hands over my face and looked up at the ceiling. "There's nothing to win. I didn't do it."

"I've got news for you, Manning, and you aren't going to like it. Your case doesn't look great. The residents of that ritzy suburb want someone to go down for this, so the prosecutor will try to wrap this up as soon as possible. You're the strongest suspect, and far as I can tell, you move from job to job and don't come from the best background."

"What's that got to do with it?"

"You're suspicious. I'm sorry." He took off his glasses and set them on the paperwork. "If you don't tell me where you were, if nobody can vouch for you, then the police are going to think you're hiding something. They want guys like you to be guilty so they can close it and move on. Give me something to work with. Otherwise, guilty or not, there's a chance you'll go away for this."

I lowered my chin, meeting his eye. Under the table, my knee bounced up and down. I wasn't naïve, not even when it came to the criminal justice system. It'd done right by me in the past, but I came from a line of bad men. Maybe based on that alone, I *should* be put away. Before I really did hurt someone the way my dad had. For fuck's sake, I'd almost taken advantage of Lake that night. Maybe I deserved this, but either way, being charged with a crime I didn't commit seemed like a cruel joke.

I'd already given Grimes my story, though. At least what I was willing to share. I opened my hands on the table. "I got nothing, man."

381

Grimes nodded slowly, studying me. After a few seconds, he peeked in the file and back at me. "Who's Lake Kaplan?"

Time as I knew it came to a screeching halt. The air in the room evaporated, fluorescent overhead lights became blinding. Lake was off-limits. Period. How the fuck had he even gotten her name? My hands twitched with the urge to grab Dexter by his mayo-stained lapels.

"I take it by your silence you recognize the name," he said.

"Where'd you hear it?"

"She left a message with my office a few hours ago." He opened and closed the arms of his glasses. If he was preparing to gloat, he didn't seem happy about it. "I called back, but nobody answered. The machine belongs to a family."

Fuck. Fuck. *Fuck*. Goddamn stubborn Lake. I knew she'd try to help, but I'd hoped the threat of making things worse would be enough to stop her. The thought that Mr. Kaplan could've picked up the phone made me sweat. I wiped my palms on my scrubs. "Please don't tell me you left a message."

"Lake mentioned it was sensitive, so I didn't. She sounded young, Manning. So now I have to ask why a young girl has information I need."

I looked at the table. "She's nobody. My girlfriend's little sister."

"How little?"

"Sixteen."

"I see." He proceeded slowly, as if deliberating over his words. "What's her involvement?"

For what felt like the hundredth time in three days, Lake's face came to mind, her big, blue, gullible eyes, the way her chin ended in a point, like a heart. She'd looked terrified when I'd last seen her. Then hurt when I'd dismissed her to get Tiffany. Making her feel like a kid was the only way I could get her to leave.

Somehow, I'd dragged a girl, who was younger than Maddy would've been if she were alive, into my mess. I laced my hands together. "Nothing else to tell."

"Whatever you say stays between us, Manning. If . . . something happened with her—"

"Nothing happened."

"But if I know what occurred in those two hours, I can start building your defense. I need the truth."

"I told you. Nothing . . . fucking . . . happened."

"All right, then." He scooted his chair closer to the table. "We have to discuss your options before they call us up. The way things are headed, I think we'd better talk about the plea bargain the prosecutor is offering."

I lifted my head, drawing my eyebrows together. "Isn't that if you're guilty?"

"If you're likely to be convicted, then it's best to take a deal to soften the blow. Less time, for one."

"But I'm innocent."

"This is no longer about innocent versus guilty. It's a game, and you need to play."

"That's bullshit," I said. "The law's the law. I didn't break it."

"We can argue mistaken identity," he continued, "but since the victim ID'ed you in the line-up, and she claims she turned the lights on, I can't promise it'll turn out how we want."

"She picked me out?" I sat forward. "The other guys weren't as tall as me. Maybe she's remembering it wrong."

"Maybe. I'll need more time to look over all this." He scratched his jaw. "Luckily, you have no priors. The max for attempted robbery in the state of California is four-and-a-half years."

I laughed from my gut, harder than I had in a long time. "This is a huge misunderstanding."

"The D.A. is offering to reduce the charge to first-degree burglary with a low-term sentence of two years. With good behavior, you'd be out in less."

Whatever he was talking about went in one ear and out the other. I crossed my arms. "I'm not going to jail for something I didn't do."

"Then we go to trial, but we risk ending up with a longer, more severe punishment. I'd *definitely* need to know the details of what happened that night—all of them. And I won't be the only one snooping for information." He tapped the top of the file. "I believe you didn't break into that house. I *don't* believe your story."

This conversation hadn't gone anything like I'd expected. I thought I'd explain to my lawyer that this was a case of wrong place, wrong time, and be home by tonight. Now, we were talking jail time. I was in deep shit. I squeezed my hands together until my knuckles were a sickening, bloodless white. "If I tell you what happened, it stays here? You won't try to make me say it in court? Because I'll lie if I have to."

Grimes held up his palms. "You have my word."

The room suddenly seemed half its size. I inhaled. I didn't want to see the look in Dexter's eyes when I told him, but I held his stare. I deserved to face my mistakes, and maybe that wasn't all I deserved. Fact was, I *had* done something bad. And bad people got locked up all the time for one thing or another. "Like I said, Lake is Tiffany's younger sister. Tiffany's my girlfriend, for lack of a better term. Lake, though . . ." I couldn't put into words what she was. As if I even knew. "She's my friend."

"Be straight with me, Manning. She's sixteen."

I flattened my hands on the table. I'd have agreed to almost anything for a cigarette at that moment. I'd never felt more deserving of one. "I had a younger sister."

"Had?" Dexter sat back. "I'm sorry."

"Having Lake around reminds me of how it used to be. With Maddy. You don't just stop being an older brother."

Dexter gave me a moment. "If that's true, and it's nothing more, then we might be able to use that to our advantage, show your character."

"It *was* true . . ." I said slowly. "At first, Lake was uncomplicated. Genuine. Trusting. She brought back small things about Madison I hadn't realized I'd forgotten." I had the urge to look anywhere but at Dexter. To bash my head against the table and wake myself up from this nightmare. I'd made these decisions, though. I couldn't just pretend I hadn't. "It's not that anymore. The more I get to know her, it's something else. She's not like the rest of us. She's good."

"Are you saying something happened?"

"I'm saying what I feel for her comes from an innocent place. I would never hurt her. If anything, I wanted . . . I *want* to protect her. To keep her pure."

"But you had sex with her," he concluded.

"No. God, no." I ran both hands over my face. "We went for a drive. We don't get much time alone, and somehow we'd ended up with this one night. We were only in that neighborhood with the lights out to see the stars. Never even stopped the car. On the way back, we almost hit a coyote so I pulled over. She got out and jumped in the lake. She wanted me to chase her. To give in. She wanted me, and fuck, I wanted her back, but it's no excuse. In the truck, we got a little too close. I almost went where I shouldn't. But I swear, that was all, and I ended it right before the cop spotted us. Lake hid in the back while I talked to him."

"She hid. Fuck." Dexter took it all in. "He didn't see her?"

"No."

"Drinking?"

"Not a drop, either of us."

"No sex at all? Were you inside her at any point?"

"No, fuck no. We didn't even kiss." To hear it put so clinically, my stomach churned. "I know I lost control, but I'd never take advantage of her."

"Does anyone else know? The sister?"

"Not unless Lake told her, but she promised me she wouldn't. I'm sure that's why she called. She's probably scared."

He chewed on his bottom lip. The room got so quiet, I heard his watch ticking.

What I did with Lake, it could've been worse, but what people thought held more weight than the truth. Even if we swore she'd ridden in the bed of the truck the entire time, people would think the worst. Blame me for taking advantage of a young girl. And some might blame her, too. They'd look at her differently. Her *dad* would see her differently. That changed a person, and I didn't want her to change, didn't want her to feel the stares, to think she'd done anything wrong, or that she'd disappointed her family.

Lake was untouchable. I'd make sure it stayed that way. "I won't bring her into this," I said. "Even if it saves me."

He looked up. "You can't go away for driving around with a minor. If you were with her and she corroborates that, then you couldn't have been at the house. Basically, she's your alibi."

If she were called to the stand to tell the court what'd really happened that night, she'd be traumatized. But *I'd* be fucked. I hadn't forgotten what Mr. Kaplan had said at dinner about his "friends in the legal system." If the burglary charges were dropped, no doubt he'd bring his own against me. He'd find a way. Maybe even statutory rape, and I'd serve a decade before I put Lake through that. I opened my mouth to tell Grimes as far as the courts were concerned, I had no alibi.

"But," he said, frowning, "since the cop didn't see Lake, he'd either assume you were lying or that she'd hidden. So even if the jury believed her story, they'd draw their own conclusions as to why she'd hide from a cop."

"You're agreeing with me?" I asked. "We can keep her out of this?"

"I think that's best," he said hesitantly. "I'm concerned her testimony could actually hurt us." Dexter picked up my file, straightening it on the table. "We'll have to find another way."

27
LAKE

The clock on the dashboard changed. 12:53 P.M.

Tiffany had been the perfect person to get us here—driving over the speed limit was her default. But we hadn't left the house early enough, and traffic had slowed us down. I had only seven minutes to find Dexter Grimes and tell him what I knew. I wasn't sure if it'd help or hurt, but at this point Manning's lawyer was the only person who'd be able to help me.

Tiffany pulled into a parking spot, and I jumped out of the car.

"Slow down," she said, unbuckling her seatbelt. "I don't know where to go."

"Neither do I." I slammed the door shut and hurried across the courthouse's parking lot. It was smaller than I expected. During the drive, I'd built it up in my mind as some large, scary place.

"Lake!" Tiffany caught up with me at the entrance since we had to go through security. "Don't ditch me," she said. "Dad'll kill me if I come home without you."

Maybe she was making a joke. I couldn't tell. My stomach hurt, and my mom's pumps kept slipping off, already rubbing against my heels. "It's almost one."

We went through the metal detector and retrieved our purses from the conveyor belt. "Maybe they'll be running behind," she said.

"Maybe they won't."

In the lobby, the line to talk to someone was too long. A large calendar on the wall displayed a list of names, so I went there instead.

Tiffany stood next to me, scanning it. "There he is," she said, pointing. "Sutter, M. Courtroom eight."

I turned to her. "But where would his lawyer be?"

"I have no idea."

I bit my bottom lip, looking around us. Men and women in suits hurried down the hall in both directions. The clock above reception ticked down . . . four minutes to go.

I took off for courtroom eight, our only shot, the click of my slippery heels echoing off the walls. A week ago, I'd been on a horse, hugging Manning's middle while the sun warmed us, inhaling the scent of pine trees-and-Manning with every breath. He'd helped me conquer my fear, but he'd also taught me something about myself. As I checked the numbers over each courtroom, I realized what he'd said was true. The sick feeling in my gut told me this was my Ferris wheel, my Betsy Junior. It was as bad as boarding an airplane. I had no control over Manning and me, and I never really had. Whatever choices I'd made that night, they'd led us here, but that wasn't me being in control. That was my selfishness. I'd pushed and pushed Manning, trying to get him to see me differently. To want me. To love me. This was my fault. I had to show up for Manning, no matter what happened; it was the only thing I could control in this moment.

Tiffany and I arrived at the same time, pulling open the door to courtroom eight together, all brown wooden pews and worn carpeting inside.

Manning stood before a judge in an orange jumpsuit, his back to us, a head taller than anyone in the room. The judge, elevated above the rest of us, looked down at Manning and spoke words I barely registered. " . . . count of attempted robbery in the first degree . . . felony . . . do you understand the nature of the charges?"

The brown-haired, suit-wearing man next to Manning looked over his shoulder at me. *Dexter?* I mouthed to him, but he just glanced at the ground and turned forward again.

Manning nodded once. "I do."

The judge shuffled some papers. "Are you entering this plea freely and of your own will?"

"Yes, Your Honor."

"Do you understand that by pleading guilty, you're giving up your right to a trial?"

"Yes, Your Honor."

Guilty? I must've misheard. My ears rang. *Not* guilty—that's what he'd said. I took a few steps farther into the room, my heels sticking on the threadbare carpet. Tiffany grabbed my elbow to pull me back.

"I understand there's a plea bargain on the table," the judge continued. "The prosecutor will now state the terms of the agreement to the court."

A man at the table to Manning's left stood. "Your honor, we're offering to reduce the charge from attempted robbery to burglary in the first degree with a low-term sentence of two years."

The judge looked at Manning. "Do you understand the terms of the plea agreement?"

"I do."

"Two *years?*" I asked aloud. A few people looked over at me.

Tiffany tugged on my elbow while the judge asked questions I didn't understand. "Let's sit," she said.

I ripped my arm from her grip and walked toward the divider separating the gallery from the court. Tiffany hurried after me.

"Mr. Sutter, how do you plead to the charge?" the judge asked.

Manning didn't even hesitate. "Guilty, Your Honor."

Tiffany and I looked at each other. *No.* He had no reason to plead guilty. It must've been a mistake. It had to be. I went for the gate, but Dexter turned, put his hand up to stop me, and shook his head.

"The court will accept your plea of guilty . . . sentenced to two years for a felony charge . . ."

I gripped the sides of my head, covering my ears. "Manning," I said. "Please don't."

Manning turned as quickly as he could, his hands cuffed in front of him. My vision blurred with tears, but our eyes met, his imploring me.

"What are you doing?" Tiffany asked him. "You're not guilty."

"Ma'am," the judge said. "Please don't communicate with the inmate."

"It's okay," Manning said immediately, his voice hushed. I didn't even think he understood what he was saying. He came to the wall. "Everything's okay. You shouldn't be here."

A man in uniform started toward us.

Dexter checked over his shoulder. "Time to go, Manning."

"Not yet," I said, but my voice came out as a whisper. I had to undo this. All of this had started because *I'd* gone over to talk to him on the wall, because *I'd* forced him to let me in the truck, made him drive me around when we should've gone straight back. "I can help—"

"It's okay, Birdy. I've got this," Manning said calmly, leaning in. "You did good."

"No I didn't." My voice and hands shook. We were so close. I wanted to feel his stubble on my cheek, to have him whisper in my ear that this wasn't happening. He couldn't even touch me with his hands shackled. "This is my f—"

"I did this to myself," he said. "It was the only way. You have to trust me."

"But you're innocent."

"Be good, Birdy." He looked at Tiffany. "Thank you for—"

"*Defense,*" the judge said. "That's enough. Communicating with the inmate is grounds for arrest."

"Come on, Manning," Dexter said.

The man dressed like a security guard grabbed Manning's arm. "Let's go, inmate," he said, leading him away.

Tiffany's chin wobbled. "Can I come see you?"

"Your sister needs you," he told Tiffany over his shoulder.

Her contorted expression eased, smoothing out. I looked from her to Manning just as he disappeared into the back.

Dexter stayed with us. "It was the best-case scenario," he said. "The odds were stacked against him."

"But he's innocent," I said. "I was—"

"I know," Dexter cut me off sharply. He looked me in the eye. "It doesn't matter. It's over. If we do anything more, *it can only hurt him.*"

My chest tightened. I had to steady myself on the divider. Manning had told me to trust him. Dexter clearly knew about me already. The information I had could make things worse, I understood that—I'd only hoped the opposite was true.

Dexter handed Tiffany a business card and a clear plastic bag with hardly anything in it.

"What is this?" she asked.

"Manning said to give it to you. His apartment keys are in there." Dexter shook his head. "I don't think he has anyone else."

I took the bag from her. There was a pack of cigarettes, keys, some loose papers, a ring, and . . . the bracelet I'd made him. I swallowed back another wave of tears as I took it out. It was worthless, just a few intertwined wax strings, but they hadn't even let him keep that. This was all that'd been on him when they'd arrested him—which meant he'd also been carrying around the huge and chunky ring at the bottom of the bag. I wasn't sure what it was or if it meant anything to him. The other morning as we'd walked into Reflection, he'd said he'd wanted to give me something. Maybe this was it. I put both the bracelet and the ring in my pocket before Tiffany could take them.

Dexter had to go. Tiffany and I, out of options, walked back outside. The California sun felt angry, blinding. By the time we reached the curb, I was limping from the blisters the shoes were giving me.

Tiffany noticed. "Wait here," she said. "I'll get the car."

I took off the pumps. Away from Manning, Dexter, and Tiffany, my nose tingled as tears leaked from my eyes. Guilt weighed on my shoulders. I never would've jumped in the lake if I'd known how his sister had died. I never would've gotten in the truck if I'd known an innocent man could end up in jail. I'd made some huge mistakes, and I didn't even have the luxury of reaping the punishment myself. The man I'd hurt, the man I loved, had to do it for me. If anyone deserved to be led away into that ominous back room, it was me.

Tiffany's BMW pulled up to the curb. When I didn't move, she rolled down the passenger's side window. "Get in."

Barefoot, I crossed the pavement and slid in next to her.

We sat in silence a few moments, her staring through the windshield, me out my window at nothing but the building's beige stucco walls and chipped brown roof.

Tiffany turned off the car.

I looked over at her. "What're you doing?" I asked.

She kept her gaze forward. "Did you have sex with him?"

My mouth went dry as the car shrunk around us. Sunlight harshened a film of dust on the dashboard. "What?"

She turned to me. My sister's eyes were as familiar as anything in my life, but I didn't remember them ever being the glacial shade of blue they were now. "I saw you get into his truck that night. So did you?"

"No." My voice shook. It never occurred to me someone might've seen, least of all her. That'd been over three days ago, and she hadn't said a word about it. "I swear, I didn't. All we did was go for a drive."

"Why should I believe you?" she asked.

"I wouldn't lie to you, Tiffany. We drove around and came back. He didn't burglarize any house. We didn't . . ."

"Say it."

"We didn't have sex."

She grabbed the baggie of Manning's things from the console and threw it at my feet. "What the fuck am I supposed to do with his shit?"

I picked it up, the keys jangling. "I . . . I don't know. He has no one else. I guess we—"

She snatched it from me. "There is no *we*. Are you going to go to a landlord and explain this? You can't even *drive*." Her voice broke. "He wouldn't even talk to me in there. He only had a few seconds, but *you* took them. All he said to me was 'your sister needs you.'"

There was nothing else to say. How could I ever explain what the last five weeks had been for me and Manning? That I'd felt justified in the decisions I'd made to try to keep him for myself? "I'm sorry."

"Sorry won't get him out of prison." She started the car. "Look what you've done, Lake. You made a colossal mistake, and now my boyfriend has to pay the price."

We pulled away from the curb. I watched the courthouse in the side mirror until it disappeared— gone, just like summer. Just like Manning.

I stared at nothing in the reflection long after we'd driven away, until I could no longer see through my tears.

Tiffany's words played over and over in my head. *Look what you've done, Lake.*

BOOK TWO IN THE
SOMETHING IN THE WAY SERIES:

SOMEBODY ELSE'S SKY

LEARN MORE AT
WWW.JESSICAHAWKINS.NET/SOMETHINGINTHEWAY

TITLES BY
JESSICA HAWKINS

LEARN MORE AT JESSICAHAWKINS.NET/BOOKS

SLIP OF THE TONGUE
THE FIRST TASTE
YOURS TO BARE

SOMETHING IN THE WAY SERIES
SOMETHING IN THE WAY
SOMEBODY ELSE'S SKY
MOVE THE STARS

THE CITYSCAPE SERIES
COME UNDONE
COME ALIVE
COME TOGETHER

EXPLICITLY YOURS SERIES
POSSESSION
DOMINATION
PROVOCATION
OBSESSION

ACKNOWLEDGMENTS

For their patience, encouragement, and mastery, I have to first and foremost thank my editors, cover designer, & cover photographer. This story has lived in me so long, I worried I wouldn't be able to tell it right, in written form or visually. I don't think anyone on my team knew what they were getting into. Elizabeth London, I would be lost without you. Thank you for talking me through this story over and over and for encouraging me with '90s-tastic gifs. Letitia of R.B.A. Designs, you not only nailed it, but you did it on your first try. I bow down. I'm thrilled to have your magic touch on the covers to come. Lauren of Perrywinkle Photography, I didn't think there was a chance in hell I'd get to see the characters in my head on the cover. You were that chance. Your talent has blown me away for years, and I'm proud to finally have your work on my books. Lake and Manning have come alive under your direction. Thank you. Katie of Underline This Editing , you were one of the few to help shape this book, and thanks also to Tamara Mataya Editing for your eagle eye and for a running commentary that kept me laughing when I needed to.

Behind the scenes, my publicist had nearly nothing to work with and managed to do her job splendidly anyway. Thanks, Melissa, for never making me feel nutty when I know I'm acting that way. You're a sounding board and a friend. My author pals and peers are support systems whether they know it or not (I hope they do). From sprinting vampires to covert cover advice to shop-talking, I'm inspired and motivated by them on a daily basis. My reader group and street team are my happy places. Period. To get "face time" with readers every day is priceless. To know you're rooting me on, sharing yours ideas, laughing at my mishaps & tpyos, letting me into your personal lives, and showing each other pictures of how you see my characters—it brightens my world like you'll never know. I love you all!

ABOUT THE AUTHOR

JESSICA HAWKINS is an Amazon bestselling author known for her "emotionally gripping" and "off-the-charts hot" romance. Dubbed "queen of angst" by both peers and readers for her smart and provocative work, she's garnered a cult-like following of fans who love to be torn apart...and put back together.

She writes romance both at home in California and around the world, a coffee shop traveler who bounces from café to café with just a laptop, headphones, and coffee cup. She loves to keep in close touch with her readers, mostly via Facebook, Instagram, and her mailing list.

CONNECT WITH JESSICA

Stay updated & join the
JESSICA HAWKINS Mailing List
www.JESSICAHAWKINS.net/mailing-list

www.amazon.com/author/jessicahawkins
www.facebook.com/jessicahawkinsauthor
twitter: @jess_hawk

65850076R00243

Made in the USA
Middletown, DE
04 March 2018